Carter Finally Gets It

By Brent Crawford

Disney · HYPERION BOOKS
NEW YORK

First Edition
10 9 8 7 6 5 4 3 2 1
Library of Congress Cataloging-in-Publication Data on file.
Reinforced binding
ISBN 978-1-4231-1246-4
This book utilizes portions of dialogue and lyrics from the musical
stage production of *Guys and Dolls* written by Frank Loesser.
Used by permission of Frank Music Corp. (ASCAP).
Visit www.hyperionteens.com

To my boys

end of summer

1. Girl Power

In the back room of the Pizza Barn, with only two weeks before the start of high school, my boys and I are at the Freshman Mixer. The awesome kids from Merrian Junior High (us) are supposed to "mix" with the degenerates from Hawkus Middle School (them). We knew it was going to suck. What we didn't know was how hot the Hawkus chicks would be and if any of them would be down to *mix* with us. And free pizza is free pizza, so here we are!

The Hawkus kids have taken over the front room because they're lame and got here early to stake out their territory. We, on the other hand, rolled in fashionably tardy and have been stuck in the arcade for two hours. I don't mind a bit. I love the video games here; they're the ancient, stand-up kind. They're older than anyone here, only cost a quarter, and because we're trapped like POWs, it doesn't look uncool to play them.

On my second trip to the buffet, I scope out the Hawkus crew. The chick selection is like the pizza: cold as ice, picked over, and not very appetizing. The dudes look mean, though. One kid in particular is really big and cool-looking; the other kids are gathered around him like he's giving out autographs. But he's not talking, he's just staring at me and my pile of Hawaiian slices. He looks pissed, like the last time he saw me, I kicked him in the nuts or I stole this pizza from his grandma. Whatever his problem is, it looks like trouble.

I retreat to the safety of the back room to find the old Punch-Out game open for business. I scarf down a slice and pop my last quarter in the slot to kick some digital ass. I wish this boxing ring were real and I could walk up to that big punk out there and give him what the game calls a MIGHTY BLOW! Right to the jaw. I think I know him from somewhere, and I'm sure I don't like him.

I blast the first boxer in my game (Glass Joe) with a flurry of MIGHTY BLOWS! and drop his ass. As the game tries to figure out who my next opponent will be, I casually cruise the room with my eyes. Our girls are looking a whole lot better now that I've seen what else will be on the menu at Merrian High. I never thought they were dogs or anything, I just thought that I'd have more options. Like Taco Bell is awesome, but you shouldn't eat it every day. You need some KFC, Pizza Barn, or Subway for a balanced diet. I need variety in my chicks. Not because I'm some player; I've never really talked to a girl that I was interested in before. I mean, I've talked to girls, like "Can I borrow a pencil?" or "What time does school start?" But never anything smooth, like walking up to them with a rose and saying, "This bud's for you, baby" or "I like your shirt . . . I'd like it better on my bedroom floor." I just need a little practice.

But I'm almost in high school; I'm overdue for a surge in confidence and maturity. I've grown five inches in the last four months, so I've got a new perspective on things. Who's to say I won't experience a growth spurt in the smoothness-with-ladies department? I might magically become *the man* in two weeks. Two weeks?! I jerk the controls of the game and slam my fist on the punch button. This is ridiculous! I should have been practicing all summer. All I think about is girls, and I don't do anything about it. How can you dream about something twenty-four/seven and not take action? I've got to get over this now! I need to MIGHTY BLOW my shyness in the face!

In between the Vice City and Ms. Pac-Man games, I see Amber Lee (hands down, the hottest girl in my class) trying to get coins from the change machine. She's usually guarded by her friends Bitchy Nicky and Chubby Abby, so you can only get close enough to give her a nod or a "S'up?" in the halls. But she's all alone at the moment, unsuccessfully shoving a dollar bill into the old, picky machine. We started calling it the Devil Machine in seventh grade because it only gives you quarters if your dollar bill is perfect, faceup, and shipped directly from the U.S. Treasury that day. My game's not even close to over, but I see a window of opportunity that I've got to jump out of. Starting high school with a hottie on my arm would make things a lot easier.

I walk over with purpose. This must be the wave of confidence and maturity washing over me now. No need for practice, it's game time! I'm going to say something incredibly funny about the Devil Machine or the U.S. Treasury. I'll start simply with "Won't give you change?" I might lean on the Ms. Pac-Man machine, I might cross my arms, I haven't worked it all out.

Like a viper, I approach my prey from the rear. Her long hair spills over her pink tank top, probably just long enough to brush the tops of her boobs. It might be long enough to cover the whole boob, like one of those shampoo ads where the chick is naked but you can't see anything important, because her hair . . .

Dang it, Carter, focus on the task at hand! "Won't give you change?" That's your line, now say it! Be cool, be confident, but don't be cocky. I'm always spacing off—I'm afflicted with attention deficit disorder. Although it's a disease, my mom won't let me take the medicine. My best friend, EJ, over at the X-Men game, he takes the Ritalin. And you can tell when he forgets to take the stuff. Whew! He's like a rocket ship without a pilot. He has ADHD, though. It's a little different—you spaz out on top of the spacing off. I just space; I don't spaz. I'm old-school ADD. My mom says, "You're a dreamer, and there's nothing wrong with that." She makes me write things down to combat my disease. I jot down everything that seems important on my arm or hands. Some days I look like a Hells Angel I have so much stuff to remember.

I should have written "Won't give you change?" on my arm, because it's not flowing out like I want it to. I'm standing behind her like a friggin' stalker, but she hasn't noticed, so I'm still cool.

I'd love to stay on task, get my homework done, ace the test, get straight As, be the kid in class everybody tries to cheat off of. But the world seems to have a different plan for me. Why would they put windows in classrooms if I wasn't supposed to stare out of them? Why does Amber Lee have to wear short shorts, have tanned, shiny legs, and rock Reef flip-flops with pink toenails? Am I not supposed to gawk at her short shorts and wonder why there's no visible panty line? Did she forget to put underwear on this morning? I'm a pretty forgetful guy, but I always remember. Are they a new high-tech underwear that can't be detected by horny fourteen-year-old boys? Or are they the mother of all panties, the undergarment surely conceived by a god who loves to torment me: the G-string (Victoria's Secret, fall catalog, pages 12–15) a.k.a. butt floss or crack warmers. That's the only logical explanation back here.

The only thing standing between her butt cheeks and me is paper-thin denim and four little words: "Won't give you change?" Here we go! I fill my lungs with pepperoni-scented air and courage, but her panty line (or lack of) is short-circuiting my brain and scrambling the signals being sent to my mouth.

"W-w-w-w," I stutter. The W's caught! "W-w-wuh-woo," I continue. You've said it a thousand times. It's a simple word, just spit it out. The rest of the sentence will flow from the "won't." Take a deep breath, focus your energy, relax, and say the damn thing!

"W-w-w-wu-whh, woo," I stammer. She can't hear me, thank God, and nobody else is watching. I know this because, if they were, they would be pointing at me and pee-ing their pants.

I have a slight stutter; I've always had it. It's my older sister, Lynn's, fault. When I was a baby and just learning how to talk for myself, I would point at things and try to sound them out. I'd gesture toward the round object and say, "B-bu-buh." But before I could make the word for myself, Lynn would yell out "BALL!" and wreck my natural progress. She was everywhere! Like a swooping, toddler ninja, she would just appear and yell, "Hat!" or "Cookie!" when I wanted something. After a while I stopped using the hand signals and tried to identify the object without her knowing. However, I'd feel her watching and try to speed up the process in my tiny brain, and I'd s-s-stutter! My parents always laugh about it: "Baby Carter would try to so hard to get those words out, and little Lynn just wouldn't have it!"

Really great parenting, I'd say: torture for sport! And here I am, thirteen years later, creating a wind tunnel in the Pizza Barn arcade room because of it.

"W-whh-wou," I continue to stammer. She finally turns around to see who's blowing on her.

She smiles at me (thank God) and asks, "Carter, what're you doing?"

Won't (or any other word with the letter *W*) is not going to work for me. So I cut to the chase, nod my head as coolly as possible, and mutter the word "Change?" That's it, boy! Nix the fluff. "Change!" That's what you want!

"OhmyGod, you're waiting for the change machine?" she says. "Sorry, my dollar is retarded. You go ahead."

Dang it! I don't have any money. Language isn't working, so action will have to do. I grab the dollar from her like a mugger in a dark alley and move toward the Devil Machine. I see a corner that's bent and a hairline crease— either one could be the problem. I run the bill over the side of a table to smooth out any imperfections. I think I've got it, but you can never be too careful with this machine. I look like a total expert. My buddy Nutt's older brother, Bart, says that women like it when a man takes charge. Well, I'm in charge of everything here . . . except my hand. Which is shaking like I'm trying to develop a friggin' Polaroid! Stop screwing this up. This is it, Carter: you can kick open the door of high school holding hands with Amber Lee, or you can be a loser and die a virgin! It's up to you.

I summon Bruce Lee, Jackie Chan, Dragon Ball Z, and all the masters of discipline. I need strength through calm and serenity. I have to quiet the demons in my hand. *Stop shaking, you worthless, good-for-nothing club, or I'll cut you off with Dad's chop saw!* I lift the bill like a feather, and with all of my focus I slide the dollar into the old machine and, *Zher—Zer—Zhar!* Four quarters fall out. Yes!

"Oh, thank you, Carter," she cheers.

"Cool," I say as I hand her the quarters. "I-I-I start football tomorrow."

Girls love that. Football. You could be the biggest geek in the school, but sign up for football, and all the sudden you're cool. It's the only reason I play the stupid game.

"Yeah, cheerleading too," Amber says. "Oh, it's gonna be sooo hot."

"YEAH, HOT!" I reply, way too loud. Dang it! Watch the volume. You're doing fine. We're having a conversation, and I'm fully participating! She's wearing a tank top that says "Girl Power" right across her boobs, and I'm not affected by it at all. Amber doesn't have lady boobs yet. They're still girl boobs, but with mucho potential. Sooo nice. Boobs don't freak me out as bad as they did in seventh grade, but they can still short-circuit the mainframe from time to time.

Girl Power is officially controlling my mind at this point. Amber Lee could rule the world with her powers! Girl Power could start a revolution. I'd totally join. Dang it! I haven't said anything for like, a whole minute. I'm just staring at her chest.

I've got to come up with something else to say or she's going to think I'm retarded, so I blabber, "Um, like, hey, d-du-do you w-w-want to go to the pool? Or see a movie or something, sometime? In general, or you know, like, with me?"

I just said it. Holy crap! All the TV I watch is finally paying off. Just like in a movie, I'm the cool guy! . . . I think . . . I thought. But I may see something I don't like. Is that panic? Panic in her beautiful green eyes? She hates me and would rather eat a turd than go to the movies with me.

She laughs. I must be making a painful face.

I laugh too. "Ha-ha!" Yeah, just joking! Of course I'm joking; why would I want to go out with you? I've only been in love with you since the first day of sixth grade.

"No," she says softly. "Carter, I, uh, my dad won't let me go out with boys."

"Oh, y-yeah, it's cool," I reply as unfazed as I can. My insides, however, are screaming from the pain of rejection. I shoot her a weird thumbs-up as if to say, "No sweat. I'll just get in touch after college, maybe."

Amber walks away from me and out of the arcade really fast. My heart sinks into my stomach, out my legs, and right through my Pumas. It went away, and it'll never return. In the second Indiana Jones movie, a pharaoh type of guy shoves his hand into a slave guy's chest and pulls his still-beating heart out, and then shows it to the guy. According to Mr. Trimmer, my health teacher, and the Discovery Channel, if somebody sticks their hand inside your chest and pulls your heart out, you're a goner before they can show it to you. But that is wrong! Because my still-beating life force is flopping around the dirty carpet, heading for the door. This sucks and it hurts! I want to cry. I want to vomit up my pizza. I'll never see her panties or what gives her the Girl Power. That realization hits me hard, but then EJ turns around from the X-Men game and punches me in the arm really hard.

He yells, "High score, douche bag! Beat that."

There's nothing like being called a feminine hygiene product to keep you from crying.

2. Slappy, the Pool Boy

EJ and I lock up our bikes in front of the Merrian Pool and stroll through the side gate like we own the joint. It's packed. Only twelve days left before the big day, and everybody is soaking up the last rays of freedom. I hate the long lines at the diving boards, but I like the additional hotties on the lounge chairs.

I love the Merrian Pool like no place else in the world. I'm kind of a big deal here because I came in second at the all-city swim meet, and I'll be a junior lifeguard next year. I hang out here so much it's like I'm working already, but I don't get paid, and nobody does what I tell them to.

We peel off sweaty T-shirts and give a nod to our boys Nutt, Hormone, Doc, Levi, and Bag, who're already going off the diving boards with some older dudes. Amber Lee is holding court on the lounge chairs with Bitchy Nicky, Chubby Abby, and the rest of the Merrian Junior High chicks.

As I kick off my grass-stained Nikes, I hear a familiar screeching sound coming through the fence. I turn to see EJ's mom yelling, "Emilio . . . EMILIO!!! You put on your sunscreen!" through the chain links. My jaw drops at the thought of his imminent humiliation, but he just coolly turns his back and walks toward the dive well. Nobody's called EJ "Emilio" since kindergarten, so no one knows who the crazy lady is yelling at. Only I can spot his bright red ears giving away his mortification. She's a surrogate parent to me—has fed me, helped me with homework, cleaned up my vomit, taken me on vacations—I dare say I love the woman. But I follow EJ's lead and completely ignore her existence. She futilely hollers, "You're not to have any soda today, young man!" to no one, and eventually backs away in defeat.

I've seen my mom's car in the parking lot a few times this summer, but she never gets out and embarrasses me. Parenting seems to be a learned skill that requires constant effort on the kids' part. I have Lynn to thank for my folks' coolness. She's such a psycho that they're scared to death most of the time and don't mess with me. When she was in seventh grade, a teacher put her in charge of the "fashion police" during an assembly just for fun. The fun stopped when she arrested and interrogated twenty-three girls, then called the Merrian P.D. for backup. Compared to her, they think I'm a perfect child. I can't walk in the house, crack open a beer, and pop in a porno or anything, but I've been riding the mile and a half to the pool by myself since I was nine.

I give EJ a subtle fist bump as we watch Nick Brock, a six-foot-five, two-hundred-fifty-pound, All-American senior linebacker go off the high dive. He bounces down so low, everybody gasps in anticipation of the board snapping in half. It doesn't; instead it shoots his massive frame into orbit. He pauses in midair—like gravity stops working when you're that high—then pulls his muscle-bound legs into his huge pecs, falls back to earth, and busts the biggest cannonball of all time. *BOOOM!* The splash covers the deck, and everybody's stuff gets soaked. Everyone "Oh"s and "Ah"s accordingly.

"You know we'll be going to school with that guy?" EJ whispers in disbelief.

I don't like to focus on such things, so I let my eyes drift up to the lifeguard stands, where the hottest chicks in the world are perched for our protection. They have real names, but we call them Pam, Yasmine, and Jemma. The city of Merrian may own the pool, but these girls rule it. Last year the city introduced a new swimsuit for female guards. The one-piece grandma suit wasn't cutting it anymore, so they broke out the two-piece model. An official bikini! Since then, fat girls who want to lifeguard have to start working out or find a different pool. Teenage guys from all over the area show up at Merrian Pool now, like it's church. Religious attendance, absolute devotion, and everybody wants to get saved. Cracking voices holler out, "Praise the Lord!" all day long.

Pam's on duty in the dive well. Her real name is Kammie Sparks. She's Bag's older sister and she's positively the hottest girl I've ever seen walking around talking to people. She's permatan and buff. She stretches the LIFEGUARD written across her chest so tight that we all wait impatiently for the day when her boobs finally bust out of their Lycra jail and make our wet dreams come true.

Pam sensually wipes Nick Brock's splash off her thighs and looks down at EJ and me gawking up at her. "What's up, Heartbreaker?" she asks me.

That's what she calls me. "Nothin' much," I say, rubbing my chin to make sure I don't have any drool on it.

"Where's your girlfriend?" she asks, knowing full well I don't have one.

"Oh, she's out there somewhere," I reply.

Pam is soooo far out of my league that I can talk to her without stuttering. I love to gawk at her, but for some reason I can be myself around her.

"You'll be a heartbreaker someday." She laughs.

I wouldn't break her heart for a million dollars.

"So, is today the day?" she asks.

"What, the day I get a girlfriend?"

"Is today the day you're finally going to do that gainer?" she inquires.

A gainer is a reverse flip into a can opener, and it separates the men from the boys at the Merrian Pool. I can do a front flip, back flip, side flip, twisting flip, one-and-a-half, and I've landed a double twice, but most attempts of a gainer have resulted in a *SMACK!* Flesh meets water, hard, fast, and flat. I love nothing more than seeing one of my boys bust one, but I can't stand it myself. Two things I can't handle: pain and humiliation. The smack delivers both.

The gainer keeps me up at night. I've tried and tried, but I always chicken out. I nicked my head on the end of the diving board last year, so the thought of cracking my skull open and spilling my brains into the water is very real for me, and it puts the air brakes on every time. The older guys and lifeguards can all do it. My buddy Bag can bust a gainer off the high dive, and he gets mad respect because of it. EJ was close to doing one off the low dive in July, but he smacked really hard and hasn't attempted one since. I hadn't given it much thought, but today would be a great day to land a gainer.

As we step to the back of the lines, the Skeleton drops an insane, style-filled gainer with a huge splash off the high dive. His real name is Paul Skelton; he's Yasmine's boyfriend. He's tall and skinny and has a skull tattoo on his back. The Skeleton was a lifeguard last year, but he's working construction this year because it pays more, and dating Yasmine is expensive. He's still the undisputed king of the diving boards, though. He can do a triple flip off the high dive—need I say more?

I make my first attempt off the low dive, and nobody suspects a thing. I jump high, throw my arms back, arch my spine, suck my legs into my chest, and totally chicken out. I pull myself out of it, twist and flop into the water like nothing happened. Slight smack with the legs, but it could have been worse. I get out of the water slowly and look around. EJ's eyes are all big. Of course EJ noticed. My mom says we share a brain.

He asks, "Dude, are you really goin' for a gainer?"

I don't even look at him when I reply, "Yep," and go to the back of the line.

"All right, let's do it!" EJ says.

I didn't ask for a partner, but it's okay. It's just more fuel on my fire. Now it's definitely ON! But the second attempt is another victory for my inner chicken. EJ goes right after me, and it's not pretty, but he throws his arms back, arches his spine, sucks his knees into his chest, rolls over, and flops into the water feetfirst. He's done it! No can opener, so it's not technically a gainer, but a reverse flip at the least.

Pam yells, "Yeah, EJ! Gainer!"

I want to yell, "Not technically!" But he's my best friend and I'm not a hater, so I let it slide.

I guess I'm proud of him too, but I can't just ignore the crime that's been committed here. The outright theft. My thunder has been stolen! Now I must do it. I stand on the board and think it through. The approach, the suck, the roll, the potential for smacking, the odds of brain damage, the possibility of humiliation, and the undeniable opportunity for glory.

I meditate about a second too long, and people have taken notice that I'm about to do something of note. Everybody gets really quiet. I'd better do something. My public is waiting. I make the approach, I bounce down and jump up as high as I can. I throw my head back, arch my spine, and suck my knees up perfectly. This is it! No turning back. You got it! Oh, but it's rolling a little slower than I'd like. I'm laid out flat, looking for the water. Not seeing the wa—*SMACK!* My back hits flat. My flesh screams. I hear the "Ohh"s from the lounge chairs. *Don't cry, dude!* I swim to the ladder in painful disgrace. That'll be the last attempt of the day. Owww! I'm walking back to the line behind the low dive, thinking about doing my famous twisty flip to redeem myself, hoping my back isn't half as red as it feels, when I hear someone behind me say, "Awesome, man!"

It didn't come from my friends. We don't do compliments or encouragement. We "burn," we "dog," but under no circumstances do we support one another. It was the Skeleton.

"You're soo close, bro! This next one is it, dog!" he says.

"Uh, I don't know," I say with hesitation, feeling the nerves in my back scream, "No way!"

"You can't stop now, man!" the Skeleton argues. "I've

seen you do every trick in the book. All you need is the gainer, right?"

He knows me. The Skeleton knows my potential, and he wants me to be great. "You gotta go off the high dive, dog!" he says.

"What? You're crazy, dude!" I say. Did I just call the Skeleton crazy? No stutter or anything; it just flew right out.

"Yeah, you under-rotated," he says. "You'd have landed that last one easily off the high dive. You could even stick the can opener if you bust off of the high!"

The Skeleton let the "crazy" comment slide, but he's serious. And he has a point. "Y-y-you think?" I ask. He might be right. No need to rotate faster if you raise the bar eight feet or so. I would be a legend if I stuck a full gainer off the high dive on my first attempt. Nobody would even remember EJ's weak-ass reverse flip.

"Yeah." The Skeleton nods. "Go for it!"

He says, "Go for it!" not so much like my dad's encouraging "Go for it." But more like, "I'll kill you if you don't 'go for it.'" I slowly climb the ladder, trying desperately to control the shaking in my body. My hands and feet are busy climbing, but my chest's like a paint mixer at the hardware store. When I get to the top I say, "It's cold," in case anyone notices the tremors. Ninety-two degrees, but I'm chilly.

I hear the Skeleton ask EJ my name, and then he starts the chant I've always wanted to hear: "Car-ter, CAR-TER, CAR-TER!" The girls on the lounge chairs sit up. Pam's calling out my name with everybody else. "CAR-TER, CAR-TER, CAR-TER!"

I'm not thinking at all when I take the first step toward

greatness. I make the approach like somebody's behind me with a bazooka. I spring off the board like a rocket being shot out into space. I stiffly throw my head back. I suck my legs up into my chest with every scrap of power in my body. I roll over and open my eyes. Yes, there it is! The water. I'm not going to die. I can hear the people gasp at how cool I am. Then it happens . . . the seed of doubt shoots up and springs out.

The seed yells, *Carter, what are you doing? A gainer off the high dive? You just turned fourteen, who do you think you are?*

I hit the air brakes. I press the chicken button as hard as I can. But gravity has my number and it's calling! I flex every muscle in my body trying to stop. Pam's squeal turns to a terrified scream.

A familiar voice yells, "Oh, God!"

The voice is my own, and this is going to be bad. I hear more screams from the onlookers, and then all sounds are drowned out by the *SSMMAAACKK!!!*

My face hits the water the exact moment my chest, stomach, thighs, and feet smack down. Perfectly level. Arms out, legs spread like an inverted, retarded snow angel in the middle of summer. I don't even think I'm wet. I just bounce off the water like it's concrete. The sting in my back goes away instantly as the entire front side of my body screams in pain. I'm sure the flesh has just ripped off my stomach.

I'll just float here for a minute and try to collect myself. Oh, this isn't good. I'm hurt! Not just my pride, either; my will to live is broken. I can't move. If I move, I'll cry. The wind is knocked out of me . . . all of it! I need air, so I lift my head out of the water, breathe in the shame, and let out a wail. "Aaahhhh!!!" I sob like a five-year-old girl. I choke on some water and look up at Pam, who's standing beside her lifeguard chair staring down at me with concern.

She gives me a nod as if to ask, "Are you okay?"

My crinkled-up face, coughing lungs, and teary eyes have to be giving her the *Hell NO, I'm not gonna make it, Pam. Come and rescue me!* look.

She springs off the lifeguard stand like a big-breasted angel coming to save me. She swoops underneath me and slides her tanned arm across my throbbing chest. She pulls my lifeless body to the edge of the pool without any assistance from me. I'm way too busy making an ass of myself in front of a hundred kids, less than two weeks before I start HIGH SCHOOL! I take a break from my agony and shame to feel the greatness that is Pam's boob on the back of my head. This isn't the way I would've liked for it to happen, but feeling a boob is feeling a boob.

I climb out of the pool and grab my stuff. Some smart-ass yells, "Bu-bye, Slappy!" as I limp toward the exit gate. This little black mark is going on my permanent record. Not any sort of document the school hangs on to, but the kind of thing my boys will break out years from now to have a good laugh at my expense. Maybe someday I'll be able to laugh about it with them, but today isn't that day. I unlock my bike in defeat and try to regain feeling in my face. The bright red of my back is only matched by the purpley blues radiating from my front.

My dad always says, "When you fall off a horse, you've got to get right back on." And I will get back up on that horse/high dive. Next summer.

3. Kickin' It

I wasn't lying to Amber Lee; I really am on the football team. Not because I like it or anything. Every summer, like a zombie, I just sign up. I wanted to play when I was little because of the "costume" (cleats, shoulder pads, and black makeup under the eyes), but that wore off after the first week. Running around in ninety-degree heat with a giant plastic hat and twenty pounds of protective gear will do that. All of my friends seem to love it, and people are always sort of impressed when I tell them I'm on the team. I never mention that I don't play very much and I'd really just like to be the kicker. If I were the kicker, I could come to practice one day a week and just show up for games. I'd save the day with my clutch fifty-yard field goals and get carried off the field after every game.

As it is now, I'm not the kicker. I'm the second string right guard (like the deodorant) on the line. I've always been a lineman because I was a "heavy" kid. Mom preferred the term "stocky." A guy at a clothing store called me "husky" once, and it made me cry. I'm not really heavy, husky, or stocky anymore these days, thanks to my growth spurt over the summer. With five extra inches I'm looking more like "tall guy" than "stocky boy," so I shouldn't have to be on the line anymore. There's no glory on the line. I want to be the quarterback, the running back . . . the KICKER! I want people to watch me. To know that I'm on the team. Not just because I'm in the team photo and I wear my jersey on game day, but because they saw me make an unbelievable catch, pass, tackle, or kick. They heard some other kid telling another kid about how awesome my moves were. They saw it in slow motion on the six o'clock sports report, where the newsman said, "Carter was unstoppable!" or something else menacing like that. Kids will talk behind my back about how cool I am, and I'll look at them like I'm all annoyed, but on the inside I'll be stoked when they gossip about my greatness.

For now, though, I only play in the games if my buddy Hormone gets tired or hurt. And then I simply go out and try to smash into the kid who lines up in front of me. That's it. That's the game as I see it. Coach chatters on about "strategy" and "teamwork." He draws Xs and Os on the chalkboard and blathers about "plays" and "holes," and I have no idea what he's talking about. I space off and think about that movie *Holes*, and how it would suck to dig holes all day in the desert. If I were the quarterback or like, a running back, though, I would know all of the plays and exactly when and why the Xs and Os go where they do. I'd pay attention to every last detail and I'd focus on it all day long, so I could be the best. But since I only have to smash into the kid in front of me, what's the point?

This season is going to be different, though. Because I've got a plan. We start weight training tomorrow, and I'm going to work out three hours a day, seven days a week, until I'm GINORMOUS! I'll crush anybody who comes up against me, and if that doesn't work, I'm also going to be the kicker for sure.

For phase one of the football plan, I ride my bike to an open field by my house with three old footballs and a makeshift holder in a laundry bag. The holder is supposed to mimic a guy holding the ball after it's hiked. I built this triangle device out of a blue plastic oar that came with my inflatable boat. I cut it into three pieces and duct taped it all together. It works a lot better than EJ ever did, but I'm pretty screwed the next time I want to use that boat. I'll just row around in a circle with my one oar. But by next summer I'll be so famous as a kicker that no one will care that I'm rowing in a circle all the time.

My contraption works so awesome, I'm probably going to make a whole bunch of them and sell them to the NFL for millions of dollars. I mean, how much money would they save by not having to pay a guy to hold the ball for the kicker all the time? How many kickers out there right now are waiting for their holder to show up? And he might not hold it steady if and when he does finally show up. He might try to make a Charlie Brown joke when you go to kick it (Bag), and pull the ball away just as you're about to blast the sucker fifty yards. Instead of glory, you fly up in the air and smash down to the ground on your butt in agonizing, humiliating pain. Or he might run off after only three kicks to chase a butterfly (EJ). If you're going to be a famous kicker, you can't have distractions. You've got to be focused.

So the ball's all set up. I take three steps back and two steps to the left, like they do on TV. I stare the ball down like it's an old enemy who has come a great distance to fight me again. I'll smash the WILSON off this ball! I'll split the stitches. This piece of leather is going to regret the day it was made into a football and not, like, a coat or pair of shoes. (It may not actually be leather, it's probably Naugahyde or pleather or something.)

After about ten minutes of staring at this stupid ball and getting psyched up, I realize I've been standing here spacing off and staring at a football for ten minutes. I take my first step with great purpose; the second step is even better than the first. I plant my foot really close to the ball. I cock my foot back like the most powerful ninja of all time. I close my eyes and swing my leg through with all the force I have. I feel my foot collide hard with something other than Naugahyde, and I hear the crunch and tear of duct tape. I open my eyes to see my kicking contraption flying through the air in pieces. It flies for about five yards and tumbles to the ground in a heap. The ball is just lying there untouched. Whoops. I guess you've got to keep your eyes open.

I should just pack this crap up and go to the pool, but that would be pretty weak even for me. So I tape the device back together and set it up again. I keep my eyes open this time and kick the ball about ten yards, straight to the left. An imaginary referee laughs at me and makes the sign for "No good." Ugh, this is pointless! I'm going to the pool. But as I'm packing up my balls, I hear my mom's voice (she's not following me or anything, I just hear her in my head. Like the imaginary referee). "Carter, nothing good comes easy," she says. "Adversity is just opportunity in work clothes."

The next ball goes about ten yards again, but this time it's straight. And straight is good! The imaginary referee lifts his arms high above his head and yells, "It's good!" It's not far enough to be good for much, but it's a start. And each time I kick, the ball's going a little bit farther than the last. It's not going fifty yards yet. I don't think it's going even twenty. To be honest, I'm not sure how far a yard is, but if I practice every day, I'll be hitting them from fifty yards easy.

4. GINORMOUS Struggle!

Pre-football workouts begin for incoming freshmen. The older guys have been working out all summer, so we've got a lot of catching up to do. The coaches show us how to lift the weights properly, but I don't need any help. My dad and I have worked out at the community center five times already, and I've seen about a million Bally commercials on TV. Those chicks are hot and strong, and they do NOT work out in the Merrian High gym. All we get is an occasional softball chick.

We're only supposed to do two body parts each day and start out "light" so we don't hurt ourselves or get burned out, but I want to get jacked! Going light will never get me huge. So I'm doing all of the exercises . . . today! And if you want to get GINORMOUS, you've got to go heavy! That big, mean-looking kid from Hawkus middle school who stared me down at the Pizza Barn is using the big weights like the older guys, but the rest of us freshman are just using the bar or like, the littlest bitty weights. We look sooo weak.

"We're not gonna get anywhere just lifting the bar, dude," I explain to EJ, who seems to have his doubts. "If you want to be a wuss, then let's do the small weights. People will always pick on us, girls will never talk to us, but we'll always have each other, dog," I say.

EJ has no argument for that, so we start loading up the bar. I think a safe place to start is with the second heaviest weights. And we're kicking it off with bench press. "How much ya' bench?" We're about to find out. I lift the bar with one hundred and fifteen pounds on it. JEEEZZZ! It's heavier than I thought it'd be. My arms are starting to shake like a Tickle Me Elmo doll. I'd better put this bar back where I found it.

Then EJ barks out all the encouragement I need: "Let's go, you pussy!"

With that I try to lower the weight slowly to my chest. The *lower* part I did really well, but the *slowly* part is going to take some work. The bar crashes into my chest like my arms aren't even there. It knocks the wind out of me. All of it!

"Uuhhh!" I wheeze in pain.

My spotter seems to think something is funny back there. EJ laughs and tries to lift the weight off me, to no avail.

"Lift it off me, punk!" I whine, still trying to push.

"I can't, dude!" he says through the laughter.

"You've got to help me!" I scream, and kick my legs.

Even I think that's funny, and now I'm laughing. EJ stops lifting so he can do an impression of me. "You gotta help meee!" he wheezes through the shakes and tears rolling down his face.

I'm starting to panic. He tries to squat down and lift the weight with his legs. But with just gym shorts on he's basically sticking his nuts in my face and jumping up and down laughing.

"Dude, get your nuts out of my face!" I cry out.

This gets the attention of a few other kids, who are now looking our way. This is not what I had in mind by "getting pumped." I'm just trying to breathe at this point, and I stop pushing. Which is a big mistake, because the bar rolls toward my neck. I'm turning blue, and so is EJ, from laughing so hard.

Then, out of nowhere, Nick Brock throws EJ out of the way and lifts the bar off my neck with one hand. He slams the weight back onto the rack and points his muscular finger at my red face. "Quit jackin' around, you twerps!" he yells, and goes back to his thousand-pound workout.

Dang it! I'm even redder from embarrassment than from lack of oxygen. EJ was the one who was "jackin' around." I was just trying to survive.

"Let's do this, EJ," I say as I load the bar with tiny weights.

I'll show Nick Brock I'm serious. I'll do every pully and press thing. I'll lift every weight (the little ones) in this place! I want to make sure Nick Brock sees I'm not "jackin' around"! And I won't be a twerp for long.

The next morning

Oh God. I can't move. Dang it! I'm paralyzed. I've paralyzed myself. "MOM!!! Mommy??? Mom, I can't move!" I yell to nobody.

I'm going to have to do this alone. I'm so alone. I am sooo sore! I think my muscles are going to rip off of my bones if I move even an inch. I try to sit up, but my stomach is just a worthless ball of pain. I roll out of bed, crash onto the floor, and crawl toward the hall. I finally get to the bathroom but can't support myself to pee. I've got to sit down and do this chick style. Owwww! The muscles in my butt don't like the hard toilet seat one bit. My dad must have heard me screaming, because he's waiting for me when I hobble down the stairs.

"What's the matter with you?" he asks.

"I . . . Muscles . . . Ahh . . . Huge. Pain," I attempt to explain.

He gives me a handful of Advil and tells me to stretch as much as I can. Stretch? If I stretch, the muscles will come off. I have "Workout—Get Huge" written on my hand, but I think I'll go to the pool instead.

5. Tig Ol' Bitties

I didn't even have to ride my bike to the pool today because Hormone picked me up in his NEW CAR! The car's not even close to new, and he doesn't have a driver's license, but his dad said he was sick of driving him around, and got him this little Honda CRX. (Having divorced parents isn't all bad.) It only has two seats, but somehow Hormone, Nutt, EJ, Doc, Levi, and I have squeezed in, and we've still got to pick up Bag.

We all limp through the front gates, and I'd swear that Amber Lee, Chubby Abby, and Bitchy Nicky are checking me out as we hobble past the lounge chairs. Only one day in the gym and I'm already getting noticed. My chest is one big bruise, but it's looking pretty swollen too. They're checking out my pecs! Either that or my trunks are up my butt or something.

I struggle to get my shirt off, when EJ points at my chest and asks, "Hey, are you sore right here?"

Before I can respond—*WHAAAMM!*—he punches me in the left pec as hard as he can. Oh, it hurts sooo bad. I can't make a noise loud enough to express my feelings, so I just kneel down on the concrete. My boys howl with laughter. I plan my revenge.

❀   ❀   ❀

We swim around for a little bit to get the blood flowing and then hit the snack bar. Bitchy Nicky marches up to our table like somebody has pissed her off, and in a loud cheerleader voice demands, "Carter, I need to talk to you."

"S-s-sh-sure," I reply, wondering what the hell I've done.

My boys say nothing, but suspicions are up, and questions will abound when I return.

We walk toward the baby pool, and she informs me, "You know, Carter, I have a friend who's into you."

What the hell? I thought I'd killed her dog by the way she stomped up to us. "Yeah, w-w-wh-who?" I ask, but I know who it is. Amber Lee's been kicking herself for shooting me down. She's decided to disobey her father and run away with me.

"Yeah, my friend Abby thinks you're the bomb," she says with a smile.

Abby? Who the hell is Ab . . . ? "Chu . . . Abby, huh?" I ask my feet.

Chubby Abby? She's on the drill team. Drill team is where girls go when they get cut from the cheerleading squad for being too fat. Abby is not one of the fattest ones, but she's not exactly skinny, either. She's cute, though. She sang at the talent show in seventh grade. She was awesome at first, but twelve- and thirteen-year-olds are not the supporters of the arts she had hoped. We started to throw things at her, and she ran off the stage crying. Man, I don't want to go out with Chubby Abby. I want to run away with Amber Lee!

"Uh, cool," I say, trying not to make a face.

"Do you like her?" she asks, like a junior detective in a bikini.

Of course not! My friends will totally make fun of me if I go out with Chubby Abby.

"I-I-I dunno, yeah, I mean sure, Abby's cool," I say.

Why did I say that? I don't want to get poor Abby's hopes up and then shatter them when she finds out I'm not into her.

"Are you going to Maria's party tonight?" she asks.

"Yeah," I say.

"Well, we'll see you there," she says, and then scurries away. She's wearing a towel around her waist, but you can still tell Nicky has a nice butt. Why couldn't it be Nicky who's into me?

I totally brought this on myself. I had English and home ec with Abby last year, and I was always talking to her. Chicks think that just because you're talking to them you want to get married or something. I was always cracking jokes and making her laugh. You see, Abby doesn't scramble the mainframe or cause the stutter, because I'm not into her! I'm not trying to impress her with my razor wit. I'm not worried about what she thinks. I wish I could like her, because she dresses really cool and she can crack a mean joke as well. She used to call Ms. Porter "Ms. Porno" right to her face. Abby's real smart, so nobody would think she would bust a porno joke. She'd say it under her breath, like, "Ms. Porno, I don't get where the adverb is." And when Ms. Porter got to yelling at some kid with her lisp, Abby would put up an imaginary umbrella to protect herself from the spray. I started doing it too, because that's funny. In home ec, I'd pretend to be the Swedish Chef from *Sesame Street* and yell, "Morgan-A-Morgan-ah-MORG!" as I was chopping vegetables up and shooting them all over the room.

The teacher would yell, "Carter! KNIFE!!! Knife, Mr. Carter!" But Abby thought it was funny. If I liked her, I'd never have busted a *Sesame Street* joke in front of her.

I sheepishly walk back to my boys, who turn into a flock of hens before my eyes. We're some of the toughest guys in our class, but you'd never know it today.

"S'up with that, Carter?" EJ asks, full of suspicion.

"Was she asking you about me?" Nutt asks.

"No, nothin', she just told me that Chubby Abby's into me." I shrug like this happens every day.

A gasp flies into the air. I know what's coming next: they're going to start crowing on me and making fun of Abby. But that doesn't happen.

"You know Chubby Abby isn't so chubby anymore," Bag observes.

"Yeah, she's still got those tig ol' bitties, though!" Nutt adds, and high-fives Bag.

I don't remember Abby having . . . wait a minute! Abby does have pretty big boobs. I was staring at them on the second to last day of school last year. I'd forgotten all about them. How is that possible?

"That's hot fresh meat, dog!" Doc yells.

Nutt does a little dance, squeezes some imaginary fruit, then sings, "Ol' Carter's gonna get that juicy juice. He's gonna get that juicy juice!"

We all laugh at him for being such a tard, then walk back to our spot by the diving boards, right past Abby, Nicky, and Amber. They don't seem to notice us. Which is weird because we basically do a drive-by shooting. Shooting a thousand looks at Abby's boobies. And damned if they aren't tig ol' bitties! And she isn't so chubby. She's solid and nicely featured in a brown bikini. Her boobs must have gotten warm or something, or her gawk alert is going off from seven guys not so subtly staring at her chest at the same time. She turns beet red and rolls over onto her stomach, and lo and behold, baby's got back, too! It's as if she's saying, "You think my fun bags are nice, Carter? Check out the junk in my trunk!"

I didn't talk to her or anything, but I did bust my double flip off the low dive. No smack. She had to have been impressed.

6. Lynn's Holy Grail of Chick Knowledge

School starts in nine days, but I'm going to my first high school party tonight! It's just going to be freshmen (and Maria's parents too), but it's completely different. I'm going to have sex tonight, I'm pretty sure. I ransack my closet trying to find the perfect ensemble. I try on a couple of things, but everything I own is so junior high. It's got to be perfect. It's got to scream "SEX!" I want to stand out. I want to be a new man. A man chicks can't resist.

Mom and Lynn found out about the party because I have "party at Maria's" written on my hand. They must have sensed my wardrobe struggle, because Lynn just burst into my room and threw a new shirt at me. It's simple and cool, and it matches my Nike Shox. She tells me I have to wear jeans with it and to stand up the collar, but I tell her, "That's gay."

She smiles and replies, "No, Carter, writing 'deodorant' and 'party at Maria's' on your hand . . . that's gay. Who's the girl?"

"W-what? I don't know anything about any g-g-girl," I stammer.

"Carter, you've been getting dressed for an hour, and you have an entire tube of my gel in your hair—Who is the girl?" she demands.

I tell her how Nicky said that Abby's into me, and she gets all excited. "Oh my God! I have step class with Abby, she is sooo cute," Lynn squeals. "Wow! I can't believe she likes you."

I hear a crashing sound from downstairs, and my mom yells, "What's not to like? Carter is charming, smart, confident, funny, handsome . . ." and all that crap she's always spouting.

"Whatever, just be cool and don't lunge at her or anything," Lynn orders.

"I'm not gonna lunge at anyone," I reply (I don't think). "I don't even really like her; she's too—"

"Too what?" Lynn barks. "You'd better not say *fat*, because she's not. Abby's skinnier than I am, and I'm not fat! Abby's more like, voluptuous."

"Voluptuous" must be the female equivalent to "husky" for guys.

I'm thinking about writing "no lunging" on my hand as I back away from the conversation and stroll out the front door.

"Hey, playboy," Lynn says as I pull my bike out of the garage. She has a strange expression on her face. If I didn't know her better as a scourge of humanity and the permanent thorn in my side since birth, I'd think she's coming at me with genuine concern.

"Just because Nicky says Abby's into you doesn't give you the right to be a jerk. Abby isn't some slut you're just gonna have sex with," she explains.

What? Obviously she doesn't know the Abby I saw this afternoon at the pool.

"She's a cool girl, and if you really don't like her, don't mess with her," she continues. "You should like her, though, because Lord knows when another girl will be delusional enough to express interest in you."

If this is just going to be an abuse session, my friends are waiting for me to do this very thing at a party. I throw my leg over the seat, but Lynn grabs my handlebars, looks me in the eye, and drops her Holy Grail of Chick Knowledge on me.

"Just talk to her," she says. "If you feel yourself trying to brag or be impressive, just stop and ask her a question— a question about her! Ask about drill team. Ask about her singing. Find something about her that you think is especially cute tonight and compliment her on it. Not her boobs or her butt, Carter! Just stick to her clothes or jewelry for tonight. Her hair and her eyes come later. And even if her shoes or toes are cute, don't say anything about them. Some girls think it's weird if you like feet. So avoid the subject. And only one compliment, two at the most! You don't want to cross over into stalker territory. If you run out of things to talk about, just ask her another question. The question is your bread and butter. Got it? Don't try to get her drunk or drag her into some back room, bathroom, or shed!"

We may be crossing over into some personal stuff here, where guys have treated her with less than respect. She notices that I've spaced off, and flicks my ear back into the moment.

"Ouch!"

"Just don't be a horn dog," she continues. "Abby's meeting you at a party; you're not on a date. You've got to play it cool if you want to get anywhere later. Don't seem too interested. Let her come to you a bit, but don't seem like you're uninterested, either!"

"Defense!" I say.

"What?" she asks.

"Like, in football or basketball when you play defense, you're just reacting to what the other guy is doing," I explain.

"Yeah, that works, but try not to use sports metaphors in romantic situations," she suggests.

"Okay," I reply.

"This is tricky stuff," she says. "Your little ADD brain might short-circuit during the process, but if you can find the balance, you'll get a hell of a lot farther a hell of a lot quicker."

"You mean I can have sex with her sooner if I do all this stuff right . . . right?" I ask.

"Focus!" Lynn barks. "Blow her off a little bit. Talk to your friends some, and then talk to her some. Be cool. Talk about school, football, movies, and above all . . . HER! Don't talk about farting, sex, or video games. If you get lost, ask another question. Now, if it's going well, kiss her good night. Don't try to suck her face all night, though. And if it *is* going well, you *have* to kiss her good night. Don't chicken out! If you do, she'll think that you don't like her. When you feel it's time, take her by the hand and get away from your friends."

"But how will my boys know that I made out with her?" I interrupt.

She flicks my ear again and asks, "What do you care what those dorks think?"

I shrug and say, "I don't care what they think; I'm just saying it would be easier to prove like, in a court of law or something, that I made out with a chick if I had eye witnesses. But I totally get what you're saying. When it's time to get busy . . . break out."

She shakes her head, pinches the bridge of her nose, and seethes, "You know, you don't deserve this information."

"Probably not, but please continue," I say politely.

"Okay, where was I?" she asks.

"Take her hand, get away from . . ." I respond.

"Right. Hand holding: if your hands are sweaty, try to wash them with soap and very hot water before any hand holding; it cuts the sweating in half. Now, about the kiss. Don't grab her by the face and shove your tongue down her throat! Focus on the lips. You don't want any slobber or tongue action anywhere outside of the lips. Nobody wants a baby calf coming at them with a foot-long tongue. Try to close your eyes if you can. If your eyes are open it means you don't trust her. But if you start to get dizzy, go ahead and open your eyes—you don't want to fall down. Always give a peck before tongue. Maybe two pecks if she's really nervous. But don't do three! Three pecks just means that you're scared and you don't know what you're doing."

I raise my hand. After a moment's deliberation, she nods that I have the right to ask a question.

"Yeah, I'm wondering about the 'no grabbing of the face,' and the 'no shoving of the tongue.' Because that's exactly what Nutt's brother, Bart, and Bag say to do. Bart even showed us a make-out montage on his laptop, and every time Keanu, Brad, or Tom kiss a chick, they lead with the hand, secure the face, and shove the tongue."

She takes a deep breath and asks, "What is Bag's full nickname?"

"Uh, Scumbag," I reply.

She calmly says, "Please don't take advice from a guy named Scumbag, and if you ever get near Bart again, check yourself for lice."

"Got it," I humbly reply.

She pops my collar up and says, "You're not in junior high anymore, Carter. What you do affects me. I've worked way too hard to be as cool as I am for you to come up and ruin me. So just do exactly what I've said and you'll be fine . . . and have fun!"

7. Steppin' Out

Her speech is over, and I pedal off toward Maria's house. My head is reeling! How am I going to write all of that on my hand? I'll have to be the Jedi-Zen-Carter tonight if this is going to work. I'm frustrated and confused and pedaling so fast up a hill that I start riding a wheelie. I've never been able to ride a wheelie before! It's either the workouts or I'm so nervous that I'm uncommonly strong. Whatever it is I just pushed the pedals around four times before the front wheel crashed back down. AWESOME! If I can get five around, I'll quit football and start training for the X Games. I squeeze the front brake to bust a phat endo, and flip myself onto the concrete face-first instead. *WHAM!* Dang it.

A Chevy minivan blasts its horn and screeches to a stop two inches from my face. That was almost bad. Then it goes ahead and gets really bad. The driver's window rolls down, and Yosemite Sam sticks his head out the window and yells, "AYE! Get out of the road, dumbass!" His red handlebar mustache flies up from the force. He gets out of the van and stomps toward me. He's much taller than the cartoon, but his hair is fire red and his eyes are bugging out of his head.

I start laughing because I'm nervous, I almost died, and I'm face-to-face with a Looney Tune. I stop when I see Amber Lee in the passenger seat. Oh, dang it.

"Sorry!" I sheepishly reply, and peel myself off the ground.

Amber rolls down her window and asks, "Carter, what are you doing?"

"Uh, riding over to Maria's party, bustin' a couple tricks," I say.

"Bustin' your butt is more like it!" Her dad laughs.

Wow, that's a funny joke . . . dick.

Then he barks, "Throw the bike in; we'll give you a lift."

Oh my! I climb inside the van with my bike, and Amber looks superhot in a lacy white shirt that shows her bra. Yosemite must've relaxed the regulations tonight, because her makeup's much heavier than usual. Kind of slutty, actually. I'm thinking like crazy for a question I can ask as we role out. "D-d-do you do your own makeup?" is all I can come up with.

Her dad snarls at me in the rearview mirror.

"Why?" she asks.

"W-w-why not?" I ask, trying to keep up the inquisition.

Her dad turns around and asks, "You think she's wearin' too much makeup?"

"Daddy, shut up!" Amber yells.

"Not too much for me, I-I-I think it looks nice," I answer.

Amber turns around and gives me the nicest smile. I asked her two questions, and she flashes me teeth. Questions are sweet!

I couldn't have planned my arrival to the party any better than it goes down. About twenty kids are in front of the house. A 50 Cent track is blasting from a stereo inside as Amber Lee steps out of the van, short shorts in full effect. My boys look over as she slides the van door open for me (because of the child safety locks). I pop out with my bike in tow and give them a nod, like, "What's up, FOOLS!" I step down just as 50 is rapping about his Es-co-lade. I'm stepping out of an As-tro-Van, but my friends have to be thinking, "What a pimp that Carter is!"

Amber whispers, "Wow, my dad never talks to anybody, especially not cute boys."

I may have said, "Yeah, I have a way with parents," or something clever like that, but Amber Lee just referred to me as cute so I may have just muttered, "Cool," and ran away . . . I don't really remember.

I high-five EJ as the boys start ripping on me.

"What? You couldn't ride all the way?" Hormone asks.

"Her dad almost mowed me down with the van. The least he could do was give a brotha' a lift," I reply.

"Did he call you a varmint?" Bag asks.

Doc adds, "I heard her dad killed a guy with a tire iron!"

I was going to tell them that I heard that too, or bust a Yosemite Sam impression, but Abby steps out of the house and my heart skips a beat. Seriously, like a CD from the public library, it goes *ZZebbTTT* and skips. Holy crap, she looks hot! Where did this girl come from? This is not the chick I knew in home ec at all. She's wearing a short jean skirt and a tight T-shirt with the number 44 printed across her boobs. Her belly button's exposed and it's all good. My brain's having trouble keeping up with all the new signals. I think I've gone cross-eyed for a second, because the 44 just said 4444.

From football, I know that the number 44 is reserved for linebackers and usually the toughest kid on the team, but she's stretching the number in a way no linebacker ever could. I usually run away from the kid wearing 44, but I'm thinking about getting closer to this one.

She smiles at me, and I say, "Hey Ab-Ab, you l-l-look fantastic!"

She smiles even bigger and says, "Thanks, Carter, so do you."

Way to go on the hard-to-get tip, doofus. Dang it, does that count as one of my compliments? I'm only supposed to bust that out if I can't think of a question. I guess I only get one more.

"How's the party?" and "How long have you been here?" were going to be my first questions of the night, but I seem to be stuck on, "H-hhh-haa . . ." It's her belly button; she's never broken it out before.

"H-h-haaa," I wheeze. Her button's like kryptonite! It's weakening my powers—my power of speech. I'm definitely blinking too much. EJ's just watching me like I'm bad reality TV and he's got a great seat for the show. The word "cool" may have worked earlier with Amber, so I give it a shot.

"Cool party" shoots right out. Nice!

She replies, "Yeah, Maria's house is perfect for a party."

"Have you been here before?" would work perfectly here, so I stammer, "H-h-h-ha-ho-ho . . ."

EJ busts in to save his oldest best friend with, "Pay no attention to Elmer Fudd here; he stutters when he likes somebody."

Why, you good-for-nothing son of a . . . This is why I'm

still a virgin! I shoot him an I'm-gonna-kill-you-later smile, and although I didn't want it pointed out at that moment, he's kind of right. I've gone from being totally whatever about Abby to really liking her.

"Y-y-you w-w-wanna go inside?" I ask her.

"Sure, they have Cokes and food in the kitchen," she says as we walk away.

I whack EJ in the back of the head. Hard!

Abby walks past the stereo and does a little MTV hip-hop shoulder bob to the beat of the song. Wow, my girl can dance! I need to write that on my hand for later questions.

"How's your sister?" Abby asks over her shoulder.

Dang it! I'm supposed to be the journalist here.

"Uh, she's cool. She got me this shirt," I reply.

"Oh, cool. I was just going to say I love that shirt. It matches your Shox," she says, grabbing a Diet Coke.

I start to blabber, "Naw, Abby, y-y-you really look great. Really, like awesome! Your earrings and that necklace are perfectly coordinated. It's pooka shell, right? Your whole look is fierce! The shirt and that mini are so cute together, and with your tan you look all beach chic."

Oh, good God, Carter! This isn't *Queer Eye*. Back off, you stalker!

She may be thinking "stalker," but she's all smiles. No more compliments, though. I start in on my first of a thousand questions. "How's drill team going?" "Do you have any brothers or sisters?" "Do you guys get along?" "What's that like?" "What's your favorite movie?" "How do you think U.S. foreign policy is affecting our economy?" "Do you think oral sex counts as sex? And why?" I left out the last few, but they're about the only ones. I'm friggin' Jimmy Olsen digging for clues! The funny thing is, I'm learning a lot about her. Not really from what she's saying, because I space off a lot, but more by how she's acting. She's being kind of giggly and silly. I think she's nervous. I may be making a girl nervous! I thought I knew her, but the girl she's giving me here is not the same chick I joked around with in junior high. She's looking way hotter, but she's not acting as cool. I, on the other hand, am cool as a cucumber. I even start to crack a few jokes in between questions, and she's laughing her head off. I think I have the upper hand here, and I'm liking it.

"I'm gonna go check up on my boys," I tell her, and then just walk away.

Man, I am doing really well. I stroll through the party like I'm John Mayer after a concert. I give my nods and my "S'up?"s. My high fives and my low fives. I notice my bike lying in the front yard, where I abandoned it an hour ago. I get punched a couple of times in the arm, not because anyone is mad at me; that's just what we do. EJ is talking to the big dude from Pizza Barn. I've since heard that his name's Andre, he can bench two hundred fifty pounds, and he's dating a supermodel. He's not talking again; he's just listening to EJ tell the story about how we shaved off one of Bag's eyebrows last year and how crazy a guy looks with only one eyebrow.

I punch EJ hello in the kidney. "S'up?" I ask.

"Ahh! Don't do that; I've got kidney stones!" EJ cries.

"I know, I thought that would help break 'em up, dog," I reply.

I give Andre a "S'up?" and he gives me a nod, looks into the kitchen at Abby, and asks, "Is that your bitch?"

Now, I may have just punched my best friend in the

kidney and he may pee blood tomorrow, but that was a pretty rude response to a "S'up."

"My bitch?" I ask, for clarification.

"Are you hittin' that or what?" he asks.

I look over at EJ, who's shocked by this guy's line of questioning too, and say, "Uh, only when she starts freakin' out and I have to whack her across the face, like, 'Pull yourself together, WOMAN!'"

EJ laughs, and Andre shakes his head and says, "I'll take that as a no," then walks into the kitchen and starts talking to Abby.

"What a jackass!" I say.

"Jackass who's mackin' on your girl," EJ replies.

"What the hell am I supposed to do with this?" I ask.

"Pray she's not into him," he says, while monitoring the kitchen with me.

"I know him—Where the hell do we know him from?" I demand.

"Swim team," EJ replies. "You know that kid who beats you every summer in the all-city championships?"

"That's him? That's Andre? I hate that kid! I've hated him since I was five," I respond dumbfoundedly.

"Looks like he's not a Carter fan, either," he replies as we watch him touch Abby's exposed belly button.

"That's my button!" I say as a lightning bolt shoots down my spine and I march into the kitchen to start my first fight. A fight I will surely lose. But just as I'm about to jump into the air for a flying-crane kick to the back of his fat head, Abby steps past Andre, grabs me by the hand, and says, "There you are! Excuse us, Andre, I need to ask Carter a question."

She pulls me on to the back deck and says, "That guy's a jerk."

"No kiddin'," I respond. "He called me *fat boy* summer before last at a swim meet. Twelve is a difficult age for boys, and wearing a Speedo is hard enough without some butthole commenting on your weight issues!"

Abby touches my chest and giggles. "Carter, you are hilarious."

I laugh as well, like I was trying to make a joke and I'm not still mad that he called me fat boy and then smoked me by two full seconds in the race. I chuckle a little more because she's still laughing, and I try to think of another question. I want to tell her that I was kidding about wearing a Speedo and that I'm starting karate soon, so I can kick Andre's ass if he bothers her again. But my sister's instructions are burned like an Outback steak into my brain, so instead of lying or bragging, I say, "Tell me more about drill team camp," like a robot.

She doesn't shut up for five minutes, until Nick Brock, the Skeleton, Scary Terry Moss, and a couple other seniors walk past us and through the back door of the house. They have real beer. One dude's smoking a cigarette, and the Skeleton just stuck his hand in Maria's fish tank. I don't think he caught anything, but Maria's dad is pissed and yells at them to leave. Man, I wouldn't tell those guys to do anything. I'd let them burn my house down without a peep. Her dad looks scared too, because Nick Brock is huge, the Skeleton is really tall, and Scary Terry Moss is a psychopath. You can see it in his eyes! He came over to my house last year to hang out with my sister, and he was kind of a dick to me. He pushed EJ down in grade school, and he just kicked

Maria's mailbox as they walked out the front door, confirming the rumor I heard that he knows karate. This guy is the complete menace package! And then he picks up my bike and starts to ride around on it.

"HEY! No, no, NO, Scary Terry! That's my bike!" I yell inside my head. But I'm speechless on the outside as Brock gets on my axle pegs and they ride away. He weighs two hundred and fifty pounds; my pegs can't handle that kind of weight, dude! Nobody else seems upset. I guess they can't hear the screaming inside my head. I walk out to the driveway like I'm going to do something about all this, but I just watch Brock and Terry ride into the sunset with my Redline 500a. I look back at EJ, and he kind of shrugs his shoulders, like, "Nothing we can do, dude, just let it go."

I know I have to, too. I'm so mad at myself for riding my stupid bike to a high school party. I didn't even lock it up, or hide it, or anything. I saw Abby's belly button and left my bike for dead in the middle of the yard, where any drunk senior could ride away on it.

I walk out to the curb just in time to see the seniors laughing and piling into an old pickup truck. The Skeleton carelessly throws my bike into the back, and they drive off. I should call the police, but then Scary Terry would kill me in my sleep. I feel the swell from my loss and I start to cry. At my first high school party I'm crying in the street. Dang it. I take a walk around the block to stop the waterworks and make sure nobody sees. It's time to say good-bye to my bike-riding days anyway. A bicycle is a kid's thing, and I'm not a kid anymore. It's time to grow up and stop pedaling around. I really want to go home so I don't have to go back to that party with red eyes, a puffy face, and no bike. But while my pride is strong, my hormones are way stronger. I played Abby as good as I can, and that Andre is going to swoop in on her if I don't go back. And if I don't kiss her good night, she's going to think I'm not into her. And I do not want her to think that.

As I open the front door I see her sitting on the couch with a drill-teamer named Kathy. The whole room's looking at me. I see my boys on the stairs and walk toward them, but then I bust a left and head toward Abby instead. She jumps up when she sees me turn. Kathy must not have been saying anything important.

EJ shoots me a look like, "That's cold, dude."

Abby gives me a hug and asks, "Are you okay?"

"Yeah, it's no big deal," I lie.

"That was your bike, huh?" she asks, all close to my face.

"It was my Redline five. . . . Yeah, it was my bike, but it was gettin' old," I say as the tears start to well up. No, no, no crying! There's kissing to be done.

"Oh, Carter, I'm sorry," she says as she hugs me again.

"I've got to go, Abby," I say.

"Okay, I'll walk you out," she says.

I hadn't planned it, but I think I'm being pretty smooth here. I take her hand, and we walk to the door. I see that Andre and my boys notice, so I give them a nod (pimp). Amber Lee is also glaring in our direction, which is weird, but so is the gallon of sweat that's dripping from my palm. I need soap and hot water, STAT!

We head toward a big tree off to the side of the yard, out of the high beams of any approaching parents' headlights. The last thing I need is EJ's mom seeing me make out with a girl. Dirt gets out faster from her telephone than the CNN news desk.

Both Abby and I know what we're at this tree to do. There's no doubt; I have a green light. But courage is slow to boil on my fourteen-year-old stove top, and I pester on with the small talk.

"What are you doing tomorrow?" I ask, without an ounce of interest in the answer.

"I have a step class in the morning," she replies.

"Oh yeah, my sister will probably be there, but then I'm not sure if she will or not, she didn't tell me for sure. So she may be there or she may not. She and my mom shop a lot on Saturdays. . . ." I blather on and on. What the hell? Enough with the yapping and get to the lip smacking!

"Yeah, I hope she's there, because she's really good," Abby says. "The class is better, I mean, when she's there. Lynn, like, makes the class better or something. More . . . Oh God, Carter, I'm rambling."

"Yeah, so am I, I don't know why. I'm nervous, I think. I try to just play defense, but I think you have to play offense some of the time, if you want to get anywhere, ya know?" I ask. Of course she doesn't know! I don't know what the hell I'm talking about; how could she possibly be keeping up?

"Sure, I'm nervous too. My hands are really shaking," she says.

"Oh, that's you? I thought it was me. Awesome. Um, I've got to walk home, so I better get going," I say as I start to shift backward.

Don't chicken out, Carter; she'll think you don't like her! I hear Lynn whisper/scream in my head.

I finally make my move. I slowly lean in and give her a

kiss. Just a peck. I can't tell anything by the first one, so I go in for peck number two. *Nobody likes a baby calf coming at 'em with a foot-long tongue!* echoes in my brain as I feel the craziest thing in my mouth. A wet piece of sponge or . . . tongue? A TONGUE has entered my mouth! Uuhhh—It's super weird, but pretty damn cool. It's all that I can do not to start laughing. She looks so beautiful here in the moonlight. . . . Why are your eyes open? Shut them, doofus, and don't fall down! We go at it for about five minutes. I never want it to end. It's awesome! I can feel her boobs pressed up against my chest, and I'm sure she can feel the tent I'm pitching in my Levi's. I pop my eyes open just for a second to make sure everything is cool out here, and it all seems to be going great, so I shut them again and refocus on the kiss. We stop for some reason and I give her a goofy smile. My first real kiss went . . .

"Awesome," I say like a tard. "I didn't mean to say that out loud."

She giggles and says, "Yeah, well, I had fun tonight."

I reply, "Yes, fun, I had too." (Who are you—Yoda?) "It was nice to talk to you some more." All the blood in my body is nowhere near my brain.

"I'm sorry your bike got stolen," she says.

"Yeah, I'd forgotten about that, but thank you for reminding me," I reply.

"Oh, I'm sorry!" She snort/laughs and turns beet red from embarrassment.

I give her a hug and say, "I'm kidding." I managed a joke so funny it made a girl snort, and I think that calls for another round of kissing! We reassume the position and it's all good. My tongue's getting tired after a while, and it's probably the only muscle that wasn't sore before, so I'd better stop before I overdo it.

I say, "Good night," and tell her, "I'll call ya," all smooth, but I'm not looking forward to that. I tried to call a girl once before, and it sucked. The chick wasn't home and I tried to mumble, "Yeah, uh, tell her Will Carter called," all cool, and her grandma goes, "Okay, Ricardo," and then hung up on me. The girl had no idea I called, so I vowed never to do it again. But I positively want to do more of this kissing, so I might have to give it another shot.

Fall

8. Ready or Not

High school may have started off with a bang. I may have ridden up on a Harley the first day, driven across the front lawn and into the cafeteria declaring, "I have arrived, BITCHES!" Or my dad may have dropped Lynn and me off in the Accord and three days have already flown by. It's not half as big a deal as I thought it would be, but I may have a C- in algebra already. I have no idea how that happened.

I know my drama class is super fun, and football has definitely started because the bruises on my arms make it hard to write assignments on them. I finally got to show off my kicking skills a few days ago. I shanked the first one so bad it almost hit my coach, but then I hit four extra points in a row, so I'm officially . . . THE KICKER! (And second string right guard.) Just on the freshman squad, and if I miss any kicks in the games I'll get fired, but so far I think I'm kicking ass and I love high school.

I've even called Abby a few times, and that wasn't as bad as I thought it would be, either. I just ask her a few questions and then hang up. Cake!

Freedom abounds in high school. We're allowed to go out to lunch on Wednesdays and Fridays, and all the best restaurants are super close. Only a short, seven-minute, all-out run down to Taco Bell, Pizza Barn, McDonald's, KFC, or Subway.

We've taken fast food to new heights. It's not great on the digestion to sprint for, like, a mile after eating your lunch in four minutes, but what are we supposed to do, eat in the cafeteria?

I enrolled in the drama class in case my football career doesn't work out. (Being a famous actor isn't a bad backup plan.) My boys make fun of me for it, but I look forward to going down to the drama wing all day long. For most high school activities, you have to be pretty serious, but Ms. McDougle (my semi-hot drama teacher) wants us to be silly and get rid of our inhibitions. I've always hated my inhibitions.

The big difference between junior high and high school is the kids. Because some of them aren't kids. There's a wide gap between a fourteen-year-old boy and an eighteen-year-old man. They can vote, drive, and buy cigarettes and porn. I just got pubic hair in March (finally!), but these dudes can grow beards. In junior high, if a kid wanted to start static, you just pushed each other a few times, threw up your hands, and yelled, "What's up?! WHAT'S UP?!" and hoped your friends or a teacher would jump in and stop the fight. But I hear these guys will just kill you: punch you in the face, slam your head into a locker, and leave you for dead. I think my friends would be hard-pressed to jump in if I got into a scrape with a six-foot-five senior. I've really got to learn karate.

And the girls . . . scratch that—WOMEN! Lady boobs everywhere. These girls have power and they know it! They wear jewelry and perfume. I've seen pierced belly buttons and tattoos! Belly button exposure was taboo in junior high, because weak-willed minds like mine wouldn't be able to concentrate on anything else. And while I do feel a bit more mature and a little more sophisticated . . . hot-smelling, tattooed, pierced belly buttons underneath lady boobs might just do me in.

9. What's in a Name?

Everybody who's anybody has a nickname. They started up toward the end of sixth grade. Some nicknames stick, others do not. Thank God. C-C-C-Carter was almost my nickname after a bad stuttering episode last year. Most of the names come from some sort of bastardization of your given name, like Dolla Bill (Bill Dews). Otherwise, it's if you do something of note. Like Cory Day was called May Day after he gave a kid the Heimlich maneuver in the cafeteria. More often it's when you do something stupid—those are the ones that stick. My friend Bag (Matt Sparks) went up to a girl at the movies last year, and I don't know what he said to her, but she yelled out, "You're a scumbag!" We took the liberty of shortening the name to Bag. Now it's part of his permanent record; he'll never shake it. One kid with the misfortune of being nicknamed Sloth in eighth grade moved to a town, like, four hours away and foolishly thought he'd escaped it. Someone in our class had a cousin in that town, and he was called Sloth before the teacher could even get his name out on the first day. The names just happen, and you sure can't make one up for yourself.

The guy who unofficially gives out most of the nicknames is J-Low (Josh Loos). He just says them a few times, and other kids start to follow along. J-Low can't do it all on his own, but if three guys get to calling you something like

Levi (Gene Arioli), that's your name. Nutt's (Todd O'Connell) full nickname is Peanut, from an unfortunate locker room incident in junior high, but he's just Nutt now. Doc (Billy Kasson) isn't smart or anything; J-Low just referred to him as "the love doctor" once at a football game. He wasn't even that good with the ladies before then, but now all the girls think he's "all that," and he gets chicks. A great nickname is very important.

I've been Carter for a few years now. My real name is Will Paul Carter, but even my mom calls me Carter now. It's just a lazy nickname, though. My last name? Big whoop! I've been trying to get a new one started for myself, but it's tricky. My plan was to run everywhere for a couple of weeks and then subtly drop the name Race Car into a conversation. I laid the groundwork with the running, but nobody noticed, and I never found the right moment to work Race Car into any conversations.

The opportunity presents itself one day between first and second hour. I'm hanging out in front of my locker when Bag walks up, gives me five, and says, "What up, Slappy?"

He said it right in front of J-Low, whose ears kind of perk up. Dang it! SLAPPY, from the diving board incident! This will not be my nickname. But I'm smart enough to know that the surest way to stick a nickname is to protest the damn thing. I've got to be cool. I calmly ignore Bag and turn my attention to J-Low. I need to feel out how close he is to calling me Slappy.

"D-d-did you go to your dad's this summer?" I ask him quickly.

"Yeah, it sucked. The guy's a friggin' hippie. He doesn't have a TV," he replies.

"It's summer, dude, just hit the pool every day," I say, looking away in disgust with myself. *The one subject you need to avoid!*

"Yeah, I heard about your gainer, dog," J-Low says with a smile.

Congratulations, your new name is . . . Slappy! I'm not going down without a fight, though. Drastic measures are all that can save me from Slappy for the rest of my life, so I push it and say, "Yeah, I just ran track most of the summer, myself."

EJ and Bag look at me funny, but they don't know all of my activities! I could have been a member of a late-night track team.

"You ran track, Slap?" EJ barks out.

That's two people. Dang it! If another guy uses that name in reference to me, I'm done for. And with J-Low right here, it's almost a done deal.

"Yeah, I ran . . . and ran," I say defiantly.

"Really, what events did you run?" Bag pesters on.

"Uh, like, the four hundred and the eight hundred, and I was on a relay team?" I ramble. Thank God I watched the Olympics sixteen hours a day this summer. Only three minutes to the second bell and Slappy is hanging over my head like an anvil in a Bugs Bunny cartoon.

"Yeah, called me the R-R-Race-Race Car, t-t-the team did," I say as they think it over. "Get it?" I press on. "Carter? Ya know, my name and then Race, like Race Carter?"

"That's what they called you: Race Carter?" Doc asked from behind me.

"W-w-well, just Race Car. Not the full, Race Car-ter, b-b-but, like Race Car, yeah. Because I'm so fast or something," I stammer.

I think that about does it. I've said it like, ten times already. It should be stuck, right? I better quit stuttering, though, or they're going to break out C-C-C-Carter again.

EJ chimes in. I was hoping he wouldn't. He knows I wasn't on any track team. He knows I spent every day with him at the movies, the pool, on my bike, or at Bag's house. But he probably knows that I don't want to be called Slappy for the rest of my days, either.

"They called you Race Car, huh? On this track team?" EJ asks.

"Yeah," I reply with a straight face. He just said it too. It's a tie. Two for Slappy and two for Race Car! It's anybody's name now.

"I think I've got a friend on that track team. You probably know him. His name is Ricky. Do you know Ricky?" he asks.

EJ pulls through for you sometimes when you least expect it. "Yeah, sure, I know Ricky. Ricky's my boy! He's on that relay team with me," I say in shock.

"Yeah, Ricky is, like, the best kid on the team, right?" EJ adds.

"Yeah, he's almost as fast as me, the Race Car!" I say with a laugh.

"Yeah, I read all about him in the paper. He's, like, the fastest kid in all of the Special Olympics, right?" EJ says all sly.

Dang it! I walked right into it.

"It's not the Special Olympics, dude!" I try to say over the laughter.

"You and Ricky are special friends?" Bag adds.

The guys all laugh until the bell rings. As we break our

group, slap fives, and punch each other good-bye, J-Low shakes his head and says, "You kill me, Carter," officially crushing the Race Car, drowning out Slappy, and restoring my nickname to its old, lame self.

10. He's Our Man

The first freshman football game is under way. My parents are in the bleachers. Both Abby and Amber Lee are on the sidelines. Abby's rocking the red spandex leotard as captain of the freshman drill team. She looks fine as hell as she herds the other girls into place. She's going to get kicked off the team if she gets much skinnier. If everybody is chunky, people notice it less. Their hair's pulled back tight and the makeup's on thick.

Everyone's yelling and jumping around because Andre just scored a touchdown, and I've got to kick the extra point. It's all happening too fast. Everybody gets lined up super quick and they wait for me to give the signal to hike the ball. Thank God we've practiced this a million times, and I just nod my helmet like a bobble head doll to Bag, who gives the signal to Levi, who hikes the ball perfectly. Bag sets it down and I blast it right through the goal post. Holy crap, I just scored a point! I jump around like we just won the Super Bowl, but I've got to pull myself together quick so I can kick the ball off again. I'm so important!

The kickoff went great and I'm back on the sidelines trying not to smile. The sidelines of a football game are for the purpose of looking tough and mean. I really should only be focused on the game and not so focused on Abby's butt, but this football helmet is awesome for gawking. I can point my head at the game, but my eyes are totally checking out boobs and booties underneath the face mask. Amber is in charge of the freshman cheerleading squad. Her belly button is nicely exposed, as are the other nine potential distracters of my kicking greatness. The belly buttons are all doing a little cheer just for me. "CARTER, Carter, he's our man . . ."

"CARTER, wake up, man!" Coach screams in my face. "Go kick me a field goal!"

Apparently we've got the ball back because Andre couldn't get a first down on the last play, so they need me to save the day with a clutch field goal. I think Coach knows I wasn't entirely focused on the right stuff back there, but I'm about to redeem myself by blasting the ball thirty-six yards and scoring three easy points. I'm so happy, I might poop my football pants right here in front of everybody. Oh God, THIRTY-SIX YARDS! What is Coach thinking? I've never kicked anything even close to this far. I'm trotting out like this isn't a big deal, but I'm shaking like an overcharged dildo, and my face must not be brimming with confidence, because my boys seem to have their doubts.

"Carter, you okay, dog?" EJ asks.

"Dog . . . Dude? Where? I . . . KICK, bang!" I reply.

We break the huddle, and Bag smacks me on the butt and says, "No sweat, Carter; just a chip shot, bro."

Who's not sweating? And isn't "chip shot" a golf term? Stop messing me up, Bag! My boys are counting on me. My parents are hoping not to be the parents of the loser kid who missed the game-winning field goal. My potential girlfriend is hoping to bask in the potential glory. My sister is . . . well,

I think she's at the mall, but she'll still be pissed at me if I miss, because it'll reflect poorly on her.

The cheerleaders have honestly started to cheer, "Carter, Carter, he's our man!" which flashes me back to my earlier train of thought, where I am indeed "their man." Please, focus! You've got to kick the crap out of this ball! Everybody is set. The tension is thick, or hot, or moist . . . Not sure exactly what the tension is, but IT'S FRIGGIN' TENSE! The other team is going to try to block my kick—and my legend—from blossoming.

The ball is HIKED. . . . Dang it, BAG, I never gave the nod that I was ready, because I sure as hell am not! Bag catches the ball and puts it down, I take my steps, I plant my foot. I keep my eyes open and swing my leg through, like I'm launching a missile off my foot. I blast the ball so hard and with such a *BOOM*, if anybody tries to block the thing, their hand, arm, or head will be ripped off from the force. The ball makes a hissing noise as it flies away. It's definitely got the distance, but I wouldn't exactly call it straight. Everybody's hands, arms, and heads are out of danger. Nobody blocked it. I really wish they had, though, because that ball must have flown fifty yards straight to the left. A scientist could draw a diagram and show me how a ball could go that far left, but I still wouldn't believe it. It flies over the sidelines, beyond my coach, past my parents, the drill team, and cheerleaders before finally crashing into the back of a band kid's head. Dude wasn't even paying attention to my kick (that'll teach him). It knocks his glasses off, and his funny hat and trombone hit the dirt as well. That's embarrassing.

I hear my mom yelling, "It's OKAY, SWEETIE!"

Not helping, Mother.

"You'll get the next one," Bag says as we run back to the sidelines, followed by another pat on the butt. When did it become okay for us to touch each other's butts? I guess he's trying to make me feel better, but he's just making me uncomfortable.

We stop the game for halftime, and the drill team comes out with flags to bust a move. The marching band plays a cheesy version of a Stevie Wonder song, minus a trombone player, who's still sitting on the ground trying to figure out what hit him. I'm kind of hoping Abby's flag will get away from her and impale one of the other heifers, so I won't be the only dumbass in our relationship today; but of course she's friggin' perfect.

I'm guessing I've spaced off for a second or fifty, because my nose is being smushed by my coach's finger and he's screaming, "Carter, you are killin' me, son!"

"Sorry, Coach," I instinctively reply. "I've just got to keep practicing, work on my control, and I'm sure I'll do better."

He gets in close to my face and whispers very seriously, "I wasn't talkin' about your kickin'. I'm talkin' to you, right now, about your lack of focus. I'm tryin' to wake you up from this daydream you live in. 'Cause you're gonna waste your life in it if you're not careful. Pull your head out of your ass and realize that you're lettin' your team down, and you're lettin' yourself down." He stares at me for a second to make sure I've understood what he said, then turns and blows into his whistle for us to huddle up for the second half.

I don't cry and I don't say anything to him. I'm not sure if you're supposed to talk after someone tells you you're retarded, letting everyone down, and wasting your life, so I just try to look more serious.

Andre scored another touchdown after halftime, so I got to kick another extra point, and thank God, I made it. We won the game, and I scored two points. That's two more points than I've ever scored before, but I still feel like crap.

11. Behavioral Disorder

I did as Lynn instructed and asked Abby on Wednesday to go with me to the movies on Friday night. The plan is to meet up at the big theater by her house. Lynn says it's better to meet at the movies, so you're not riding in a car with the units making small talk. Pickups and drop-offs are apparently very awkward. So I'll just ride my bike. No wheelies, of course . . . Dang it! I don't have a bike anymore, and there's been no progress on its recovery, but Scary Terry hasn't come to kill me either, so I'm still on top.

Apparently Lynn stomped up to Terry in the hall yesterday, got in his face, and demanded that he return my bike. He called her a bitch and said he didn't know what she was talking about. She then called him "a clueless loser with bad breath and no sense of style." It's nice to have someone sticking up for you, but when your guardian angel is my sister, it might get you killed.

The more I hear about Terry Moss the less I like him. He seems to have some real head problems and has to go to a special class called B.D. That stands for Behavioral Disorders. It's where all the worst kids in the school go to hang out and talk about how to battle their urges to kick the crap out of each other or to burn the school down all the time. If a kid can't cut it in B.D. class, he has to go to a special school for bad kids. I think it's called "jail" in certain circles. On the curriculum lists of what courses I could take at Merrian High, I never saw Behavioral Disorders as a class I could just sign up for. Just like I couldn't enroll in honors calculus because I wanted to, there are steps to getting into the all-exclusive B.D. program. Only so many slots and a whole slew of bad kids, but Terry seems to have made the grade.

They have the Learning Center, where they put the slow kids and the guys with learning disabilities, but not the kids with ADD. I was recommended for the L.C. in junior high, and I was devastated. But they also recommended me for a class called Seek that's just for the smartest nerds. My mom told those school psychologists to get their junk together. She wouldn't be putting her son in a special class for retards in the morning and then one for nerds in the afternoon. My brain is fragile enough as it is.

Anyway, if the school makes up these nice names for the nerds and the tards, why can't they figure out a nicer way to describe the Behavioral Disorders class? I bet they tried to call it *Choices* or like, *Problem Solving* back in the day, and some normal kid strolled in thinking he'd be all right, and the B.D. kids killed him. So they had to go back to B.D. They put Behavioral Disorders right on the door so there should be no mistake. "If you open this door, you'll find only kids with . . . behavioral disorders!"

The room is right by my locker at the end of the building, and the door is always shut. I bet it's locked too. If you let them out they'll just steal bikes, kick mailboxes, and push kids down. Apparently Lynn went through a bad-boy phase last year and tried to date Scary Terry. He's somehow popular despite being a nut bag, so she thought it was okay to go out with him. She was wrong, because the degenerate got into a fight with five guys in a Safeway parking lot while they were trying to get frozen yogurt. These dudes in a Jeep had apparently cut him off for a parking space, and he went crazy. He had a baseball bat in the backseat and started hitting their car. My sister is a busybody to the core, so she tried to break up the brawl, and of course she got popped in the face with the bat. Terry didn't hit her. He was unconscious by that time, because the five guys got the bat away from him (shocker). I'm sure it seemed like a good plan in his crazy-ass head, but unfortunately, both he and Lynn ended up in the hospital.

When the 'rents and I picked her up from the hospital, she was hopped up on some funny-ass painkillers. If she could have stayed like that for the rest of her life, it would have been A-OK with me. And I know brain damage isn't supposed to be hilarious, but she was like a drunk comedian; even the nurses were laughing. She kept yapping about "hot homeboys" and their "hot, hot dogs" and "strawberry milk shakes!" She was killing me, but my mom was crying because her daughter was babbling like a slutty tard in a hospital gown. For all we knew she was going to be like that permanently, but once those pills wore off, she was a raging bitch again.

Apparently Scary Terry's parents were worried about their troubled son when he was in seventh grade and getting into too many fights, so they signed him up for karate classes to instill discipline in him, or some such crap. Another way to look at it is that you've taken a kid with anger issues and trained him to kill more efficiently. The only reason he's not a black belt is because he's always getting into fights with the owner of the karate school. I heard he wins sometimes, too.

12. Silent but Violent

I dust off my sister's old bike for my date with Abby. It had tassels hanging from the handlebars until a couple of minutes ago, because although I'm secure enough to ride a hot-pink Schwinn girl bike (at night, as long as nobody sees), I'll never be confident enough to ride anything with tassels.

I have enough lawn-mowing/college money to buy my ticket and Abby's too, if she's an old-fashioned type of girl. Which I hope she isn't, because then I'll have enough cash for the concession stand. EJ and I usually do the "double feature." We pay for the first movie and then sneak into a second one. We always buy snacks as payment for the stolen screening, because who would stop somebody walking into a theater with a big tub of popcorn, Milk Duds, and a huge cherry Coke? It's like we've just arrived! We've seen three movies in a row before, but it was tough on our ADD.

I ride the old pink Schwinn like a rented mule. If someone spots me, they may think, Is that Carter on a girl bike? But before they have a chance to confirm their hypothesis . . . I'm gone! If I were racing Lance Armstrong tonight, he would be losing. I blaze through red lights and stop signs. I'm about to blast past the Taco Bell when I slam on the brakes. I check my watch and realize that because of my breakneck pace, I'm going to be really early. And what if Abby isn't into popcorn and Milk Duds? I'm going to get hungry, and my stomach will be growling when it's time to kiss good night. I can definitely spare ninety-nine cents for a burrito. I bust through the drive-thru, and of course it's a cute girl a little older than me who hands me the Burrito Supreme. She gives me kind of a laughy smile. Maybe she thinks I'm cute because I'm doing the drive-thru on a bicycle, or maybe she's thinking I've escaped from a lunatic asylum and stolen this pink girl bike as my getaway vehicle. I break out before the Taco Belle can pass any more judgments. I wolf down the burrito in fourteen seconds, almost breaking EJ's record, and ride off, fast. I lock up the pink cruiser in back of the theater and walk around front, to see Abby standing under the marquee looking super hot in a simple black dress.

"What's up, Momma?" I ask, trying to sound like a rapper in a video. But I think it sounded really stupid as it came out, and I wish I could take it back.

"Just waitin' on you, Daddy," she replies with a level of cool I never knew a girl could possess.

"Wow, you look really great," I say. "Are you going somewhere after this?"

She turns red. "Oh, Carter, you jerk! I'm totally overdressed! I knew I would be. . . ."

"No, I think you look awesome. I actually had a suit and tie in my fanny pack and was going to change into it, but then I remembered that fanny packs are gay and had to throw it out. I'm sorry," I say.

She laughs. Lynn's voice echoes in my ear: *Not too many jokes, Carter! Comedians don't score with the ladies. Get to the questions!*

I start with, "What movie do you want to see?" I really

want to see The Rock's new movie, because he's awesome. He's funny, but that's not why the ladies love him. But Lynn said, "Absolutely no action movies, idiot!" So I guess I'm going to have to see a Drew Barrymore cheesy chick flick or something. And please, God, don't let her be into horror movies! I can't handle them. I had to sleep in my parents' room after the last one, and I'm just getting too old for that.

She replies, "Anything but that cheesy Drew Barrymore mov—"

I cut her off with my lips. I probably just broke a rule about kissing before the date starts, or interrupting with my face, but I don't care, she is awesome. "Sorry," I say as we softly break the kiss.

She's totally flustered when she asks me, "Um, what, what movie do you want to see?"

Huh? I can't lie to her, because Lynn says, "When boys lie to girls, we always know!" So I say, "I heard The Rock's new movie is good."

"Yeah? Who said it was good?" she asks.

Dang it! I lied and she totally knew it. "Okay, I heard it was good from the announcer on TV. He says, 'It's nonstop action,' and that 'The Rock really shines!'"

She laughs and says, "Well, they do have this movie called *Red Betsy*. It won the Sundance Film festival. I read this article about it, and it sounds amazing."

I try not to make a face as I say, "Cool." Ugh, if somebody wrote a whole article about it, it's going to be all talky and complicated and totally SUCK!

She walks up to the window before me and buys her own ticket. Awesome, now I have enough cash for snacks! But that Burrito Supreme is sitting like a brick in my gut.

I think chewing is not only good manners, but your stomach prefers it.

She tells me that she doesn't like candy, which I think is funny because I've seen her eat her weight in M&M's back in home ec. I don't laugh out loud or anything, because her recent dislike of candy has led to her looking really good in bikinis, red spandex, and black dresses. So no snacks for us!

I'm starting to get into this movie about a dude who builds his own airplane, and his crazy mom, when I feel a little rumble just above my belt line. The tremor goes south and is trying to brew itself into a monster fart that will ruin my chances with Abby. No way, pal! If I were here with EJ, I would love nothing better than to rip a stinky-ass Taco Bell fart just as the movie is getting good. But tonight is a different deal. I squeeze my butt cheeks together like a maximum-security prison trying to hold in a crazy prisoner who wants to escape and murder an innocent fourteen-year-old girl on her first date. This sucker is not getting out! I like this girl, and I like this movie. SQUEEZE! The fart passes and goes back to whatever part of your body farts go when they fail to complete their dastardly mission. But I know it'll be back.

The movie is awesome. Nothing is blowing up or anything, but the main guy's really funny and is getting into all kinds of adventures with the ladies in his town, and his dog is funny too. I'm feeling really proud that I'm on a date with a cute girl and enjoying an art film, when I have to fight off another sneak attack from the prisoner in my bowels. I beat back two more escape attempts after that, but my stomach is hurting. I'm starting to think that the Taco Belle was smiling at me because she knows better than anyone how terrible it is to mix freeze-dried beans, sour cream, low-grade meat, processed cheese, yellowy lettuce, and brown tomatoes with a nervous stomach.

I can't survive another attack. I've got to let this fury out. I jump up and squeeze past Abby like my shoelaces are tied together.

She whispers, "Are you okay?"

"Yeah, I just gotta go potty . . ." I whisper, shut my eyes as tight as my butt, and pray she didn't just hear that. Silence is golden, dude. I bolt down the stairs and just get around the corner when I give birth to a monster! It's quiet, thank God. But as all Taco Bell farts are, it's awful! "Silent but violent," Bag would call it. It takes like thirty seconds to exit my body, and a great weight has lifted—WHEW!— I'm still watching the movie from the hallway and I'm ter-rified that this smell is going to fill the theater and kill everyone, but I don't think it's possible for a fart to travel fifty feet. I hang out in the hall for about a minute and a half, so it looks like I'm peeing and not taking a grumper. I bust a couple of jumping spin moves to separate myself from the stank. (My boys and I came up with The Farting Ninja Spin last year, and it works.) I go back to my seat a stink-free happy fella.

I'm watching the dude have an argument with his mom, who's just died, and I'm thinking that this is some-thing I'd probably say to my mom if she ever died and came back from the dead to nag me. It's really sad. I feel the tingle in my forehead, the pinch in the nose, and finally the watering of the eyes. OH NO, CARTER! Fart all you want, but please, please, please don't cry on your first date!

Think about football, think about how nice Abby's boobs look tonight. That works, but then I imagine how funny it would be for a guy to start crying on his first date, and that gets me laughing. There's nothing I can do. I'm totally cracking up. A lady in front of us turns around to see who the insensitive prick is who is laughing at the death of this dude's mom. Abby shoots me a look because everybody's all sniffling and her date is over here giggling.

I finally get it under control, and Abby must be grateful, because she softly grabs my hand. Dang it! I should have washed my hands when I was pretending to pee. The dude's making a final plea to the love of his life and apologizing to her for wrecking everything . . . Uh-oh, another fart! I've only got a couple more minutes. I have to fight it off! I squeeze my butt cheeks and Abby's fingers with all my might. Abby jerks her hand away, and I realize I was crushing the poor girl's digits as I was trying to save her life. I then accidentally place my hand on her inner thigh. Actual hand to almost private part contact! That did it. The mainframe lost focus and . . . PRISON BREAK! Coach is right; my lack of focus is hurting everyone! It was silent but it's a doozie. I pull my hand away from her thigh and try to move the air around us away from Abby. Is it possible to catch a fart and throw it away from innocent bystanders? I'm subtly blowing the air to my left, hoping this fart will jump on the jet stream I'm creating in the theater. Oh, it's strong and *refried stinky*. I think Abby's being spared, but I steal a glance over at her just as her face crinkles. Then it contorts into bug-eyed shock.

"Ohh, nasty!" she whispers. She's been hit with the fury of post–Taco Bell syndrome. She sits up straight, grabs her stomach, then doubles over and pukes everywhere. The stream splashes off the nosy lady in front of us. Her neck and hair are covered, and she bolts. Vomit is everywhere. The only smell worse then my Taco Bell bomb is the stink of Abby's regurgitated Weight Watchers entrée. Oh gross, I hate puke! But I feel responsible for its presence, so I hold her hair back as she burps and gasps for air . . . because that's the kind of guy I am. She lets go of a few more servings of chicken à la king before she finally stops. Jeez, no wonder she didn't want snacks; this girl was full! I lift my feet off the ground just a couple of inches so as not to get any of her "points" on my Shox.

The movie's over, and I have no idea if the chick took the dude back or whether they live happily ever after or not. If I'd missed the last couple minutes of The Rock's new movie, I would know that he had saved the day. But with these damn art movies, she may have told him to drop dead and that she was really a man after all that. I'll never know because we have to get out of here! It stinks really bad, and I don't want Abby to have to hold my hair when *I* start puking.

She's not talking; she's so pissed at me for farting on our first date she'll never talk to me again. And she's totally going to tell everyone, and I'm going to have to transfer to a religious school where they can't judge me. Dang it, I'm never going to have sex! I'm definitely not getting another good-night kiss. Actually, I don't think I'd be interested even if she were offering.

We're walking out toward the parking lot when she starts sobbing. "Carter, you have to say something! I'm so embarrassed, I want to die!"

"What, why? Just because you puked back there? Nooo," I reply.

She laughs. "Oh, Carter, don't make jokes."

"I'm not joking, you shouldn't be embarrassed. I'm the one who detonated the T-bomb and made you ralph," I confess.

"No, that wasn't you. It was that big guy next to me! You didn't smell the first one because you were in the bathroom. I had to cover my face with my shirt. But that second one. It was just so strong and vile!" she cries.

I was honest. I told her it was me . . . once. But I see no reason to beat the point to death. She's in much too fragile a state right now to listen to who did what and when, so I just let it slide . . . literally!

I give her a kiss on the cheek (I don't want to get too close to her puke shooter) as her mom pulls up, and I say, "I'll see you on Monday," because I want the memory of this date to die down before we talk again.

"Okay," she says as she shuts the door.

I give her a wave as they drive away, and then drop another earth shaker. Man, I need to see a doctor!

I flip off the Taco Belle with both hands as I ride by, but then I realize I'm hungry and still have a couple bucks burning a hole in my pocket that could start burning a hole in my colon instead. I've got football practice tomorrow, and nothing's funnier than ripping a Taco Bell bomb in the huddle. Nobody can scream or run away, because Coach'll freak out and yell, "You boys need discipline!" and we'll have to run until we puke, so they just have to stand in the stench and cuss under their breath, "Who the . . . ? Aww!!! Not cool!" I never thought I'd actually look forward to football practice, but here I am.

13. Kindergarten

Sometimes I can't sleep. I just can't shut down the mainframe. Images zip around in circles. The trick is to take some deep breaths, try to clear my brain out, and focus on one thing. Girls in bikinis usually does the trick, but tonight even that isn't working. I know better than to bring naked girls into the picture. They get me focused, but not on sleep.

I can lie awake for hours sometimes, staring up at the cottage-cheese ceiling from a bed that's clearly too small for me. My feet hang ten inches off the bottom. I don't fit anywhere.

I was thinking about hairstyles earlier, and a joke Abby told me about leprechauns before the movie. Then I tried to figure out why Andre doesn't like me for a while. I smash my head into the pillow a few times, and now I'm focused on what Coach said to me during our first game. How life is going to pass me by because I'm always dreaming. I wish I was dreaming right now. I think I do a pretty good job of hiding the fact that I don't know what's going on most of the time. I really do try hard, but then I *forget* to try hard for a second, and it all falls apart.

I've been in high school almost a month, and it's nothing like I thought it would be. Life just goes on. I thought there would be this click in my head and everything would make sense. But so far, nothing! I'm the same stupid, scared kid I've always been. I feel like I did on the first day of kindergarten. Like, all those other kids knew what was going on, and why we washed our hands fifteen times a day . . . and what the hell happened to snack time? I can't keep track of my books and assignments, no matter how much I write on myself. Everybody else seems to have it all figured out, and I'm totally lost, following the pack and praying no one notices what a tard I am.

I can't stop thinking about how I'm going to do a better job at everything—tomorrow. I need to get more focused. What I need is sleep! If I had more sleep, I'd do better. I wish we could still take naps.

I don't think my sophistication and maturity are coming. Could I be sent back to junior high if they find out how defective I am? Can they do that? Who is "they"? Would Abby date a guy who got demoted to eighth grade?

The other kids seem to know where they fit. If they're a dork, they seem comfortable with it. They dress and act accordingly. If I were a dork, I think I'd be okay with it. If they're a jock, they just think and talk about sports. I play sports but I don't think I'm a jock. Guys like Nick Brock are jocks, so how can I be? A girl called me a *prep* once, because half of my collar was sticking up after gym. But I'm not prepping for anything. I take an art class but I'm not artsy, I take drama but I'm not a theater geek. The band dorks think I'm the devil because that trombone player I drilled with my first field goal starts shaking and blowing the wrong notes every time they practice on the football field. The smart kids think I'm stupid because I fail a lot of tests.

And the dumb kids think I'm a nerd because I talk a lot in class. I just want to fit in. I don't want to walk around in some dream. I want to fall asleep! I want to feel comfortable. I want a new nickname. I want to be stronger, but I don't want to be so sore all the time. I want to shock people. I want people to think about me as much as I think about them, and I worry that I'll always feel this way. Like I did on the first day of kindergarten.

14. Look Out, Varsity

On top of my sleep troubles, the varsity football team lost their third game in a row, so we have to run fourteen hundred-yard sprints as punishment. One painful long-ass sprint for every point the other team beat us by. Now, the term "us" is confusing to me. "Us" apparently means "me" when it comes to this running crap, but the "me" part of "us" knows good and well "I" didn't even play in that game. "I" barely watched the damn thing! "I" was in the bleachers talking to my friends, goofing around, watching cheerleaders, and eating hot dogs. Apparently what "I" missed was that we got creamed by fourteen points, and we have to run these sprints because of it. And if anybody is caught "dogging it" or "loafing," we have to start over. And we did, twice! The varsity linemen are way beyond husky—they're huge—so a hundred-yard dash is no joke for them. But these guys need to take my acting class fifth hour and learn how to at least pretend like they're giving it their all. You'd think I didn't have a scrap of energy left after just one sprint. After two sprints I give an Academy Award–winning performance in *On the Verge of Death at Football Practice*. Huffing and puffing, moaning and groaning, I double over, wince my eyes, and show my teeth like a rabid dog. Nobody can accuse me of "dogging it."

I'm acting up a storm over here! But after twenty hundred-yard sprints, dogging it or not, I'm beat. No acting required.

I was shocked to hear that the varsity kicker, Allan, missed two field goals and an extra point during the game. The guy never misses, EVER! He can hit from almost fifty yards, but for some reason he choked and missed every kick he tried. So after the twentieth sprint, Coach yells, "All right, men! Now that we've worked on the conditioning problem, let's work on the kickin' problem!"

I know this isn't going to be fun for Allan. Everybody is exhausted as we head for the goalpost to watch him kick. The varsity special teams crew slowly lines up for the field goal. The holder gets into his stance. Allan marks off his steps. Nick Brock squats down and gets ready to hike the ball. You'd think these guys were trying to kick a field goal from the top of Mount Everest the way they're sucking wind.

Coach yells, "Whoa, whoa, Allan, you think you're my kicker after Friday's game? How many kicks do you get to miss and still keep the job, son? Carter, get in there."

Everyone gasps and looks at me. But why? Oh my, did he just say what I think he said?

"CARTER, you're killin' me! Get in there," Coach barks.

Oh God, my heart's in my . . . I don't even know where the damn thing went off to, but it's beating way too fast. I trot out, utterly confused but remarkably focused. Focused on not passing out. Everybody is still huffing, puffing, and watching me. Allan is looking at me like I killed his dog.

"If Allan can't get it done, maybe Carter can," Coach

yells. "This boy hit a field goal and an extra point in the freshman game, so he's your new varsity kicker."

I should point out that I actually missed a field goal and the marching band lost a trombone player, but I'm too freaked out to talk. "Will Carter, varsity kicker!" I like the sound of that. Andre is the only freshman to play on the varsity squad. I can totally see myself wearing that letterman jacket. I'll order it two sizes too big, so it's not too small when I get GINORMOUS! I'm trying not to giggle as the holder shoots me the *Are you ready?* look. I'm not, but I give the nod like, "No sweat, dog. Let's rock!" (I hope that's the look I gave.)

As high-pressure kicks go, I think this would have to rank up there with ten seconds left in the Super Bowl type of pressure. I am fourteen years old! Some of these guys are like, twenty-five and killers. The holder has a goatee . . . FOCUS! Here it comes . . . FAME! I drive forward, cock my leg back, and kick that ball as hard as I've ever kicked one. As hard as anyone has ever kicked a ball. I hear the *BOOM* as my foot collides with the leather. It would've flown sixty yards, easy . . . if it hadn't been blocked by Nick Brock's back. *SSMMAACK!* Right into his huge muscle-bound kidneys.

"OOUUCCHH!!!" The big man squeals as he falls to his knees. Everyone else goes "OHHH." I would tell him sorry if I could remember how to speak.

"At least he's kickin' straight!" Coach yells. "He got a hold of it too, don't you think, Brock?"

Nick sort of whimpers an unintelligible response. Then Coach looks over at Allan and sneers. "You see how he's doin' that? Kickin' it straight? Give the freshman another one."

It takes a while for Brock to get back into his stance. He grabs the ball and snarls at me from between his legs; the holder shoots the look to me again. I raise my eyebrows as if to say, "I don't know about this, dude," but the ball is hiked (a bit wobbly this time) and set up. I take my time. I've got to get this ball off the ground. No grass burners! No back slappers. I've just got to kick it harder. And I do. I DRILL it!

The *BOOM* sounds like thunder, immediately followed by the *SSMMAACK* of leather meeting a large amount of flesh at high velocity. *Wham!* Right into Nick Brock's giant kidneys again. Dang it!

"HAAAAHHH," Brock squeals as he falls to the ground clutching his stinging back.

Man, I should have been practicing more. I should have been meditating during the hundred-yard sprints, just in case. I'm so mad at myself. Not nearly as mad as the two-hundred-fifty-pound dude screaming on the ground in front of me, mind you.

The varsity guys are laughing and so is Andre. I'd swear Coach is trying to hold back a chuckle, but it's probably just gas, because that guy doesn't have a funny bone in his body.

"Least he's consistent. There ain't a kicker in the NFL could make that kick twice!" Coach laughs. "Or would want to. Let's wrap it up before this freshman takes anybody else out. Brock! Get up, you candy ass!"

I guess that's the end of my letterman's jacket. Man, I would have looked cool.

15. Rumble, Young Man, Rumble

I've made the decision not to be tardy anymore. All I've got to do is plan ahead and stop socializing in the halls. I want to be at school for as little time as possible, and because of my tardy ways, teachers are making me come in after school, and before school, and ruining my lunch in retaliation. There's even talk of me going to Saturday school. Hell no! I'm now bringing all the right books with me to the right classes. You can imagine the discipline it's taking for me to remember which class is coming up, and coordinating which books go where. I haven't made it yet, but it's sixth hour and I've been perfect so far today. Only two more classes and two more books (health and science). I just might do it.

I'm looking down at my left arm to see what's written on my wrist about science class—I took a shower this morning, and I can't tell if it says "quiz" or "pizza"—when who should pop out of the Behavioral Disorders classroom like a crazy rabbit out of his cage? None other than Scary Terry Moss. And guess who runs right into him?

BAM! I drop my health book and slowly look up into his crazy eyes. "What the hell, muthafucka?" he screeches.

This is not good.

"S-S-Sor-Sar . . ." I stammer. The word "sorry" will just not come out. But guess what does fly out of my death-wish mouth?

"You stole my bike, you A-HOLE!" Oh, Carter, why is your mouth open? Who did you just call an a-hole? It feels like I just stepped off a cliff.

"You little punk ass. You Lynn's sucka-ass brotha? You tell her some smack 'bout how I gangked a BMX from a freshman party? I oughta stomp yo ass!" he yells.

I just stare at him. No blinking. No breathing. Just heart pounding. I'm pretty sure that's your only job when you fall off a cliff: just fall. Just stare at the ground and wait for the *POP!*

"I'd like to see you try, you pussy!" someone sneers. Who the hell said that? Did I say that? I look around, and there's EJ standing beside me with his nostrils flaring, daring Scary Terry Moss to stomp my ass. EJ, nooo!

EJ rolled up on me the first day of kindergarten and asked, "Do you want to be my friend?" We have been through thick and thin since that day, but I'm wishing I'd told him to go take his medication and beat it. But I didn't. I told him we'd be best friends forever, and it's too late to back out now.

"Please don't help, E," I mutter under my breath. "I got everything under control."

"Oh, that's it, FOOLS! Now it's ON! " Terry yells as he rips off his shirt and starts jumping around. I never knew he had a tattoo of a puma on his back. What the hell is going on? Then he does this Jet Li–looking, spinning, roundhouse kick in the air. Wow, that was so lame! Yet really intimidating.

This hallway was empty a second ago, but now it seems like the whole school has gathered to watch Scary Terry end my young, foolishly lived life. EJ right by my side to the very end. All of my boys, Abby and Amber Lee, even Pam and Jemma have magically appeared to watch me die. I'll die a virgin!

"I'm sick of this jerk," EJ whispers back. "If Terry gets in one more fight, he gets kicked out of school for good!"

EJ's still pissed that Terry pushed him down in grade school.

"Just fight him and put us all out of our misery!" EJ pleads.

"What are you talking about, you retard?" I ask.

"You call me retarded, fat boy?!" Terry yells, and shoves me into the lockers.

The back of my head smacks into the hard metal, and my face turns purple as I yell, "Nobody calls me FAT, especially in front of girls!" and I shove his skinny ass, hard!

"Ohhh, OH no you didn't!" he screams. "Nobody touches the TERRY!" Then he starts punching himself in the face. This kid really is crazy! I may not even have to fight him. He's doing it for me, and I'm winning!

Just then, a big bald teacher comes flying out of the Behavioral Disorders room. He's obviously heard the "Nobody touches the TERRY," and the shepherd instinctively knows something is amiss with one of his black sheep. He's in crisis mode, and this is not the first fight he's been around, because he's breathing all heavy but his voice is calm when he says, "Terry? Terry, calm down! You have worked way too hard to throw it all away on something this silly. Walk away, Terry! Do it NOW!"

Yeah, Terry, walk away, please! Keep the bike. Forget what I said, or that I dared to "Touch the Terry"! But he's still hopping, yelling, and punching himself.

"This kid just got me so mad, dog!" Terry yells back at the teacher.

"Whatever the problem is, you're the one who pays the price," he responds.

Uh, I believe it's my dad who's going to have to pay the doctor bills and buy me a new bike, but the teacher does have a point, because Terry's beating himself like a stepchild.

"He tryin' to punk me with my ex-girl Lynn, talkin' 'bout how I stole a bike!" Terry screams. "I never gangked no bike!"

"You did too! You stole my bike, A-HOLE!" I yell out. Jeez, I'm like a Chatty Cathy Doll: just pull my string and I'll say, "You stole my bike, A-HOLE!"

"Keep quiet, young man!" the B.D. teacher barks at me.

Now wait a minute. I may not have a behavioral disorder, but I've got a behavioral issue with this crazy kid stealing my bike and calling me fat boy. Don't tell me what to do, baldy! Now I'm getting fired up, but Terry's calming down.

"I'm gonna get you, you little punk! I ain't stompin' you today, but I know where you live, bitch! And I'm gonna jack you up!" he says, all bug-eyed.

Well, this isn't good at all. I procrastinate on most things, but I don't want to have to worry about where and when this ass-stompin' is coming. I can't believe what I'm contemplating. The rest of the school needs me to dispose of this kid as bad as I do, so here we go. . . .

"W-w-wh-why wait?" I say quietly, giving him a little

shove. "You scared, Terry? Is that w-w-why they call you Scary Terry? 'C-c-cause, you're scared of freshmen? Maybe I'll s-s-stomp your ass, b-b-bitch!"

The teacher yells, "Terry Moss, if you assault this boy, there's nothing more I can do for you."

I maybe feel sorry for Terry for a second, because he's yelling nonsense and crying, but EJ picks up my slack and adds a well-timed kissing noise to push Terry over the edge. It works—*WHAM!!!*—Terry smashes EJ's face in with a Bruce Lee–looking karate punch. EJ's lights go out before the fist lands.

"You didn't say nothin' about hittin' that boy," Terry says with a laugh as EJ crumbles to the floor.

The teacher lunges for Terry, but it's too late. I'd cocked my thick-ass science textbook back somewhere between EJ's kissing noise and his knees buckling. I swing as hard as I can. Terry's face scrunches up as he realizes what's coming. The book connects with a loud, hollow *POP!* His eyes roll back into his head, his knees cave, and he falls. "Down goes Frazier! Down goes Frazier!" David knocked out Goliath with a pebble; I got Scary Terry Moss with the twenty-second edition of *Intro to Science*! He and EJ are lying on the linoleum like two preschoolers down for their afternoon naps. Except EJ's gushing blood from the mouth. (Did I mention he has braces on his teeth?) Abby's eyes are bugged out and her mouth is wide open. No one is cheering or anything. Everybody's just staring at Terry like he's a bear that's been tranquilized.

I'm sitting in the principal's office and I can hear EJ screaming as the nurse detaches his lips from the braces. I can see that Terry's face is swollen and he's openly crying as the cops walk him past and out of the school in handcuffs. I feel bad for EJ when he hobbles by with an ice pack on his mouth, but I'd feel worse if I needed the ice for my own face. Terry didn't get an ice pack. I guess you don't get much T.L.C. on your way to jail.

I'm suspended for three days, and Principal Banks tells me, "This'll go on your permanent record."

Oh well, I'm thinking about giving the rest of my lawn-mowing/college money to Nutt's brother, Bart, for a used porno, and I'm failing math, so I guess Harvard's out anyway. My personal record has a big new mark on it as well, and a fight at school is about as good as it gets! This is the kind of glory that gets brought up at a reunion twenty years from now. And three days' out-of-school suspension? Can it get any better?

"That means no football practice," Banks tells me, all stern like he's dropping the harshest punishment of all. It takes all of my strength not to jump up on his desk and sing, "HALLELUJAH! HALLELUJAH!"

"That's four football practices, you know," Banks adds.

"What?!" I ask, all confused. Please enlighten me as to how this keeps getting better!

"This afternoon and all three of your suspension days. You can't hit other people with textbooks, no matter the provocation," he says.

I'd like to inform him of the service I've just performed on his behalf. How much grief I've saved him down the line with Terry Moss no longer on his watch list. But I'm doing pretty well by just keeping it zipped.

I stroll into Coach's office to give him the good news,

and he puts the icing on the cake. "Carter, you're killin' me. You're gonna miss too much practice for me to let you play right guard in Saturday's game, but we'll need you to come in and kick for us."

I could kiss the old codger on the mouth. I've got three days with nothing to do but practice my kicking! I'll see if I can squeeze it in. I'm going to be pretty busy with video games and TV, though. My parents have to sign a notice of suspension, and they can call Principal Banks if they need any information. Well, they won't, because they aren't going to find out!

The funniest thing is, EJ didn't get suspended. He just got hit. You don't get suspended for defense. He has to go to school tomorrow and football practice this afternoon. Some people (EJ) may not find it funny, but to me it's hilarious. EJ'll see the comedy when I bring it up at that reunion in twenty years.

16. La Famiglia

The final bell of the day rings, and my boys head off to football practice. My dad doesn't pick me up for another three hours, so I go to see what normal kids do while I'm getting yelled at and smashing into other dudes in stinky shoulder pads. I feel so free.

I'm also a star. Kids are talking about me behind my back. I think I grew another inch. I kiss Abby for a while in front of the drill-team room. If Lynn saw us, she'd kill me, but I'm making my own rules today! Abby's really into the kissing too. She's dating a bad boy now, and she's fired up about it, breathing heavy and grabbing my back. I might go get a tattoo—or just grab a cinnamon roll and chocolate milk from the cafeteria.

It turns out that kids don't do much of anything after school, so I'm walking around the senior parking lot, kicking a rock, basking in my glory, and watching my boys trudge up the hill to practice. I'm on top of the world as I shoot my milk into a Dumpster and work out my vacation plans.

My arm/list is filling up fast when Nick Brock's truck rolls up behind me real slow. The rumble of the engine is the only thing louder than my heartbeat. Brock is one of Scary Terry's best friends, and he's skipping football practice to murder me! I knew this was all too good to be true. The tinted window lowers, and he gives me a nod. If I run, he'll just catch me. He's real fast.

"You need a ride?" Brock asks.

So that's how it is? It's going to be a Mafia-type hit. I'm supposed to just get into that truck and get driven to some swamp to get whacked? No way, José.

"Uhhh," I reply.

"Get in," Brock says.

Like a soldier who knows he's got to face the firing squad, I climb into the old truck. Maybe he'll do it quick if I don't fight. He doesn't say anything as we drive out of the parking lot. I'm like a puppy being driven off to the vet for a "little procedure." We drive past the practice field, and I make eye contact with EJ. His bloody, swollen lips drop open in shock. Time slows as I say farewell to my old friend. He gives me a sad wave. I press my hand to the glass. Nothing he can do for me now. I've never wanted to be at football practice more than I do right now.

"I've got to go to the chiropractor today," Brock says. "Can't practice."

"Y-y-yeah, me too," I say stiffly. "Not the chiropractor, but the no practicing."

He looks over at me and gives me a nod, like he might not kill me or he's thinking about where to dump my body after he does. We drive in silence until I can come up with another brilliant question.

"Did you hurt your back?" I ask.

He replies, "Did *I* hurt my back?"

He's either messing with me or he's retarded, so I say it again really slowly and point to his spine, "Did yooou hurt yoour baack?"

"Nooo . . . you did," he says plainly. "You kicked two footballs into it, remember?"

Oh, he's definitely going to kill me, and he's not going to do it quick, either. He's going to put my foot into a meat grinder and hook my nipples up to jumper cables! Of all the guys in the world you'd never mess with on purpose, Nick Brock has got to be at the top of the list. And this is the dude I keep pissing off!

He makes a slow right turn toward downtown. We angle onto an old gravel alley in between big brick buildings. He looks me in the eyes and says, "I heard what you did to Terry this afternoon."

This is it. The hat trick. I've hurt him, and I've done harm to *La Famiglia*, and now I must PAY!

"Yeah, he's a nut job," Brock continues. "It's great that you stood up to him. That's the only way a guy like that respects you. He kicked my ass twice before I fought back, but we've been friends ever since."

Wait, wait, wait! Skinny Terry Moss beat up Gigantor Nick Brock? Impossible. Brock is the toughest human on earth. He has the toughest haircut, the toughest truck, he even smells tough, like motor oil and tobacco or something. He wears work boots to school!

"Hit him with a textbook, huh?" Brock asks.

"*Intro to Science*," I reply.

"Ohh, that's a big one." He laughs.

I don't know where he's taking me. We're in an old part of the city, nowhere near my house, but I don't think he's going to kill me anymore. Unless he's a cold-blooded psychopath who can just joke around with a guy before taking him out.

"He probably won't bother you again," Brock says.

We bust a left onto a paved street, and I contemplate the word "probably." We're just cruising down the street in his badass old truck. Carter and Brock. Butch and Sundance. Bert and Ernie. It even smells cool in here. Like a woodsman and a mechanic.

"Smells good in here," I say. Dang it, jackass! Not an acceptable thing to say.

"Yeah, my dad smokes a pipe." He laughs. "Ya know I overheard your sister talking the other day, and I wanted to let you know, I didn't know that was your bike we took."

"Oh yeah, that . . . Uh, that's no big deal," I lie.

We pull into a pawnshop down on Grand Street. Brock says, "Give me a sec," gets out of the truck, and limps inside the store.

I'm just chillin' in the truck with my arm hanging out the window, hoping someone might recognize me. Maybe he's in there buying a CD or a gold chain. Brass knuckles or, like, a chain saw . . . I don't know what you buy at a pawnshop. Man, it really smells good in here. I wish my dad smoked a pipe. My dad smokes cigarettes, and that's just annoying because he's killing himself and there's no great smell left afterward. Maybe I can get him to switch. If I had money, I'd go get him a pipe at this pawnshop. I wonder if they have pipes. I wonder if they'd sell one to a fourteen-year-old.

Brock emerges from the pawnshop with an old friend: a chrome, Redline 500a. My bike! I jump out of the truck with a huge grin. It's like a reunion after a hostage crisis. Brock doesn't smile or anything; he just gives it back to me.

"So you wanna ride it home or do you need a lift?" he asks.

It probably would look cool if I just rode off, but my house is really far from here, and how often do you get to roll with Nick Brock?

"I-I-I'll take a ride, if you don't mind," I say with a smile.

"Yeah, no sweat. You live by the park, right?" he asks.

"How did you know that?" I ask as I climb in.

"I went to a huge party at your house a couple years ago," Nick says. "Your sister was a freshman, I think. It was a rager."

That little punk! I bet it was when we all went to my grandma's funeral. She couldn't go because she was supposed to be at a cheerleading thing. Oh, this is good.

"I didn't know we had a party," I exclaim.

"How could you not? Your house got trashed! She must have repainted or something." Brock laughs.

"What?" I ask in disbelief. My sister's pretty crafty, but how could she have gotten away with this? Who helped her? Oh, my brain hurts. It's not every day a little brother gets the upper hand. In fact, I don't think I've ever had an upper hand. How do I handle this? She'll be my slave. She'll clean my room until she leaves for college. Every time she goes to tell my mom some stupid thing I've done, I'll just say, "Whoa, let's party, Lynn!" or "I sure do miss Grandma." She's mine.

"How is your sister?" Brock inquires.

"She's real good, when she takes her medication," I reply. What the hell is he asking about her for?

"Really?" he asks.

"Naw, man, she's not on any medication. She should be. If doctors knew what I know, books would be written," I say jokingly.

"What do you mean?" Brock demands.

"She'll just be all cool one minute, giving me advice and stuff, and then she'll flip out and start ordering me around and acting psycho."

"Yeah, but that's just chicks, dude," Brock says, all wise like Mr. Miyagi.

This guys knows a lot, but he knows nothing of the depth of my sister's well of craziness. If other girls were as crazy as she is, the human race would never reproduce.

"Is Lynn seeing anybody right now?" he asks.

"Seeing anybody? Like, does she have the gift of sight?"

"No," Brock replies.

"She sees dead people!" I whisper, hoping to get off the subject of my sister. "Uh, did you like that movie?"

"No, seriously, who's she dating?"

Wait a minute. Am I getting my bike back and a ride home to pimp out my sister? I just might be offended if I weren't so stoked to be in Nick Brock's truck and to have my bike back. He used to date Pam; why would he be into Lynn? He may be able to bench-press a thousand pounds, but she'll break him like a piece of uncooked spaghetti. Man, I don't like this at all. Sorry, Romeo, but your Juliet is a nut!

"Yeah, she's seeing some dude at church," I lie. *It's for your own good, big fella.*

"Oh," he replies, all sad.

Man, we don't even go to church; I'm just the best liar ever.

"What church do you guys go to?" he asks.

"Uhh, t-t-the one over by Hawkus Middle School," I say quickly. It's the only church I can think of—I used to skate in the parking lot. But now Brock is going to walk in on Sunday and murder every guy between the ages of fifteen and twenty, trying to find Lynn's fictitious boyfriend. It'll be a massacre, and the blood will be on my hands. That's just bad Jesus karma! Or maybe Brock is just making conversation.

We pull up in front of the house, and I get my bike out of the back. As I set the wheels down, the front door rips open and Lynn comes flying out all red and flustered. Her shirt is on backward and she has yogurt on her chin. Oh, that's funny.

"HEY, you got your bike back!" she says. "That's great! You're really lovely, Nick."

Did she just say "lovely"? Yep, she's beet red because she had no intention of saying "lovely." Awesome! Then she runs up to me and goes for an awkward save. She gives me a hug, but we don't ever hug, so it's all weird.

"Yeah, I love ya, li'l bro!" she says, all loud. And then messes up my hair.

Who says "li'l bro"? And gives hugs and says "lovely"? Not my sister.

"Nick, that is sooo sweet, I can't believe you got his bike back," she squeals.

Well, he *was* involved in stealing the thing in the first place.

"It's no big deal," he replies.

"No big deal? Oh my God, Carter loves that bike! It's like his life. He was going crazy without it," she blathers.

"No I wasn't," I protest.

"Shut it!" she says under her breath. "Don't you have homework or something, you little nerd?"

"Your shirt's on backward," I whisper with spite, and point at my chin a few times.

Her mouth gets all small and intense as she wipes her chin, turns redder, and seethes, "I think Mom needs to talk to you about your improper use of textbooks!"

"Yeah, either that or she wants me to call Grandma or something; I haven't talked to her in a while," I say.

"Get out of here!" she finally barks loud enough for Brock to hear. The guy needs to know.

I cruise into the kitchen and pour myself a big bowl of Cap'n Crunch, thinking about where my bike and I will ride tomorrow. I'm just finishing the last of the sweet blue milk when Lynn slams the front door. The floor trembles as she thunders closer. "CARTER?!" she screams. "What the hell is happening?"

"Huh?" I ask.

"Why is Nick Brock getting your bike back? And why did you fight Terry Moss at school?!"

"I ran into him on accident and he wanted to fight," I say.

"He's a psycho; I can't believe you survived. What happened? Tell me everything!" she orders.

"Well, I was walking—"

"Shut up!" she interrupts. "Nick just said some guy at church is lucky to have a girl like me. Why would he say that?"

Dang it, Brock, you ginormous blabbermouth!

"Because he asked if you were seeing anyone, and

I told him you were dating some dude at church."

Her face starts to twitch as she asks, "What?! What church?"

"What did you want me to tell him, that the only guys you hang out with on Saturday nights are Ben and Jerry?" I reply, all snide. Man, if I could fight with other people as smooth as I fight with my sister, I would be unstoppable in an argument. (I might not just stand there and yell, "You stole my bike, a-hole!")

"That's pretty good, Carter!" She laughs. "So what did he say about me?"

This is weird. She used the words "good" and "Carter" in the same sentence. And it wasn't "good-for-nothing Carter" like you'd expect. And she seems impressed that I stood up to Terry. This is quite a day.

I try to get things back to normal when I say, "Brock's looking for a subject to study in his psychology class, and since everyone thinks you're the biggest nut bag in school—"

"No he didn't!" she says, all giggly and openmouthed. "Did he really say that?"

Who the hell is this chick, and what has she done with my sister?

"You've got to tell him I broke up with this church boy. Um, because he was too weak for me, and that he should ask me to homecoming," she squeals.

"Who the hell am I, Cupid?" I ask. "I don't exactly hang out with Nick Brock. I'm a freshman, he's a senior, and he'll kill me if I cross the imaginary force field that separates us."

"I don't know about any force field, but if he finds out there's no church boy, and that you lied to him, he will kill you. You started this fire and now you're gonna put it out. Got it?" she orders.

I just stare at her and think about how I've got the upper hand and she doesn't know it.

"Oh, he's so hot, isn't he? He's so sweet, and he smells sooo good," she blathers.

"Uh, he's not that sweet. I've seen him knock guys unconscious at football and smile about it. And that smell is his dad's cancer pipe. Did you know he called me a twerp? And before he returned my bike, he stole it!" I yell.

"You'll do it tomorrow!" she orders.

"Oh, I can't. I'm suspended," I say, all cool.

"You got suspended?" She laughs. "Mom and Dad are gonna kill you!"

"No they're not, because they don't know about it, and they aren't gonna find out. And you're gonna sign the note for 'em."

"No, I'm not. I'm totally telling Mom," she says.

I get all serious and say, "Ya know, I'm very disappointed in you. You know who else would be disappointed? Grandma. Grandma hated tattletales."

"Why do you keep talking about Grandma? She's dead, moron," Lynn barks.

"Did she die? Are you sure she's dead? 'Cause you saw her body at the funeral, did ya? Did ya see it, party girl?" I ask.

She looks at me like a lawyer on TV and asks, "What do you know?"

"Everything," I reply like a badass sheriff. "Oh, I GOTCHA!"

Her eyes narrow, and a bit of steam drifts out of her red

ears. She knows she's caught, and for the first time in our lives she'll have to negotiate with me. After two minutes of tense debate, the terms of our arrangement are set. She won't clean my room or do me any favors except sign the notice of suspension and not tell the 'rents about the fight or any events pertaining to said fight. I will refrain from any language concerning Lynn, Grandma, or parties in connection to one another. If any terms of our agreement are broken . . . Full disclosure! The dam will break and knowledge will flow.

I'm not super happy with the deal, but I'll do better next time. Man, I hope there's a next time. It's really cool talking to my sister like we're equals or friends or something, because she's really fun to hang out with. She really is a psycho, and I'm not the only one who thinks it, but she's got tons of friends. You have to be pretty cool to pull that off. I don't want us to hug and kiss all the time like some weird cult kids, but a conversation every now and again would be kind of nice.

17. Love in a Movie Theater

Abby calls because she's worried about me. That's how chicks do with outlaws. They call or they bake cakes with files in the middle so their man can bust out of jail. Next she'll get "Carter Forever" tattooed on her lower back. That would be so hot!

EJ's number pops up on the other line, and I want to ask him about his lips, so I make quick plans to meet Abby at the movie theater tomorrow after school, and hang up (pimp). EJ sounds like Buckwheat, and I can barely understand him, but I know he's jealous. He's jealous I got suspended, but more so that I didn't get punched in the mouth. I tell him all about how Nick Brock got my bike back and how I rode in his truck. He tells me that he heard Pam tell her friend all about the fight and how we both sounded tough.

"To hink, Ham and er ig oobs are talkin' out us," he babbles.

"Awesome," I add. "We should get in fights all the time, huh?"

"Uh ugh, doo, my liss look like Ick Yagger. I'n not getting in any ore fighs, doo!" EJ passionately garbles.

Well, I'm not getting in any more fights if EJ isn't going to be there to take the punches.

The first day of suspension is like a dream. It's a beautiful fall day, and I tell my dad that I'm so stoked to have my bike back that I don't need a ride. I pedal around the neighborhood, practicing wheelies until both parents take off. I watch some TV, take a nap, and make sure not to eat anything that would cause anyone to fart or vomit tonight at the movies. I was going to kick some footballs and do some homework, but time really flies when you're doing stuff that you want to do. I look at the clock after *Oprah* and realize school's already out. How the hell did that happen?

I ride like the wind and get to the movie theater just as Abby's walking into the parking lot. I ride up behind her all slow. Should I scare her, like "BOOO!" or should I be all like "Heeyyy," nice and smooth? She's wearing a short skirt, her legs are strong, shaved, and shiny. How do you get legs to shine like—

"WHOA!" Almost wrecked into a fire hydrant. A fast swerve into the grass saves the day. This is why they don't let kids my age drive cars. In a car, I would have driven across three lanes of traffic and taken out a bus or something because of my gawking. On a bicycle, however, the only one in danger is me.

She hears the "Whoa!" and turns to see me recovering from the near collision. I go for a lame save by jumping off my bike, shooting her an eyebrow raise and a "S'up?" She climbs on my axle pegs, wraps her arms around my neck, and we "carpool" the rest of the way. So awesome.

She says she wants to see The Rock's new movie, but once the lights go down we don't watch that movie for a second. I couldn't tell you who was in it or what it was about, or anything. We could be at a Drew Barrymore movie, and The Rock may be an extra in it, for all I know. The only plot worthy of my attention is this bra. Who designs these things, Brink's?! It's got flaps, straps, hooks, and loops. It stretches when you need it to stay still. It's got this metal barrier under the boobs to prevent me from going commando underneath the whole operation. It must be made out of Kevlar and elastic, because there's no getting to these boobs! I grab at the lock sideways, up and down, push, pull, twist, jerk. Nothing works.

After twelve rounds, Abby sticks her hand behind her back and flicks it open one-handed! She must have pushed some kind of safety switch or something. She's hasn't had these boobs for very long and she's already a pro with the bra, so there's hope for me. I'll just focus and practice.

I've obviously done something excellent in her presence and I'm being rewarded. If I could put her boobs on my trophy shelf they would be my most prized award. I'm breathing so heavily Abby has to tell me to "Shhh" a couple of times. You'd think I'm running a marathon and not just getting some boob. I try to pull her shirt up so I can have a look at them, but she throws down the karate-chop block. That move is apparently off-limits.

I think getting boob is called first base, but I don't play baseball so I'm not sure. What's really hurting my brain is trying to figure out if her short skirt is a green light to steal second base or not. Second base is touching on her panties, private parts, and all that, I'm pretty sure. Is it a green light or is it just a fashion choice? Do I go for it or not? Oh man, this is a tough one. What if I shove my hand up there and she's not into it and karate chops me in the nuts? Or maybe it's like the first kiss. If she's wearing a green light and I don't go for it, she'll think I'm not into her, or I don't like her that way. But that's ridiculous!

I place my hand on her knee like some sort of ultra-cautious leg doctor probing for irregularities. It's a nice knee, but her joints are not my focus right now. I have other ideas about legs. Like, where they're coming from and where they're going. The examination is going well with my right hand. My left hand, however, has not left her boob, and I hope it never will. I lost all feeling in my lips an hour ago and I've run out of saliva. I need Gatorade!

The movie sounds pretty good. This is probably the part where you'd think The Rock is going to fail, but he finds some deep down strength that pulls him through, and he manages to save the day. I'll have to come back and watch it without Abby. In fact, I'm never seeing a movie I'm interested in with this chick again. Don't get me wrong, this is way more entertaining than anything I've ever seen. I've worked my way up to the upper part of the knee, but I wouldn't call it quite thigh yet. I need some of The Rock's courage, and quick!

I think the movie is about over, because the fighting noises and loud music have stopped. The Rock's making his final jokes and wrapping things up. I've got about three minutes to steal second base. It's go time! I slide my hand up, and up . . . and UP! I open my eyes and stop the kissing because Abby appears to have stopped breathing. About a minute left. Now or never. If a trembling body and a distant blank stare is a green light, then I've got it! I'm going in. Under the skirt. I'm in! I'm here. This is it. WOOO!!! I've made it. What the hell do I do now? It's definitely warmer under here, like a denim treasure cave. I'm like a blind doctor on his first day at the hospital. I believe my patient has gone into shock. She's not blinking or breathing. Her checkup is over, I guess, because the credits are rolling and she jumps up. Maybe she has to pee? I can only hope to pick that bra lock apart as fast as she just put it together.

The walk out of the theater is kind of weird. Should we hold hands? What am I supposed to say? "Did you enjoy the film?" or "Gee, thanks for letting me grab at you for the last couple hours."

I'm kind of dizzy when I ask, "Uh, do you want to see another movie?"

She seems dizzy too, and replies, "Huh? Uh, no, no I need to go home."

"Yeah, you have school tomorrow . . . Sucks to be you!" I laugh awkwardly. "I'm planning to get up at the crack of ten thirty!"

She doesn't laugh. She doesn't even seem to have heard my joke. She quietly says, "I have to go."

"Okay, well, I'll see ya," I say, as she walks out the door with her head down. That was weird, but I don't know what I'm supposed to do here. Do I chase her down and make sure she isn't crying? I should at least give her a ride home on my axle pegs, but my stomach is killing me and I'm so dizzy that I'd wreck the bike for sure. My mom always tells me, "Just be yourself," and I don't feel like chasing her down and listening to her cry (if that's what she's doing). What I feel like doing is seeing the next showing of The Rock's new movie and getting some candy and a huge cherry Coke, because my mouth is dry as dirt from all that kissing!

18. Post-Traumatic Stress Disorder

Suspension days fly by even faster than summer-break days. I'm back in school. I hoped there would be a parade in my honor for removing Scary Terry from the general population, but everybody seems to have forgotten how awesome I am. J-Low called me Ali once, but nobody else picked up on it, so it's the same old, same old. One inconvenient difference is that I start shaking when I get close to the Behavioral Disorders class. Which is a problem because it's right next to my locker.

School's a pain in the ass even when you vaguely understand what the hell is going on, but when you've been out of it for three days it's practically impossible to keep up. We're studying Shakespeare in English. Which is ironic because I thought I spoke English until Ms. Holly broke out the Shakespeare. If that's English, I don't know anybody who speaks it. If I started talking Shakespeare jibber-jabber, I'd get my ass handed to me. That ain't English! And you can tell me all day long how Shakespeare's a genius, but that doesn't change the fact that he sucks. I was supposed to read *Romeo and Juliet* on my break. And I did try, but you can read that junk for like two hours and all you've finished is one page. I have to reread the same line a thousand times before

I realize that all he is saying is "I love you" or "You're a punk, let's fight!" Just say it, man. Make your point. I don't have the time or the attention span for all this "Withering, carrion lark" crap! Fortunately, I've developed a system for feigning interest. I just look right at the teacher and nod my head from time to time. I might even add a quiet "Huh" every once in a while when the teacher's voice goes up in pitch. If you look out the window and space off, they catch you every time, but if you space off while you're staring at the teacher's mouth, they never suspect. I'll even write down a thing or two every now and then. Mind you, my notes never have anything to do with what the teacher is babbling about; it's usually a funny story I want to tell EJ or Abby later.

I'm watching Ms. Holly's mouth at the moment, not a clue what's coming out of it. She could be speaking Chinese for all I'm getting. Her mouth is HUGE! It's like her whole family are all giants and she's the smallest one, but her mouth is the same size as the rest of her giant clan. I bet she could eat a whole sandwich in one bite. She's a sight to see just talking regular. But when she gets to blabbing that Shakespeare, her face is like a cartoon character, flapping, spitting, chomping, and squawking, "Thee, Thou, Thoo, Thuist!"

"Mr. Carter," she says, "you seem especially interested in the works of Shakespeare. What do you think Romeo is trying to say here?"

Dang it, I went too far! You see, I'm such a good actor now, that I can go from pretending to pay attention to accidentally looking like I'm fascinated. I bet Robert De Niro has the same problem.

"Mr. Carter?" Ms. Holly asks again.

"Uh, well, it, it's tough to say. I-I-I think, he's really

talkin' about . . . love?" I say with insecurity. Just a shot in the dark.

"Very interesting," Ms. Holly says. "He's in the fight of his life with Tybalt, but you think he's talking about love?"

"Yep, Romeo is all about the love," I say. *Stick to your guns; she said it was interesting, not wrong.*

"Fantastic, Carter! He's explaining his love for Juliet and how that love must include her kinsman Tybalt. Love is what this speech is all about! It's being masked with physical violence and posturing, but that's very insightful of you to see through it," she says.

No, lady, that is very lucky! See why the dumb kids think I'm smart? I do stuff like that all the time. I'll fail the test on Tuesday, but today I'm "fantastic" and "insightful"!

I've made it four hours, but my books are getting heavy and I need my calculator and history folder. I don't want to, but I've got to go back to the scene of the crime. It's crazy, but I don't think I can go back to my own locker. I know Scary Terry's in jail, but what if he isn't and he's down there waiting for me? What if the other B.D. kids want a piece of me for getting rid of their leader? Or that bald teacher is pissed at me for disobeying a direct order and dropping his favorite nut ball? I'm trembling as I come around the corner. I think I have post-traumatic stress disorder. You can still see the dents in the locker where Terry kicked it. I feel the same choking fear. I can see Terry punching himself and EJ standing next to me. I can feel the other kids staring at me, and that same adrenaline rush, like a heart attack. The bell rings and I'm just standing here all alone in the hall, trying to pull myself together.

I need a little push, and I get it. A soft hand on my back

makes me jump. It's Abby. She gives me a sweet look and asks, "You okay?"

"Yeah, yeah, just gettin' my books," I say as cool as I can.

I look at Abby and how pretty she is today and how cool it is that she walked up just then. I grab her hand and walk the last three steps to my locker.

"You sure you're okay?" she asks.

"Yeah, I'm good. You okay?" I ask like a dope.

"Yeah, sorry I acted like a freak after the movie," she says.

"What?" I ask. "You didn't act like a freak. I mean, you didn't vomit; I think we're really improving!"

She laughs and kisses me on the cheek like an angel who let me touch on her boobs and panties. She's really great.

She turns away and says, "I'm late for gym, so . . ."

I give her a wave and say, "Okay, I love you."

What the . . . ? *Oh NO, CARTER!* It just slipped out with my post-traumatic retardation! Oh, that was dumb. Abby turns beet red. It just flew out, like when I say it to my mom or something. I guess when your heart talks for you, it doesn't send the signals to the brain for evaluation. I didn't even get the chance to stutter it. "I love you." There it is, out of nowhere. Like a rogue ninja who breaks away from his master. There's no getting him back!

Abby looks up at me with wide eyes and a gaping mouth, staring at my shocked face. I must look like she did when I stole her second base.

"Carter, I . . . I love you too," she replies, and kisses me on the lips.

DANG IT! How did we get here? This place isn't even on my map. Two dates and she's locked me up! Do I have to meet her parents and all that junk? I'm going to have to go shopping with them on Saturdays. I thought attention deficit was a tough disorder, but this post-traumatic stress is the granddaddy of all disorders! My brain was M.I.A. and I declared my love for someone.

What if my boys find out? Romeo is not a good nickname. And it's coming for sure if word gets out.

Still, the kiss Abby gave me was probably the best one I've ever had. The best it ever could be. (If I'd known it would be our last, I would have tried to make it last longer. I would have slipped her tongue or something. Just a slow soft peck will be all I'll have to remember her by.)

As she turns away, I see a shadowy figure watching us from the stairwell. I'm a little worried it's a teacher about to swoop down on us for Unlawful PDA. Or Lynn watching me break one of the cardinal rules by smooching in the halls. She hadn't mentioned it, but I'm pretty sure saying "I love you" after two dates is a NO-NO!

The shadowy figure, it turns out, is going to get me into a hell of a lot more trouble than any teacher ever could. The figure is one of my favorites, in fact. Amber Lee waits for one of her so-called "best friends" to float past her, before slinking toward me.

"Isn't that sweet. The two of you kissing in the hall," she says.

"Yeah, we p-p-probably shouldn't do that," I stutter.

"No, you guys are cute. Are you two getting serious?" she asks.

"W-w-wwh-what? Me and Abby? Naw! W-w-we, we're . . ." I stammer.

"You're just hanging out?" she says.

"Yeah, sure, hanging out," I lie. I don't know why I said that. It just flew out like the "I love you" did. Post-trauma is no joke, kids.

"So, are you guys just, like, friends or what?" she asks.

"Yeah, totally . . . w-w-we, we're friends," I reply. That is not a lie! Abby and I are friends.

"Friends who kiss, huh?" she asks.

"Yeah, that too," I blabber.

"Carter, you're a player, aren't you?" she asks.

"No," I reply.

"So, are you taking your little friend to homecoming?" she asks.

"Abby? Uh, no. W-w-well, I'm not really sure," I reply.

"So, like, you could take me if you wanted to?" she asks.

"Yeah, I could do that," I reply. This is just a hypothetical line of questioning, I'm sure.

"You should then. My dad thinks you're cute and harmless. So do I. So you could ask me to go to homecoming, and I can say yes to you," she says.

"Really?" I reply in shock. Not the smoothest of responses, I know.

"Yeah," she says.

"Cool," I respond with a nod.

"So, you should . . . ask me, Carter!" she orders.

"You wanna go to homecoming . . . with me?" I ask.

"Yes I would, thanks for asking," she replies, all sly.

What the hell is happening here?

"So call me and we'll figure out what to wear and what time you should pick me up," she says.

"Uh, okay, I got my bike back," I say.

"I am not riding on your axle pegs to the homecoming dance, Carter!" she snaps.

"No, no! Of course not. I was just saying. Like, I thought you'd want to know. But like, for a joke, me in a suit and you in a dress, on my pegs. Ha-ha, can you imagine?" I blabber.

"Yeah, I'll see you, Carter," she says as she swishes away. Man, she is fine. What the HELL? I'm back at school for five minutes and all hell has broken loose! This is the life of an outlaw! Juggling chicks, breaking rules, and breaking hearts. Oh God, what am I going to do about Abby? What am I going to do about my sister when she comes at me with a machete for telling a girl I love her and then asking a different girl to homecoming in the same passing period? I really do love Abby, I think, but I've been in love with Amber Lee since the first day of sixth grade. If Abby really does "love me too," she'll want me to be happy, right? She'll be really excited about this.

I just stand there frozen through most of fifth hour and try to get a handle on the situation. On the bright side, I'm not worried about Scary Terry anymore. He's the least of my problems at the moment. I wouldn't even mind it so much if he came out of that B.D. room and punched me in the jaw. It's about the only thing that could stop my mouth from running today.

I show up at Mr. Rumpford's math class three days and forty minutes late. He seems to be aware of my dilemma by the hopelessly lost look in my eyes. He doesn't even waste his breath, he just motions for me to take my seat and continues to write on the overhead projector. The isosceles triangle means very little to me on a regular day, but today I'm in a love triangle, so it's pointless.

19. The Setup

We're getting dressed up in our stinky pads and cleats for practice, and the boys are all over me.

"You stole my bike, A-HOLE!!!" Hormone laughs.

"If you kicked footballs as hard as you swing textbooks, you'd be in the NFL, Carter!" Bag says.

"Cahta drougt ah hunk!" EJ babbles. We all look at him.

"What'd you do while you were suspended?" Nutt asks.

"Just chilled out, saw The Rock's new movie with Abby," I reply.

I thought they might ask me about the movie, like, "Was it funny?" or "Was it action-packed?" But I don't play football with film critics.

"Did you get some during the movie?" Bag asks.

"Did you grab up on those tig ol' bitties?" Andre asks.

The whole locker room stops what they're doing. They're all staring at me.

"Tell me you got a look at 'em," Andre continues.

"Yeah, I-I-I sort of did," I say quietly.

"YEAH!" the room erupts.

"Those things are nice, huh?" Nutt asks.

"They're like two handfuls, right?" Doc squeals.

"Did you get that bra off?" Levi pesters.

"Yep, they're nice," I reply.

"YEAH!" they yell again.

"Did you go down her pants?" Andre asks. Man, this guy's like the *National Enquirer* today.

"Naw," I say, all humble.

They groan with disappointment.

"'Cause she was wearin' a skirt," I reply.

"YEEAAH!" they roar. "He went up the skirt!"

I thought I was the only one who hadn't done any of this stuff, but they all seem really interested, like they may not be the experts I thought they were.

"Short skirt?" Hormone drools.

"Real short," I reply. What am I supposed to do, lie? It was short! I'm not bragging, I'm just sitting on a bench in my underwear stating the facts.

"Did you grab on that PUNANI?" Andre asks.

I shrug and reply, "Uh, I . . . I think so."

"Waddaya mean, ya think so? Did ya get up in there or not?" Andre demands.

Well, first of all, I don't really know the definition of "punani," and I'm not sure what all is meant by "up in there," but I don't want to disappoint anyone, so I yell, "Hell yeah, I got up in there!"

"YEAH!" roars out one last time before Coach comes in and yells at us to get to practice. Thank God! What a bunch of ninnies. I always wanted to be a stud, but that sucked. I walk out of the locker room and see Andre talking to some band kids on the way up to the field. Which is weird because Andre never talks to anyone, especially not band geeks. As I walk by, I could swear a girl pointed at me and said, "That's him!" I could be making that up in my head, though.

We did the whole practice thing, and I got to kick. I muffed a bunch of them because I didn't practice like I was supposed to. "Carter, you're killin' me!" follows every shank. We have a game tomorrow, so we have to go into the football classroom and talk about "the game plan," and Coach draws his Xs and Os on the chalkboard and talks his face off about focus, intensity, and blah, blah, blah. I actually have no idea what we do in this room, because it's air-conditioned, and the windows look out onto the field, where the cheerleaders practice their yelling and jumping, and the drill team works out their dance moves. I'm pretty focused on the drill team today.

I see Abby. I see Amber. I see a storm brewing as a couple of band girls walk up to Abby and start yapping. Huh . . . There are a lot of hands on hips, head tilting, and fierce nodding out there. I wonder what those chicks are saying to Abby, because the other drill team fatties are herding around her. They're all touching Abby on the shoulders and stuff. And then the crying starts. Why are those bitches making Abby cry? Are they finally giving her the boot for getting too skinny? Is this the "Eat Up or Get Out" talk? I don't like seeing Abby cry. It hurts my chest.

Abby and the herd stomp over to the cheerleader practice really fast. She walks straight up to Amber Lee. She must be asking if she can join the cheerleaders now that the drill team has dropped her. She would look great in one of those belly button–exposing short-skirt-jumper deals. Abby is really fired up and crying hard. Amber is just shaking her head. It must be too late to join up, or they're all out of belly-button costumes.

Bitchy Nicky and a few cheerleaders join Abby and the drill teamers. They break out fast, leaving Amber behind. They're stampeding toward the building like there's a sale at the mall. They look pissed. Maybe they're coming to see if there's one more cheerleader getup in storage. They're getting closer to the window that I'm staring out of. There must be twenty of them, moving fast! A cloud of dust trails them. My heart is pounding as they roll right up to the football room window. Most of the guys have noticed them coming as well, and Coach has stopped blabbering. I can hear Abby crying.

Bitchy Nicky puts her hand on her hip and yells to the closed windows, "Carter! CARTER!!! We know you're in there, Carter!"

She's cheerleader loud and her tone is deafening. All the guys turn to look at me. I might throw up. Coach looks pissed.

"CARTER? Carter! WE NEED TO TALK TO YOU!" Nicky yells again. "NOW!"

"What the hell is this?" Coach asks me.

"H-h-ho-how should I know?" I reply. My eyes are as big as basketballs.

"Get up here," Coach says, motioning for me to come closer.

He opens the window. Abby's cries fill the football room as Coach asks, all nice, "What can I do for you, ladies?"

"Coach, we need to speak with one of your players. We need a word with Car-ter," Nicky responds.

"Yes, I get that," Coach says as he turns away. "The whole building gets that."

Tears are rolling down Abby's face, and two girls are having to hold her up. Oh, I'm a bad guy! And not in like, a cool way.

Coach grabs my shirt and whisper/yells, "What the hell is goin' on? What'd you do?"

"Well, I may have told that crying girl out there that I loved her after we went to second base together at the movies . . . I think?"

He rubs his forehead and asks, "What do you mean, 'you think'?"

I whisper, "Well, I thought oral sex was third base, and I know we didn't do that, but Nutt's brother said third base was when you touch, uh . . . pubic hair?"

Coach looks like he wishes he hadn't asked me that last question, and I'm not sure I actually answered it, so I continue, "Um, but what I think the real trouble is here, Coach, is that I might have asked a different girl to go to homecoming with me."

Coach fights back a smile and simply says, "You ain't too bright, Carter."

"No, sir," I reply.

"Well, we've got a game tomorrow, and those girls aren't going away on their own," he says.

"Yeah . . . Wait. What? No way!" I reply. *You're not throwing me to the wolves just so you can go over your crap game plan!*

"Yep," Coach says empathetically. "You made your bed, now stick your head out that window and lay in it."

I thought he'd at least help me out with a diagram on the chalkboard. Like, I'm the one *0*, and there are twenty *X*s with ponytails and weapons, but he just shoots me a snarl and gives me a hard shove to the window. The guys are all giggling.

"Hey, Nicky," I say.

She looks like a lead prosecutor in a leotard. "Did you tell the whole football team that you had naked sex with Abby in the movie theater?" Nicky demands.

Abby wails! The team howls with laughter.

"What? No!" I say. How the . . . ?

Andre opens the window next to me and says, "Yeah, he did."

"No, I didn't!" I protest.

"Yeah, you did! We all heard you," Andre blabbers.

EJ runs up to the window next to Andre to defend me. "Noo, he said dat he, 'goh up in dare,' noh dat he had secs wit er," EJ exclaims through his busted lips.

That's my BOY! Coming through in a pinch.

I shake my head in agreement. "You see?" I yell, but Abby just cries harder.

"What the hell was that supposed to mean?" Nicky asks.

"WHY?" Abby cries.

"I didn't, Abby! They made me. They were putting words in my mouth!" I exclaim.

Nicky breaks in with, "Did you or did you not tell Abby that you loved her, and then turn around and ask Amber Lee to go to homecoming?"

The football room gasps.

"No! Well, not exactly . . . Amber is, uh?" I reply.

"What? What are you saying about Amber? Amber is what, Carter?" Nicky orders.

Objection: this cheerleader is badgering the witness! Coach finally takes pity on me by yelling, "All right, that's about all the time I got for this crap. I got a football game to win tomorrow. You gals can cross-examine my kicker some other time." He shuts the windows, and that's the end of that. . . . My life, that is.

20. Full Disclosure

We're having chili for dinner tonight. It's my favorite thing Mom cooks, because instead of vegetables or rice or something on the side of the main dish, we have cinnamon rolls. I don't know who told her you could swap broccoli for a cinnamon roll, but I like it—usually. Tonight I can't even think about eating. The phone keeps ringing. We aren't allowed to answer the phone during dinner, thanks to my sister. The 'rents just think it's a heavy night for Lynn's twenty-four-hour chat line, but I think there could be a few calls in there for me tonight.

"No calls at dinnertime!" my mom yells at the phone as if the person calling can hear. "Sooo, Carter, let's talk," she says all slow, and puts down her spoon. "How's school been lately?" She puts her elbow on the table and rests her chin on her fist. She's giving me the I'm-your-mother-and-I-know-something's-up look.

Huh? What does she know? I look her in the eye and try to figure out what she's got on me. . . . Dang it! Abby's mom must've called!

"I DIDN'T HAVE SEX WITH HER!" I blurt out. Lynn spits water all over the table in shock. Mom is stunned, and I think my dad's eyes are going to pop out.

"What the hell are you talking about?!" Mom

barks. The phone rings again.

Huh? Maybe that was just small talk, and a "School's fine, Mom" would've done the trick.

"I don't know! What the hell are you talkin' about?" I say.

"Who did you have sex with?" Lynn asks.

"Nobody. I'm a virgin, damn it! I'll always be a virgin! I'm gonna die a virgin!" I yell.

"'Atta boy!" my dad adds.

"Not helping, William!" Mom yells at Dad. "I was talking about you getting into a fight at school!" she clarifies.

"WHAT?" I ask, shooting a nasty look at Lynn. She has picked the wrong fella to double-cross today! Her eyes get really big as I nullify our agreement. "Fight nothin', Mom! Let's talk about how Lynn had a huge party when we were at Grandma's funeral, and how the house was so jacked up that she had to hire a cleaning crew and a contractor to put it back together!"

"WHAT?!" my parents declare in unison, shooting daggers out of their eyes.

"Is that how the doorbell magically fixed itself?" Dad asks.

"You little jerk, I didn't tell her anything!" Lynn screeches.

The phone rings again. "Unplug that damn thing!" my mom yells.

"Oh yeah, who told her then, genius?" I ask Lynn.

"I don't know, but it sounds like they didn't tell her that you got suspended on top of everything and stayed home for three days jerking off and watching TV. Did they tell you all that, Mother?" Lynn asks, all snotty.

"You got suspended?" my dad barks.

"Lynn signed the note!" I confess. Might as well get it all out.

Mom cries, "EJ's mom called to see what I thought about 'All this fight business,' and I had to ask, 'What fight business?' like an idiot. Apparently I don't know the first thing about my children! I'm just the moron who feeds them, and pays for shoes and clothes, and picks them up from the hospital!"

"You're both going to military school!" my dad yells.

"Oh, shut up!" Mom barks. The phone rings for the thirtieth time, and I'm ready to pack for military school, because that sounds pretty sweet to me.

"Oh, just answer it!" my dad orders. *Couldn't get any worse, could it, Pop?*

Lynn jumps up to see what gossip she's missed in the last fifteen minutes, and to pass on all the drama from her own dinner table. She must be so happy I go to her school now.

"It's a girl for Carter," Lynn explains, and passes the phone. *DANG IT!*

"Just see what they want and call them back, please," my mom says quietly.

"Hello?" I say into the phone, hoping it's not Abby calling to give me an earful. But it's Bitchy Nicky. Even better.

She snidely says, "Amber Lee heard what you said about her this afternoon, and we think that it would be best if she didn't go to homecoming with you."

Man, I used to think Nicky was semicool and had a nice butt, but she's really the Antichrist. "Why?" I ask.

"Oh, let's not play games, Carter! We all know that you

are a liar and a snake, and your sweet and innocent game is UP! As far as we are concerned, you are banished!" she says.

"Who is this 'we' you keep talking about?" I ask. "I didn't say anything about Amber in the locker room," I explain.

"Just stop, Carter! It's over. Abby hates you. Amber hates you. *We* hate you. Good-bye!" she says, and then— *click*—the line goes dead.

I can't move. My family's not talking; they're just staring at their only boy, who, it turns out, is really a degenerate lady-killer. They think I'm still on the phone with someone. I don't want to tell them what the call was about; I can't. It becomes pretty obvious that I'm not talking to anyone as tears start to fall into my chili. I start to shake and cry like a baby. My dad takes the phone out of my hand, and I fall into his arm. I garble, "I hate high school! You knew I wasn't ready; you should've held me back in junior high." I can't take the pressure of lying and fighting and homework and rejection and bras and going out to lunch and parties and not being able to ride my bike anymore and first base and second base and clutch kicking with varsity players who can kill me if they want to and lady boobs and lifting weights and hurting all the time.

My dad softly pats my back as I have the nervous breakdown. Nobody seems mad at me anymore, because I'm crying like a little bitch at the dinner table. I'm sobbing like a little kid who's been thrown into a world of adults and adult problems with no training whatsoever. It's too much. I've been in high school for a month and a half and I'm never going to get through it.

"Is that Amber Lee you're talking about?" Lynn asks.

"Lynn, no!" Mom orders. Momma Bear has been slack on protecting her youngest cub lately, but she's here for me now. And nobody's going to paw at me anymore tonight. But she can't protect me from the world anymore; she can't even protect me from myself. I can't ask my mom about any of this, and that thought makes me feel more alone than I've ever felt before.

21. After the Fall

I keep a low profile at school for a while and try to keep my nose clean. I haven't seen Abby in a week. She may have noticed me and broken out in the other direction. I accidentally almost ran into Bitchy Nicky when I was coming out of science class. She didn't say anything, but she threw up her hands and made a face like I was a fart roaming the halls. Andre made a kissing noise at me in the locker room after practice yesterday. And I probably shouldn't have, but I flipped him off and walked away.

I'm taking a math quiz and spacing off as usual. We've been working on the Pythagorean theorem for the past week, and this is the test to see if we get it. Well, I don't get it, but I have a funny joke. I call it Py-Fag-Orean's theorem. If this was a test about jokes I might be okay, but since Mr. Rumpford isn't into jokes, I'm screwed.

Sarah "the Caboose" Ruiz sits in front of me, and she doesn't get any of this, either. I know it because she's gotten up to sharpen her pencil twenty times. I don't mind that one bit. We don't call her the Caboose for nothing. She wears tight, low-cut jeans, and I gawk at her booty every time she presents it. Even if I did understand Py-Fag-Orean's theorem, I would still take a break from it to ogle that thing. It's like two volleyball pistons under a denim blanket.

She gets up again to sharpen the sharpest pencil in the world. Question number twenty-five means about as much to me as question five did, so I get to gawking. If her wiggly walk was a crime and I was asked to testify against it at a trial, I could give you every detail. She slowly struts up to the front and makes a smooth right turn in front of Ruddy Gill's open answer sheet. She pauses and bends down a bit to give it a closer look. She moves on to the pencil sharpener, and I move from her right cheek to her left cheek and back again. My eyes drift from the pockets to the waist, to the tops of her short legs, and right into MR. RUMPFORD'S BEADY EYES! Whoa, he spotted me spotting her booty! Dang it, you shouldn't be looking at me, Rumpford. You should be looking at Sarah and asking why her pencil is so damn sharp and why she keeps looking at Ruddy Gill's test.

He just shakes his head in disgust. Mr. Rumpford was never fourteen. He could never understand my plight. All he loves is Pythagoras and his stupid theorem. He can't understand what it takes to get me through a day in this place. He looks away, but I can see a wide smile under his little mustache. He pretends to scratch his face to hide it. No way! He's laughing. He's really cracking up at me and bends down like he's got to tie his shoe. Mr. Rumpford is a human being! He's caught my horniness red-handed and he gets it. I've never recognized a teacher as a real person before. It's almost chilling. He looks up at me still laughing quietly and shakes his head in mutual understanding. I can now see that long before he grew a mustache and combined short-sleeved shirts and neckties, he was a horn dog too!

I definitely failed that test, but I learned a valuable lesson. Teachers are people . . . underpaid, poorly dressed, lame car–driving people.

22. Back in the Saddle

Homecoming is in three days, and since I don't have a date and may never get a girlfriend, I've decided to invest in a porno. Nutt's brother, Bart, sold it to me for thirty-five dollars. It's at least twenty years old, and it's a copy of a copy of a poor-quality videotape. There's no sound and it's stuck on fast forward, but you can make out that people are definitely doing the nasty on it, really, really fast. Nutt calls it a "research tape." I watch it in the basement because that's where we have the old VCR, and nobody goes down there. The last thing I need is for my dad to stroll in and see me abusing myself to lightning-fast pornographic images. Military school will become a reality faster than those people are doing it.

I just finished my nightly research session when EJ calls to talk about shooting hoops at the community center and seeing a movie while everyone else is at the stupid dance. EJ says that dances are lame, but I know he's never talked to a girl before. How difficult would it be to go from never speaking to hanging out and dancing with one all night? I don't call him on it, I just joke about him being my "homecoming bitch" and how he'd better get me flowers.

He burns me pretty good with, "If I put out at the movies, you better not talk about it in the locker room."

I laugh, but I can hear his mom squawking in the background about how he didn't put his clothes away or how he used wire hangers or some crap, and how he's grounded for a week.

Man, she's pulled this B.S. on me soo many times! She's always busting out rules and regulations at the worst times and totally screwing up my plans. EJ drops the phone and fires off every excuse in the book, but his mom's a tough nut and EJ's cracking.

He yells, "Nu-uh, Mooom!"

"Don't do it, EJ, FIGHT!" I shout into the phone. "I don't want to stay home while everybody is going to this damn dance!" But the whining is really picking up steam and shifts to crying. I lose hope when he starts gurgling like a baby, and I hang up to save him the embarrassment.

The phone rings thirty seconds later, and I answer, "What's up, you whiny little bitch?" to bust his chops a little.

But instead of a sniveling homeboy, I get a, "Um, hello? Hello?" It's a girl's voice.

DANG IT! It's some chick for Lynn, and she's going to tell her that I answered the phone, "What's up, you whiny little bitch?"

"Uh, is Carter there?" the mystery girl asks.

"Uh . . . let me see if he's here," I say.

I collect my thoughts and try to figure out who this might be. "Hello, Will Carter here," I mutter, as cool as possible.

"Hi . . ." she says in a sultry voice.

"Hey you," I reply like I know who it is. I hate it when people assume I know their voice. My aunt does that. I talk to her once a year; I don't know her voice!

"What's going on?" she asks.

"Not much," I respond. It's not Abby, and it's clearly not Nicky, because there's no screeching. It's not Pam, but the mystery voice is super sexy.

"Do you know who this is?" she asks.

"Gisele? Look, I told you, I'm not into you like that. . . ."

"What are you talking about, Carter?" she asks.

"I don't know, I have no idea who this is," I reply smoothly.

"I'll give you a hint . . . I'm probably the only girl at school who doesn't think you're scum," she says.

"Yeah, not only does that not help . . . it's mean," I reply.

"Okay, my dad thinks you're cute. . . ." she says.

What kind of freaky phone sex is this?

She continues, "You told me that you and Abby were just friends, and that you weren't serious, and that we were gonna go to homecoming."

"Amber?" I respond like the most brilliant detective on the force.

"Rusty Dollingsworth was gonna take me to the dance, but my dad is being a dick and won't let me go with him," she pouts.

Good for your dad! That guy is like twenty years old, a scumbag, and drives his dead grandma's car.

"So now I can't go!" she continues.

"Oh, that sucks," I say. Awesome!

"So, do you still want to take me?"

Does a bear poop in the woods? "REALLY?!" pops out of my mouth before I can get it back.

She laughs. "Good, pick me up at seven."

"Okay, do you want me to wear something specific that will match with your dress?" (I am not gay; she brought it up in the hall.)

"No, just pick me up," she says, and then hangs up.

Oh man, I'm a pimp after all. I guess I've been playing defense for a couple of weeks and everything's falling into place.

I call up EJ, and you could tell he was still kind of crying. "Hey, dude," I say.

"Man *(sniffle),* I can't hang out on Saturday anymore," he says, pitifully.

Like I'm supposed to be shocked. Once his mom drops an order, there's no way around it. EJ is the oldest kid in his family, so he's in charge of breaking his parents in. But he's doing a terrible job; his little sister Emmy will curse him someday. My folks, however, have been so bent and twisted by my older sister it's almost sad. Like, I'm grounded right now, but look who's on the phone.

"Yeah, it's cool, dude," I say, all sly. "I'll just go to the dance with Amber Lee instead."

"Yeah right," he snivels. "Every girl at school hates you, dude."

"I guess one girl doesn't, smart-ass! Because I just got off the phone with Amber Lee, and she asked me to go to homecoming—for the second time!" I respond kind of mean.

"No way," he says.

"Yes way. I'm picking her up, and we're wearing matching outfits!" I say.

"What?" he asks.

"Nothin'," I say. "It's not important. What's important

is that I'm gonna get to have sex with Amber Lee in seventy-six hours!"

"Man, why are these chicks into you all the sudden? Nobody asked me to go to any dance. What the hell's goin' on?" he replies, all mad.

"Hate the game, not the player." I laugh. "Okay, dude, here's the deal: my sister told me all these secret tricks for talkin' to chicks and how to get them to put out and stuff."

"I knew it!" he yells. "What's the trick, what am I supposed to do with 'em?"

"I can't tell you, dude, it's top secret. She wasn't even supposed to tell me," I say.

EJ cries, "We've been best friends since kindergarten. You can't become a babe slayer and leave me in the dust! I don't have an older sister. I'm disadvantaged. All I got is Emmy, who can only drop preschool wisdom like, 'No pull Barbie's hair!'"

"That's probably some early girl wisdom. Nobody likes to get their hair pulled," I say. "Except this one chick in my porno; I think she's into it. I can't really tell, though. I wish they would slow down."

"Focus, Carter. Give me the secrets!" he demands.

So I tell him everything that Lynn told me, but he thinks I'm holding out on him. He thinks there's like, some magic pill. I hear there is, but it's illegal in the U.S. I tell him I have to go get ready for my date, hang up, and do some more research in the basement.

While brushing my teeth I notice some fuzz growing above my lip. Who's the man? If I'm going to be having sex on Saturday I'd better shave that junk off. And while a boy might go downstairs and ask his dad for help, a man just goes for it. I'm not an idiot. You just slather cream on your face, grab a razor, flex your abs, and scrape everything off. What's the big deal? I slide the razor up from the base of my neck to the top of my cheek. Then flick the cream off and wink at myself in the mirror. I scrape it all the way back down, and then I go sideways, from ear to ear. I can almost hear the shaving commercial music playing, and a deep voice behind me saying, "The best a man can get!" I'm the man! Man, I look cool. . . . Man, I'm bleeding! The white cream has turned pink and is dripping off my face. It's funny because it doesn't hurt, but I'm definitely cut somewhere . . . or everywhere, and bleeding like a stuck pig. Who the hell thought this was a good idea? Yeah, let's take a sharp-ass razor and push it to my FACE! I need to go to the hospital . . . now! I look like a character from the Saw movies stumbling toward my dad in the living room. He's panic-stricken at the sight of his only son with two quarts of blood dripping down his face, neck, and chest.

"Good God, what did you do?" he yells.

"I shaved," I reply with a dumb smile.

"Shave the hair, not the skin!" he yells, running to the bathroom.

He dabs a wet cloth on my bloody chin. I want to tell him that's one of Mom's good towels and not to use it. But I sort of babble "Gooo" instead and collapse to my knees. The room is fuzzier than my lip had ever been.

I don't wake up until the next morning. I'm happy to just be alive and super stoked I haven't missed the dance. We ought to sue that pretty boy from the shaver commercial. My dad told me he would show me how to shave when my cuts heal, but screw that; I'll just stay fuzzy.

Nick Brock asked my sister to homecoming. What the hell is that? He needs to be focusing on the big game, not worrying about what kind of head games Lynn is running on him. She's giddy, which is weird. She's running around all crazy and laughing for no reason. She seems to have no interest in helping me out with Amber Lee. She's way too busy yapping to her friends that Nick will be picking her up in his aunt's BMW. That's dumb. If I had his truck, I'd never swap it for some lame BMW.

"Do you think I could borrow Nick's truck?" I ask Lynn.

"What? Don't be an idiot!" she barks.

If he's not using it, what's the big deal? I drove a golf cart last summer. Amber's dad likes me; he won't care. Amber will succumb to the sex vibes of Brock's truck and she won't be able to control herself. The vibe is from Brock, but I'll be driving, so she'll have to release her desire in my direction. Wait a minute. Is Brock going to poke my sister? Dang it, I think that pisses me off. He better not, or I'll . . . Man, I hope I don't have to fight Nick Brock. My mom would not like giving me sponge baths and feeding me through straws the rest of my life.

23. Medusa at Fourteen

It's finally Saturday night, and my dad and I roll out. I'm wearing my church suit, and my cuts are barely visible. The suit was way too big for me when we bought it, but it's just right these days, and I look sharp.

"What do you know about this Nick Brock?" my dad asks.

"He can bench press three hundred twenty-five pounds," I respond.

My dad raises his eyebrows. I'm not sure if he's impressed or if he's thinking whether or not he can beat up a guy who can bench that much. As we pull up to Amber's house, Yosemite Sam is on the porch. His handlebar mustache is in full effect as he flicks his cigarette into the dirt and walks bowlegged toward our car.

"Oh crap," my dad says under his breath as he gets out of the car.

"Jeremiah Lee," Amber's dad says, sticking his hand out for my dad to shake.

"Huh, ha-ha!" I laugh out loud because I'm scared as hell, and it sounded like he said, "General Lee." My dad shoots me a mean look.

I'm not sure if "the General" is snarling or smiling when he says, "Amber's my angel. She wants to dress like a hooker, though."

My dad raises his eyebrows at me, like, "What the hell did you get me into?"

I jump out of the car to deflect some of the awkwardness. Her dad claps his hands and yells, "There he is! Mr. Slick. What're ya—runnin' for president?"

I shake my head and mutter, "No, I'm here to take Amber to the dance. . . ."

"You're gonna be a good boy, aint'cha? 'Cause I got a blowtorch down at the body shop you wouldn't like. *SHHUUUUWWW!!!*" he threatens, while acting out the use of said blowtorch.

Sweat must be shooting out of my forehead. My dad tries to keep the conversation away from blowtorches when he says, "Oh yeah, Lee Auto Body! Down on Merrian Lane. We brought our Honda in last year when my daughter plowed into a telephone pole."

I'm glad my dad is here or I'd be running down the street screaming right now.

The screen door flies open, and Amber steps out onto the porch. WOW, she looks . . . awful! What the hell happened to the hottie I see every day at school? And where did she get that green dress? A bridesmaid in 1990 is looking for it, and some football player somewhere is going to need his shoulder pads back. No wonder she didn't want me to match her outfit; it would have been impossible. What the hell is in her hair? Is that Quaker State? Why is it all piled on top of her head and then dripping down onto her face? It's Medusa at fourteen! It's like a bad dream. I'm going to the dance with the hottest girl in my class, yet her dad will kill me if I touch her, and she's been ambushed by some demented makeover show.

"You look real pretty, hon," her dad says.

No you DON'T! You look hideous. Get back in there and try again. Your dad owns a body shop. He knows fenders, bumpers, and how to intimidate, but if he thinks this is "pretty," we have strayed from his area of expertise.

After an awkward silence I jump into the backseat of the car. I can't even look at her or I'll start laughing.

Her dad leans into my dad's window like a cop giving out a ticket. "Now, she's gonna sleep over at her friend Nicky's house tonight, so she'll just get a ride with Nicky's mom after the dance."

She gives me a wink and says, "Yeah, we have to go, Dad."

What? I have to hang out with Bitchy Nicky? I thought they hated each other this week. Why would Amber have . . . ? Wait a minute. Could . . . Is this a signal? "Sleep over"? That's got to be code. And what was that wink all about? I wish I could call my sister for a translation, but I believe Amber means we will have sex very soon! What else could it mean? Oh, thank God I brushed my teeth and I've done my research. I know all the moves. I can make all the faces. I've just got to slow it all down.

We drive to the dance in complete silence. I have no questions—lots of thoughts, but no questions. I can't ask her if she wants to get a hotel room; I spent all my money on that stupid porno. And if I ask her where she got her dress, it'll come out, "Where the hell did you get that dress?" I can't give her any kind of compliment tonight because I don't want to encourage her in this direction. The thought of actual sex is scrambling my brain. I'm blinking a lot. It's, like, a hundred degrees in here.

We get to the dance, and she jumps out of the car quick. "I'm gonna run to the bathroom," she says as she slams the door.

Good news, because I couldn't stand up right now if the president walked by.

My dad looks at me through the rearview mirror and asks, "You okay, pal?"

"Who, me? Yeah, I'm good!" I say, blinking my left eye uncontrollably.

"Okay, well, take a breath, will ya?" he orders.

"Sure," I reply. Wow, that felt good. I haven't been breathing for, like, ten minutes.

"Give me a call for a pickup, be yourself, and don't do anything her dad'll kill you for. General Lee has our address," he says.

"It did sound like he said General Lee, didn't it?" I laugh and slap him five. My dad and I shared a joke. Yep, I'm becoming a man. Maybe we'll grab a beer tomorrow.

24. The Sting

The gym has never looked better as I strut inside. I give Nutt a high five and Bag a "S'up?" Bag's hands are full of caboose, but his face is on a quick break from making out with Sarah Ruiz from my math class. His sister, Pam, is here with a guy who looks like he's thirty years old. She looks hot, and he looks uncomfortable. The dude's here with Pam, and I think that's worth any humiliation. I'm here with Amber Lee, and although she's not looking her best, she's still the fox of the freshman class. I don't see her, though. She should be easy enough to spot with the two extra feet of hair and that green tracking device of a dress.

I give a nod to Andre because he's staring at me. I heard he's here with a chick from Hooker High. Hooker's our biggest rival in sports. It was named after a Civil War general, but since their chicks are all hot and easy, the name works on a couple different levels. Andre's chick wiggles off to the punch bowl in a tight red dress, and she looks like no exception to the rule. I'm glad he has connections to hot girls with nice asses from other schools, or else he'd probably be here with Amber instead of me. The guy scores like two touchdowns every single game. . . . Oh crap, Abby Alert!

Where did she come from? Why is Abby even here?

Dang it, the drill team's in charge of decorations and refreshments! She only told me about it a million times when we talked on the phone (pre-breakup). I really shouldn't play video games when I'm on the phone. Man, she looks great for someone who's supposed to be hanging toilet paper. A sexy red dress to pass out punch? Man, her boobs are doing their thing! She hasn't spotted me yet, which is good, because this could get ugly. She's going to start crying again, and then she and Amber are going to start fighting over me and pulling hair. Red dresses will get ripped off, and green sateen velvet will shred (thank God). They'll scream out their devotions. Who will win? Who will lose? Who loves me more? Oh, the HORROR!

Pam walks up and says, "Hey, heartbreaker." She has no idea.

"Hey," I respond. "Who's your date, Colonel Sanders?"

She rolls her eyes and proudly sneers, "His name is Mike, and he's in college."

"Yeah? Looks like he's been in college for a while," I say, all sly.

"Shut it, Carter!" she replies. "Who are you here with?"

"Amber Lee." I beam.

"Really? I thought she was with Rusty Dollingsworth," Pam responds.

Why would she think something like that? "Nope, my dad just dropped us off," I say.

"Oh, well, that's good. You and Abby both work fast," she says.

"What do you mean?" I ask.

"Andre," she says.

"What about him?" I ask.

"Abby is here, with Andre," Pam says, all nonchalant.

"WHAT?!" I screech as my jaw drops open, and I look back over my shoulder at Andre and the hottie he's with. That isn't a Hooker . . . that's my Abby! Son of a . . . Why are his hands around my Abby's waist? Aha! This is why he was the lead witness for the prosecution at my trial. It all makes sense. Andre set me up.

My sister swoops in from out of nowhere and pushes my mouth closed. "I guess you hadn't heard about that?" Lynn asks.

"No," I say, dumbfounded.

"Well, what do you care; you're here with Amber, right? Go dance with her," she orders, and gives me a shove in the opposite direction.

I walk through the crowd in a daze and look for my date. An R. Kelly song just came on, so it would be a good time for slow dancing. Why is Abby at the dance with that jerk? It's his fault her heart got broken. He made me tell the football team about the movie theater action. I didn't want to, but he intimidated me. Man, if he weren't way bigger than me, I'd . . . Man, I've got to learn karate!

I finally spot Amber's hair from across the gym. It's huge! It's all bobbing around. What is that hair doing? Dancing? Dang it! Amber Lee is dancing with Rusty Dollingsworth. She's not wearing that awful green dress anymore, either. She's really not wearing much. It's like a Victoria's Secret type of teddy dress (spring catalog, page 17). But why's she dancing with Rusty's dumbass on our first date? This will make a funny story for EJ to tell at our wedding. I'll just stare at them for a while, and then they'll stop, and I'll get to dance with Amber in that lingerie thing.

Rusty must be getting the hint, because he finally lets go of my date's butt and is walking toward me.

"Hey, freshman, you wanna take a picture?" Rusty asks, all up in my face.

"Uhh?" I say.

"Because a picture'll last longer." He laughs.

"B-b-but, I b-b-brought her," I stammer with great authority.

"Yeah, and I'm takin' her home! So beat it, kid," he yells.

"But, we were gonna . . . She's my date," I say just loud enough for no one to hear.

Does he not know of my legend? Was he sick the day I beat up Scary Terry Moss? He can't just cop my lady and walk out of the gym holding her hand. Where are they going? The dance just started. I follow them out and watch as they get into Rusty's dead grandma's car and drive away. I wonder what General Lee will think of this?

What the hell am I supposed to do now? I'm not going to cry or anything, but my chest is caving in. I lean my hot face on the cool glass of the gym door when the lightbulb finally switches on: Amber's dad wouldn't let her go out with Rusty, but I would do just fine for a ride to the dance. That green dress is in a trash can somewhere, along with my feelings.

"How's your date going, Carter?" a mean voice asks from behind.

I turn around to see Bitchy Nicky staring at me with the snidest look on her face. Abby is right behind her. Their dresses are tight, their hair is smooth, and the makeup is on thick. Just a couple of mean, hot assassins doing a night's work.

"Could be better," I mumble as I turn and walk past them into the gym.

I catch Abby's eye for a second, but then look away. I don't know how involved she was in setting me up, but she seems to be enjoying the results. Shouldn't she be dancing with Benedict Andre?

"Hurts, doesn't it?" Nicky adds for good measure.

Man it does, too. Worse than any smack off the diving boards, hit in football, or punch in the mouth. It physically hurts. But I keep walking through the gym and I don't look at anybody. I walk all through the school, every floor, the cafeteria, the art halls, the drama department, the science wing. It's so quiet. I wish school was quiet like this during the day. I could maybe hear myself think. I might make it through this year if everyone would just be quiet for a minute. And if I'd stop falling on my face all the time, that would help too.

25. Put It in Gere

I start walking home, but I discover my church shoes are made for sitting or standing, not walking. I have to stop at the gas station to take a break. I would take my shoes off, but I think my heels will start gushing blood.

An old-ass BMW pulls up to the gas pump and backfires. *BANG!* I look over and lock eyes with the embarrassed passenger. My sister's instinct is to give me a dirty look, but then she gives me a look of pity.

"What are you doing, Carter?" she asks through the open window.

"Just hangin' out," I reply.

She gets out of the car and asks, "Are you okay?"

"I've been better," I say.

"Yeah, I heard. I'm sorry. Girls can be mean," she says.

"Ya think?" I say.

"Get off the ground; you're in your church suit, idiot!" Lynn snaps.

At least some things stay the same in this crazy world.

Brock walks up to me, slaps my hand (ouch), and says, "Come on, we'll give you a ride home."

Again, I know that the cool thing would have been to turn the ride down. I'm positive my sister does not want me on her date, but my feet are killing me, and I don't want to call our dad for a ride. He'll just ask me what happened, and then I'll have to go over all the details. He'll forget about the joke we shared earlier, and how we were more like friends for a minute, and he'll go back to thinking I'm a dumb-ass kid.

We get to my house and I slowly limp toward the door. My pride hurts worse than my feet.

"Hey, Carter, wait up," Nick yells to me, and breaks away from Lynn.

He walks over because I can't walk to him, and awkwardly says, "Hey, dude, um, I took a dump in your basement before we left tonight. . . ."

I just stare at him. Thank you for sharing.

"Did you whack off before you went out?" he asks.

What the hell line of weird-ass questioning is this?

"Uhhh . . ." I stammer, not sure where we're going.

He looks at me like a muscle-bound child psychologist and says, "I think you may have left a porno playing in the basement? Either you or your dad?"

Oh noooo! I think about framing the old man for the embarrassing slip, but I'm so red that he has to know I'm guilty. Man, I'm a dumbass. ADD and horniness are a bad combo.

"Really?" I ask.

"Yep, *Put It in Gere*, stuck on fast-forward? That's yours?" he asks.

"Yep," I shamefully reply. "Is that what it's called?"

"Where did you get that thing?" Brock asks.

"Nutt's brother, Bart," I reply. Man, is he going to confiscate my educational video?

"Dude, I got a copy of that thing four years ago, from

my buddy Dave's cousin. Why is yours stuck on fast-forward?" he asks.

"I don't know, I bought it that way," I say.

"You paid for that?" He laughs.

"Yeah, thirty-five bucks," I reply.

"Wow, good deal, Carter." Brock chuckles. "Well look, I stuck it in the *Dirty Dancing* case, so that's where it is. You've got to turn the thing off when you're done with it, man," he says like my long-lost brother.

"Yeah, I know."

"I couldn't even tell it was porn for, like, a minute; then I recognized the damn thing. Every guy at our school must have a copy of it," he says with a smirk.

"Yeah, 'cause it's awesome!" I reply. Brock and I are really bonding.

"Uhh, not really. Don't think that anything on those tapes is real. If you come at a real girl with any of that porn crap, you won't get too many opportunities. I pitched all mine 'cause they were messin' me up," he says.

"What, because the moves are out of date?" I ask.

"No, man." He laughs and walks back to my sister and the old Beamer.

Man, that dude knows a lot about chicks . . . and he's dating my sister. Dang it!

I limp inside to throw that thing away. I don't want my mom to go down there some night to watch *Dirty Dancing* for the thousandth time and see the dirtiest, fastest, horizontal dancing of all time. I wonder how many dudes are watching this movie right now, and how I can get a copy that's not stuck on fast-forward? Focus! We're throwing it away.

26. Scrub Squad Killa

Nobody is making fun of me about the homecoming disaster. Which is worse than getting burned for it, because it means that people feel sorry for me. I try not to think about it and go back to my usual ways. Being tardy, getting by, and dragging my ass to football practice every day. All I do is wait around for the couple of minutes that we work on kicking. I'm not one of the starters on offense, so I have to be on the pretend defense when the real offense is working out their new plays. Coach calls us the "practice squad," but we call it "scrub squad," because the real offense could mop the floor with us. I usually try to do as little as possible when I'm on the scrub defense. They run the play, and the guy in front of me smashes me away from the guy with the ball. I only try hard after Coach yells, "Quit doggin' it, Carter!" Otherwise, I'm on autopilot.

The new play today is the same sweep, slant, something, blah blah we always run. The ball is hiked and pitched out to Andre. He's about to run over a few of my scrub squad brothers on his way to scoring another pretend touchdown. But for some reason, my neck gets real tight and I bust a spin move like I've seen guys do on TV. Then I swing around the end of the line like a crazy man. Nutt sees me coming and tries to block me, but I mow him down.

Andre busts around the line and sees me coming at him. He breaks left and is running toward me with fire in his eyes. The running back wouldn't normally run directly at the guy trying to tackle him, but this isn't about football. This is about Abby! I was running as fast as I could when we made eye contact, but somehow I'm going faster now. Andre ducks his head down in preparation to run me over, but I lower my body to get underneath his oncoming helmet. I hear him snarl and I let out a squeak. I hope it sounds tough.

WWHHAAMM! We collide. I have never hit anything so hard in my life, and I hope I never do again. Our forces come together like two high-speed freight trains on the same track. Something has to give . . . and it's not going to be me! I drive my legs as we collide, I blast up into his stomach. He holds on to the ball with both hands while I wrap my arms around the back of his knees. My anger boils over as I lift his massive body off the ground and drive him back down to the earth. *BOOOM!* He lets out an "UUUOHHH" as I grind my shoulder into his gut. We slide for a couple feet, and I think I may have broken my neck, but I jump up and run back to the huddle like someone is chasing me. Everyone is super quiet, staring at me. My neck may really be broken or I'm bleeding from the ears and I don't know it.

Coach breaks the silence with, "Good God, CARTER! Oh my lord!" He's jumping around and grabbing at his chest.

Well, that's it. I've finally done it. I've killed the old bastard. He always said I'd do it, and now his worthless, scrub team kicker has clobbered his star freshman running back and it's too much for him. He's having the heart attack.

"Where the hell did that come from?" Coach asks. Even

his last words will be about this stupid game. I don't respond to the question because I really have no idea.

Andre gets up slow, but he gets up. He doesn't say anything. He just stares at me. Man, he is really big. He's a lot stronger than me, and now he's really mad at me. I could've thought this through a bit more carefully.

The ball's hiked, and it's in Andre's hands again. He sweeps around to the left this time, and I'm coming for him. I'm a one-man scrub defense and this sucker isn't scoring one more touchdown! He can score all he wants in the games, and he might score on Abby, but NOT on this practice field. Not on this day! *WHAAACK!* I nail him again, even harder than the last time. We both get up slow. If this were a cartoon, I'd have little birds flying around my helmet. But it's no cartoon, it's football! I shake off the haze before the next play. And another *WWHHAAACCKKK!* awaits Benedict Andre. This practice could last all night. I'm not stopping. Another play, another bone-crushing hit. My arms are bloody, my shirt's torn, my chin is all cut and bruised. My ears are ringing, and . . . did I mention I think my neck is broken?

Coach throws every play in his book at me. I'm not cheating either, because I've never opened that book. I don't know any of these plays or where they're going. All I know is nobody can block me, and this jerk-off isn't scoring. I'm playing football! The only kicking I'm doing today is kicking Andre's ASS! Coach is loving it.

I don't know what Andre's problem is. I'd be happy to let him be the football star, and I'll be second-string whatever, but he moved on my girl. And he did it publicly. *WWHHAAACCKK!* I want blood. And I get it, too. Mostly it's my blood, but he's hurting . . . I hope. Mercifully, it starts to get dark, so Coach has to blow the whistle and end the war.

He spits the whistle out and yells, "Great practice, men! That's smash mouth football! Carter, I don't know where you been hidin', son, but I'm glad you finally showed up. You really showed me something tonight; you showed your TEAM something! You're a starter from now on!" Coach yells.

Oh, dang it! If I do this every day, I won't see fifteen. I need a chiropractor, a shower, and a stretcher. Normally I just get dressed and go home, because I rarely sweat. Today I've got dirt in my teeth and blood in my hair.

The hot water stings my cuts, and ribbons of mud and blood run down the drain. Andre turns on the shower right next to me. Punk! You can't use one of the other ten showers? We don't say a word to each other. I'm just trying not to fall down. He must know what a prick he is. He must have gotten held back or something, because, good lord, he's a whole lot more of a man than I am. But I'm not looking! How could I be looking? I can't turn my neck.

I get in the car with my dad, and he says, "Jeez, that practice was long. You guys are over an hour late. Who's the new guy?"

"What new guy?" I ask.

"I don't know, the tall guy who was beating up on Andre the last two hours. I've never seen him before," he says.

I just smile on the inside because my face hurts so bad. My dad didn't even recognize me. I want to yell, "It's me,

Pop! I'm the new guy!" but I'm too exhausted and I don't want to get his hopes up that I'm going to be a stud from here on out, so I keep it zipped. Man, I must be a lazy punk most of the time if my own father couldn't ID me.

There's no way I can stay focused like that for a whole game. Forget it. The other team will have to hurt my feelings in some way; they'll have to personally piss me off in order for me to clobber them. I'll start looking at cheerleaders or a dog on the sidelines and they'll score while I'm spacing off. My team is better off with me on the bench. There's no need to worry about it for long, though. I'll break my neck for real, and get myself a fly-ass wheelchair with hand controls and a water bottle and everything. Girls will gather around me and pat my head. I'll be the team mascot. That won't be so bad. They couldn't like me any less.

27. Arcade Backfire

EJ and I are chillin' out at the arcade on a Saturday night (pathetic). I wanted to go to the movies or sit in an ice bath, but EJ's ADHD has lots of fuel here, and there're always hot chicks at the arcade, so here we are.

"You see me gettin' wicked eye contact with the chicks at the Ms. Pac-Man?" EJ asks.

"Yeah, I do, 'cause you're staring at 'em. They're scared and trying to figure out whether or not to call security on you." I laugh.

Even though Lynn's advice seems to have blown up in my face, EJ still asks for clarification on how to use it. "What I don't get is," he says as he hip checks the Star Wars game, "how you like 'em for real, but pretend not to. But you really like 'em underneath it all, right?"

"Dude, I don't know why it works, it just does. Why don't you go practice on one of those Ms. Pac-Man chicks? Quit stalkin' 'em and go talk to 'em. Just pretend you're not into 'em and then ask a question. What's the worst that could happen?" I ask like a fourteen-year-old Dr. Drew.

"I don't know what to ask 'em," he says. "You go talk to 'em, Carter."

"Man, I'll start to stutter, and that doesn't help anyone,"

I say. "Girls hate me, that's just a fact. I'll go with you, though."

Every great pilot needs a wingman. A guy by his side who tells him how much fuel he has and how he's doing. The pilot has one job: fly the plane. Or in this case, talk to the girl. The wingman just helps the pilot out. Like a corner man at a prize fight or a coach on the sidelines.

I don't think EJ'll go through with it, though. He'll just stare at these chicks until his mom comes and picks us up. But he thinks it over for a second, rolls his eyes back into his head, and breaks for the Ms. Pac-Man machine.

"Whoa, slow down, turbo!" I say, but he doesn't hear me. The pilot makes a move; the wingman follows.

We walk toward the group of girls with great purpose. I can't believe we're doing this. I'm not even flying the plane, but my heart is in my throat. If I have to talk, the stutter is going to soar. EJ, on the other hand, is a picture of determination. Puberty is changing us all. He kind of looks like Wolverine just before his claws come out and he gets to kicking somebody's ass.

"Go easy, man. Just pretend you don't like 'em," I say.

"I got it, bro," EJ says with pure focus.

"Hit 'em with a question," I say.

"Got it," he replies.

"Breathe, dude," I add for good measure.

I'm not great at a lot of things, but I'm a good wingman. I thought we'd chat for an hour or so about what questions he would ask and how to respond to their responses, but we're just going for it! Hell yeah, just a couple of cowboys on a roundup. Yee haaaw!

We roll up on that Ms. Pac-Man machine like it's the

O.K. Corral. EJ makes eye contact with the smallest one, off to the side. That's how a lion selects his prey. My boy's got killer instinct! She's wide open. She's not the cutest one, in my opinion, which I think is super smart. She won't jack up his mainframe, and he's got a better chance at saying something cool. And she might not get as much attention as the rest of her friends, so she'll be stoked that a guy has come up to her, even if he says something stupid.

Wingman to leader: Fire when ready.

She looks up at EJ and gives him the nicest smile. He pulls the trigger and yells, "You think you're hot stuff, don't you?"

What the . . . ? Where are you going with this?

"Excuse me?" she replies, kind of sweetly.

EJ asks, "You think you're cool, don't you? Where did you get that shirt, the Salvation Army? What the hell is with your hair?"

My eyes are as big as basketballs as he fires one mean-ass question after another at her.

"You don't have a boyfriend, do you?" he continues.

It's like he's armed with self-esteem killer.

"Did your parents have any kids that lived?" EJ asks.

The girl starts to buckle, and tears are on the way.

"Are these your friends, or are they like, counselors here to observe you?" EJ shouts.

Oh, what a misunderstanding! I thought this was a clear mission, but I was so wrong. As the wingman I have to stop my pilot from destroying this girl. She's becoming more of a lesbian with every question.

He asks, "Does your grandma know you borrowed her shoes?" as I drag him away. The girl is crying pretty hard, and her friends are trying to console her. They're all giving me dirty looks, too. Thank you very much, EJ. I was worried not every girl on the planet hated me.

"Man, that didn't go very well. What do you think I did wrong?" EJ asks.

"Are you serious?" I ask.

"I was just doing what you told me to," he replies.

"I-I-I told you to go up to that girl and start abusing her?" I ask.

"You said to ask her questions and pretend that I didn't like her!" he yells back.

"Pretend YOU'RE NOT INTO HER!" I clarify. "Not that you hate her and wish she would die! Good God, that girl thought she was gonna get a boyfriend when you walked up, not years of therapy."

"Do you think I still have a shot?" he asks.

"NO, I don't!" I bark.

"You said to pretend not to like her and ask questions. . . . I did that!" he says.

I just stare at him. He means it, too. He was just doing what he thought I, or my sister, wanted him to do. Didn't question it for a second. This is why they send kids to war. Young men. Just give us an order. If you've constructed enough of a reason for us to go blow ourselves up . . . we won't question it a bit. When we get old or mature enough to ask "Why?" we aren't any good for that stuff anymore. Man, what a mess! Like a bad game of telephone, Lynn's orders have been bastardized and misinterpreted. She would be horrified to know that she was responsible for EJ giving a girl an eating disorder.

In this process of becoming an adult, I think some

people have got to get hurt. We hurt ourselves, and we hurt others. Some deserve it, while others are just waiting in line to play Ms. Pac-Man. From weight training, I know that when you stress a muscle you're actually tearing it down, and when it repairs itself, it's that scarred tissue that looks bigger and makes you stronger. So if it's true that our scars shape who we are and how we live life . . . EJ and the short girl just learned a big lesson tonight, and they'll be stronger because of the pain and confusion.

The rest of my boys were absent, so EJ was spared a lot of embarrassment. But I'll break this story out at just the right moment, and it'll be epic!

28. Grow On

My frustrations with girls, math, and staying focused continue, but football, of all things, is a big help. The more confused I get, the harder I smash into guys. I'm working out my problems the only way I can—violence! During the games I just look at Abby herding the drill team into position, and I shift my anger toward the kid carrying the ball. *WHAM!* I look over at Andre or Amber Lee and then I smash the hell out of the guy in front of me. *WHAACCKK!* I'm pretty ferocious too. I knocked two guys unconscious (one of them was me). A scorned and sexually deprived young man is a lethal weapon. I imagine the ball is my virginity and I just want to knock it loose! If I keep growing, lifting weights, and stay a virgin through graduation, I'll go pro for sure.

I'm surprisingly balanced but ridiculously bruised; it's a vicious cycle. The unfortunate kid with the ball doesn't know why I'm so mercilessly smashing his ass. If he did, he'd go over to Abby on the sideline and tell her he was sorry for what I had done, and that she should give me a second chance, and that Andre's just using her because he thinks she's slutty. *WHAAMM!* The other team's coach would go up to Amber and Nicky and slap their faces for being cold-hearted BITCHES, and for giving me the strength to smash his quarterback over and over, and for giving me the focus to kick thirty-yard field goals against his team.

Football is great for my mental wounds, but I'm looking forward to the final game of the season (next week), so my physical wounds can start to heal.

29. No Freshmen Allowed

The boys and I are chillin' at Bag's house on a Friday night, eating all his mom's food and playing video games. Bag and Hormone have girlfriends, but tonight we're practicing an old hip-hop tradition known as *bros before hos*. Where you don't let chicks get in the way of your friendship with your boys (I wish I practiced less). Eminem and 50 Cent are blaring on the old stereo. I love rap. The lyrics are "explicit," which means you're supposed to be old to listen to them. But if rap music has taught me anything, it's to screw the establishment and to do whatever the F*#K I wanna DO! My parents won't let me listen to this stuff for some reason, but at Bag and Pam's house, it's all good. Their mom works a lot, and nobody has ever seen a dad. Plywood covers a living room window, the bathroom door doesn't lock, and the lawn is like a wild–grass nature preserve. They seem to have bigger problems than what's playing on the stereo. We hang out here a lot.

Pam, Yasmine, and Jemma are getting ready for a big party tonight, so the curling irons are sizzling, blow dryers are blowing, and I think something is burning. They don't mess up our *bros before hos* night, because none of us could *ever* get with them.

Pam's boyfriend/old man has bought us all a bunch of

beer, and I take one to look cool, but it's NASTY. I don't say it out loud, but it tastes like burned salt water and Pop Rocks. So I break for the bathroom to pour it down the toilet. The door is shut and someone has hung a sock on the knob, but I just go in. The hot rush of steam hits my face like a textbook. I peer through the fog at a brownish pink figure with light and dark bits. I'm curiously drawn to it. Oh God, I think it . . . Could it be? PAM! She's just stepped out of the shower and she's wearing a towel . . . on her head! Oh GOD, she's buck naked and dripping wet right in front of me. I lose all motor function and drop the beer, shooting foam all over the bathroom. She looks toward the noise and finds me gawking at her, unable to move, blink, or breathe. She's in slow motion. She purses her lips like she's about to say, "I've always wanted you, Carter. Take me now!" At least that's what she's going to say later tonight in my dreams. But for now she's yelling and trying to cover up her privates.

"CARTER! Sock on the door! Get out of here," she yells.

I see her full lips moving, but she could be speaking Japanese for all I'm getting out of it. I'm kind of shaking and smiling because it smells so good in here, and did I mention that Pam's naked?! We stand there for a second or fifty, until she walks over to me. Water is still dripping off her boob when she calmly grabs my shoulder and turns me around. She pushes me out the door, not hard or anything, just firm. So nice, so gentle, so firm. Pam is naked and she's touching me! Just as she shuts the door, I regain a hint of my senses and blabber, "I love you."

Behind the door she says, "I know, Carter, I love you too."

Oh God, I think I'm going to pass out as I stumble toward the front door. I need air! I step out into the cool night air and wander down the streets of Merrian, trying to collect myself. I've just seen the hand of God. And although I now know he has nothing to do with her blond hair, He made a body to worship in there. I'll never be the same. How do I go on? I can't go out with some freshman chick now. Pam should take responsibility and make a man out of me.

When I finally get back to the house, everyone is jumping around in the front yard. I want to tell my boys about what I saw, but they're all too drunk to keep it cool, so I save it for later. We're all piling into Hormone's CRX, and I don't know where we're going, but I wedge myself in anyway. Nine dudes are smashed inside a car that was built for two, and we're flying down the road. I think we're following Jemma's car, but I can't really see. I can't breathe at all, but I can't freak out either. I've got to meditate. I can't focus on the fact that we're going ninety miles an hour and Bag's elbow is lodged in my throat. I've got to find a happy place. I've got to transport myself back to the steamy bathroom. Back where I felt sooo good and Pam touched me on the shoulder and whispered in my ear and . . . Dang it, I'm smashed in a car with eight dudes and I've got a hard-on. I guess nobody's noticed and we've arrived, because people are stepping on my head and I can breathe again. I climb out of the car and look up to find a girl puking in the bushes of an old house, and realize we're at a real high school party. I don't know what I thought it would be like, but it's kind of how I imagine a prison riot would be (if I ever go to one of those). Utter chaos. One of the windows gets smashed out from the inside as we walk up to the house.

"I don't think we should be here, E," I whisper.

EJ doesn't respond. He just drunkenly stumbles around the yard, looking for who said his name.

I'm positive we shouldn't be here when I hear a guy yell, "No freshmen allowed!" as we open the front door. But important information like that goes unnoticed when the music is super loud and everyone is screaming. We walk inside a house filled only with high school kids, a big dining room table, and an old stereo. There's also an aquarium, which must have had fish at one time. But it's just a tank full of water now, as the Skeleton dangles the last goldfish above his face. He drops it into his mouth and washes it down with beer. Awww, that's gross. Everyone cheers, "YEAH!!!"

I look up the stairs because there's a big commotion, and see Nutt flying through the air and tumbling down the stairs.

"NO FRESHMEN!" a big voice yells.

Oh, we're going to die! Nutt lands at the bottom with a thud and gets up slow. He shakes out the cobwebs and runs back up the stairs. Why are you going back up there, dude? You're obviously not wanted. Just hang with me and EJ over here in this corner. Our first high school party and EJ is passed out at my feet. Again Nutt sails down the stairs and crashes into a group of seniors. They've had their fill of goldfish and are considering killing Nutt. He tries to stand, but he's not doing well.

"Stay down, Nutt!" I whisper/yell as his brother picks him up by the hair. Nutt screams in pain and punches Bart right in the face, hard. Bart stumbles back from the blow, but shakes it off and lifts his little brother into the air before slamming him onto the dining room table. I've never been more thankful to have a sister as the table smashes to pieces. Lynn is a bitch sometimes, and she's pretty strong, but I don't need to worry about body slams.

I hope whoever owns this house didn't like that table, because it's toast. And hopefully they weren't very attached to their walls either because Bart just smashed Nutt's head right through one of them. *BOOM!* Ouch! I thought walls were really strong, but Nutt's head broke through that one pretty easily. Then another guy I know from football punches the wall with his hand. Then the Skeleton comes out of the kitchen and kicks a big hole in it.

"Yeah!" Everyone is laughing and cheering as these crazy punks are ripping the house apart. "Let's tear this mother down!"

EJ's starting to snore as the Skeleton punches the wall one more time, and we all learn a valuable lesson in home construction. You see, every sixteen inches or so, they put wooden supports in a wall to hold up the house. They're called studs, but they should change the name to stud stoppers, because the Skeleton found one with his fist and is crying like a baby. Good thing he's drunk. I hear stuff doesn't hurt when you're drunk, but he's screaming like that may not be entirely true.

EJ looks conscious for a second, so I nudge him and say, "If they take him to the hospital and give him an X-ray, they'll see goldfish swimming around in his stomach." EJ doesn't get it; he just smacks his lips and goes back to sleep.

Like a SWAT team, two seniors grab Hormone from the kitchen as if he's a wanted terrorist. They drag him into the dining room and smash his head through the wall. *BOOM!* Dang it!

The front door opens, and Nick Brock steps through with Lynn in tow. Everybody stops and acknowledges his presence, like he's a Mafia boss.

Doc runs for the open door, but Pam's old-ass boyfriend grabs him by the collar, high-fives Brock, and yells, "Dude, we're tearin' this house down with freshmen heads!"

He spins around real quick and—*BAM!*—Doc's head goes through the wall. My boys are going down!

Brock says, "Cool," steps over Doc, and walks into the living room.

"Why is my friggin' brother here?" Lynn barks out.

The demolition continues as Nick rolls up on EJ and me. He slaps my hand (ouch). A *BOOM* comes from behind us.

"Anybody put your head through a wall, Carter?" Brock asks.

"No." I laugh.

"Mind if I do?" he asks.

"D-d-do what?" I stammer.

Lynn looks up at him to see if he's serious. "What?" he asks her. "If anybody is gonna put Carter's head through the wall, it should be me."

EJ's eyes snap open, and he scoots away from me slowly. I'll remember this, Wingman!

"T-t-the-there's wood behind some of the . . ." I protest.

"Naw, you'll be fine, we'll just do one," he explains as he picks me up.

One what? One hole? You big son of a . . . This will definitely be my last high school party!

My sister yells out, "Nick, don't!"

Hey, that's a first. Did anybody hear that? Lynn just stuck up for me. I'm about to die, so the timing could have been better.

"Brock's got a FRESH ONE!" someone yells out as he carries me into what once was a dining room.

This will all be over in a second. Stop kicking and DO NOT CRY! It won't be so bad; I'll just have white powder and tears streaming down my face like Doc does. I go limp as he touches my head to the wall.

"Does it sound hollow, Carter?" Brock yells out.

"No, NO, I don't think it does!" I whine.

The whole room laughs . . . because apparently this is funny.

"ONE!" Brock calls out as he walks backward. "TWO!" he and the rest of the party yell together.

This is it! When they say "no freshmen allowed," they mean it. I can see now, it's not just that they don't want us here; we're in danger. It's more of a public service announcement.

"THREEEE!" they roar.

Nick squats down and drives forward with his strong-ass legs. He's going to ram me through the wall and into the backyard! At least I can leave this stupid party.

I'm hurtling forward, but suddenly it all stops and Brock throws me up into the air like a rag doll and onto my feet. He's laughing hysterically.

"I'm just messin' with you, man! Nobody smashes Carter's head through the wall," he yells through the laughter.

Wow, okay. That was a joke. Ha-ha! We're joking. Oh

man, that is funny. They should come up with a reality TV show like this. It'll be called *I'm Gonna Kill Ya!* The host rolls up and yells, "I'm gonna kill ya!" And then pretends like he's really going to do it. The contestants won't love it, but America will go crazy for it.

I'm laughing like everybody else, but more because I'm happy to be alive and not lying out in the yard. I'm glad I'm not crying and I only let a little bit of pee out when they yelled "THREEEE!" Ah, good times. High school rocks! I see why I was looking forward to this crap.

All of my friends are drunk. EJ is now puking into the fireplace, and Bag is dancing on top of him. Nutt is searching for a missing tooth. Doc looks like a mime, talking to a drunk girl about his ordeal. I hope she's drunk enough to understand whatever it is he's saying.

I want to go back to Bag's house and play video games. I want a Coke. I want my friends to act normal. Am I just being a baby? I guess I'm not adult or mature enough to understand the appeal of alcohol. It tastes awful. It makes you say and do things you would never do on your own. It makes you mean, stupid, and then you vomit. Yeah, bartender, give me another!

What am I supposed to do, though? Go hang with the self-righteous Young Life kids? Drink Kool-Aid, read the Bible, and listen to them blabber on about "the power of abstinence" and saving themselves for marriage? I'll have to jump over the campfire and yell out how I'm saving myself for the first slutty girl who'll let me do it to her! And they'll tell me how I'm going to hell for sure. I don't think I'm going to hell, but I'm definitely visiting tonight. I guess these parties are going to be like football and everything else. I'll just show up and get it done. Just another thing I hate, but I do anyway.

Lynn throws her arm around my shoulder and says, "Pretty crazy, huh?"

I just shake my head and say, "This isn't fun."

"Very few people actually enjoy these parties," she replies.

"Whose house is this?" I ask. "Their parents are gonna kill 'em."

"It's nobody's house. It's for sale. The guys just broke in," she says, pointing to a FOR SALE sign on the floor. "They couldn't get that big dining room table out, I guess. And the fish tank too."

"Shouldn't be a problem now," I say as the fish tank crashes to the ground, shatters, and shoots glass and water everywhere. "Is this illegal? Are we like, stealing this house?"

"Yeah, but these guys do it all the time," she responds.

Then I hear a very familiar squeal, and turn to see two seniors carrying EJ toward the dining room. He's weak from all the puking, but he's kicking and flailing as best he can. Just when things couldn't get much crazier, the living room fills with red-and-blue lights, and someone yells, "COPS!"

The police are here. It's about time! If I had thought of it earlier, I would have called them myself. The party becomes a fire drill on crack. People are pushing and shoving to get out the back door, out the garage, or out the broken windows. If Brock had really crashed me through that wall, we would all be home free with another back door available. I push EJ out the kitchen window and dive after him, when I hear a cop yell, "Don't move—Police!" Man, I never thought I'd hear that. And I always thought I'd stop if I did. But nobody else is stopping, so damned if I'm going down for all this.

I wipe the grass off my face and run through the backyard. I jump a fence and look around for EJ. Nutt and Bag point at a figure flying across the yard next to us. It's EJ, and he may be drunk but he's really booking it. His eyes are filled with terror, his arms are flailing, and he's screaming. He must really be scared of going to jail. That, or he's worried about the huge, snarling, rottweiler on his heels! The dog's slobbering, barking, and gaining on him. Nobody wants to get caught by the cops, but about twenty of us stop to see if EJ is going to get eaten by this dog or not.

"HAAAAHHHH, NOOO, doggie!" he yells, and runs as fast as his untied shoes will carry him. Which is normally really fast, but it looks like the dog's got his number.

"RUN, FORREST!" Bag yells out, and we all laugh.

EJ loses one of his Pumas, but he doesn't even pause. The dog must outweigh him by fifty pounds. He's just about to the fence, and that dog is so close it can almost taste EJ's ass. My best friend dives headfirst over the fence and slides for about ten feet on his stomach.

We all cheer, "Yeah, EEEEJAAY!"

But we shut up quick as that big dog takes flight. It jumps over the chain-link fence like it's not even there. Everyone sees the pending doom, except EJ, who is drunkenly laughing about his near-death experience. Silly boy doesn't know what hit him when the dog clamps down on his right butt cheek. Oh man, the rottweiler is shaking EJ around like a new toy. EJ is screaming for help, but everybody is long gone . . . except me. He doesn't stand a chance on his own, and I can't leave my wingman like this.

I run at the dog, and in my deepest adult voice I yell, "BAD DOG! DROP IT!"

The dog must have heard that before, because it drops EJ and looks up at me. Hmmm . . . What to do now? I did not think this through completely. The dog has lost interest in EJ and is now looking at me like I'm what's for dinner. For my first trick I jump the fence to get away from him, and to get EJ's lost Puma. We wear the same size, and I might need to borrow these someday. And this dog is going to make the left one his bitch if I don't. But the dog doesn't like seeing me in his yard at all, and starts to whine and bark.

"NO! NO! Bad dog!" I yell, but the dog just flexes his big neck muscles and shoots me a mean look through the fence. That worked once, but it knows I'm just a punk-ass kid who shouldn't be in its yard. I have no authority here, and we both know it. The dog takes a run at me and sails into the air. Now, who's the A-hole that built a three-foot fence for an attack dog with a five-foot vertical leap? The dog lands on all fours in his own yard as I bust a superman and land on my face in the yard where the party once raged. I jump up and sprint toward EJ, who's showing a full moon as he runs away. The back part of his Levi's is still lying on the ground. His mom could totally fix them, but then he'd have to explain what happened, and his mom would want to know where this vicious attack dog was and try to talk to its owner, and then EJ would get nailed for being drunk at an illegal stolen-house party. So it's best to just tell her, "I musta lost 'em?" Most people can't use that excuse, but EJ and I are always losing pants; I lose about four a year. No explanation; they just disappear.

I kind of forgot that we were running from the law, as well as this attack dog. But I get a heavy reminder when a two-hundred-pound cop tackles me to the ground and yells, "DON'T MOVE!"

I know he weighs two hundred because all of that weight is resting on my neck as he wrenches my arm behind my back. Ouch! What the hell? Are we filming an episode of *Cops* here, Barney?

He's yelling behind my back, "One-one-nine, officer has suspect in custody!" I guess by "suspect," he means me, and by "custody," he means in agonizing, friggin' pain, with my face pushed into the grass!

"Can't breathe, dude!" I wheeze.

"Maybe you should've thought of that before you burglarized this house and destroyed it!" he barks back, putting my wrists in zip tie handcuffs.

I hear the plastic *Zzzip*, and I can't move. The dog's barking all loud and happy like he's cheering for the cop. Shut up, dog. The cop lifts me to my feet by my wrists, and if there's a more painful way to lift someone up off the ground, I'd like to know what it is.

"OWW! I-I-I d-d-didn't . . . I'm just a freshman!" I protest.

"Well, you're in big trouble, freshman!" he says. "What's your name?"

"C-C-C-Ca . . . EJ," I say.

"Where do you live, EJ?" he asks.

"Just right over there," I nod.

"Where is that, exactly?" he prods.

This dude is going to try to talk to my parents, and that is the last thing I need. I'm still grounded!

"Just right over there, right over that hill." I nod and try to point with my cuffed hands.

I'm not lying to him; I'm honestly pointing toward my house. It is just right over that hill . . . and then three miles down the road. I'm pointing and nodding away when about twenty kids pop out from behind a garage and run in every direction.

The Skeleton points at me and yells out, "You're dead, freshman!" as he leaps over a fence and sprints away.

"I was pointing at my house, not your dumb hiding place!" I yell back.

The cop takes off after them and screams into his walkie-talkie, "One-one-nine . . . Officer needs back-door backup . . . in the rear. Suspects everywhere! Repeat, back-door backup needed. Hot pursuit!"

Three cops fly out the back door and run after the kids. I'm back on the ground, but from laughter now. *Officer needs back-door backup in the rear. Hot pursuit!* Oh, that's classic. I wish someone else could have heard that. I really wish I didn't have handcuffs on.

The attack dog is wagging his stubby tail like he wants to play with me some more. We're both confused. EJ pops out of a bush in the other yard, runs over, and slaps me in the face. *WHACK!*

"Ow! What the hell was that for?" I yell.

"What are you giving my name to the cops for?!" he barks.

"Sorry, I got nervous. It just popped out. I wouldn't have given 'em your name if I'd known you were listening."

He squints his eyes at me and contemplates slapping me again, then whisper/yells, "Let's bail!"

"No way, dude, I got cuffs on," I whisper/yell back.

EJ is laughing now because he's drunk; but this isn't funny.

"Shut up, dude!" I yell for real.

"You got cuffed and stuffed!" He laughs and humps the air. "Officer needs 'hot back door in the rear'!"

"You heard that?" I laugh.

"Yeah, let's go!" he yells.

"No!" I yell back.

"Did the cop tell you to stay? Did he specifically say you had to stay here?" he asks.

"Nooo, but I think it's implied," I respond, and show him the cuffs again.

"I'm outta here, man," EJ says, flashing me his full moon as he runs away.

I look over at the dog, whose mean look is now gone. His tail isn't wagging, and he's sort of shaking his head in disappointment, like I should've split with EJ.

"Wait!" I whisper/yell and run after my bare-assed best friend. If the cop catches me, it'll be tough to explain the look that rottweiler just gave me, and why I listened to a dog on legal matters, but I'm gone.

We look like a pair of escapees from a mental hospital, or an S&M sex convention. My shirt is all ripped up and my hands are bound behind my back. EJ has puke all over his shirt, buttless pants, and only one shoe. And we've got a long way to go.

"Dude, get behind me so no one can see the cuffs," I tell EJ, while still panting and tripping along.

"No way, you get behind me so my ass isn't hangin' out," EJ says.

"I'm not staring at your bare ass for three miles, dude!" I bark.

"You know Nicky and Abby are right about you, Carter. You're self-centered," EJ pants.

"Big words, drunkie!" I say, and knock into him.

"I'm not drunk, fag," he slurs. "I just don't want people lookin' at my junk," he snaps and pushes me.

I stumble a bit and narrowly miss running into a tree. I yell, "Don't push! I'll fall down."

An evil lightbulb goes on in EJ's eyes, and he kicks my left foot behind me as I'm running. I fight gravity for about two and a half steps and then eat it. My face skids on the wet grass and my legs flip up over my head. I hear a pop come from somewhere near the top of my spine, and I know you're not supposed to move when you've broken your neck, but I've got an ass to kick!

He tries to apologize, but he's laughing so hard he can't get it out. I finally fumble up to standing, and charge him like a bull. I ram him in the chest—and slip on the grass. I gain my footing quickly, but accidentally crash the top of my head into his chin. His teeth smash together with a CLACK, and his eyes fill with shock and tears. I think his orthodontist is going to be pissed.

"I was jokin'!" EJ cries as he cocks his fist back to Friday and punches me in the stomach. I could see it coming, but what can I do?

"Yeah, how funny is this?" I wheeze, and kick him in the ribs. This is a poorly conceived fight if there ever was one. The odds would be surprisingly even, though, I think.

I kick him in the ribs again after he punches me in the ear. We're both crying. I never thought EJ and I would fight like this.

"Ah, did I hurt your feelings?" EJ cries, and swings wildly at my head. "It's not like I stole your fat girlfriend, or blocked one of your sideways ten-yard field goals!"

Man, EJ is a mean drunk. He's got the ammo to hurt my feelings like no one else, so I run at him and ram my head into his chest again. I hope this is hurting him as much as it is me. Neither of us has a brother, so I've never thought we were especially tough. But I'm in a fight with my hands tied behind my back; that's pretty bad ass.

I jump into the air and try to give him a flying karate kick to the head, but it doesn't go very well, and I, more, knee him in the shoulder and we both fall to the ground. I boot him in the back. Why is he drunk? I needed a wingman at that party. I need to tell him about seeing Pam naked, but I headbutt him in the shoulder instead. I need to tell him about how scared I am at football practice. I need to tell him how much it hurt when Amber Lee set me up at the homecoming dance. But instead I kick him in the stomach because he left it wide open. He rolls away from me, and I go for a headbutt to the kidneys. I bring my head down with vicious force, knowing that if I connect properly he'll pee blood tomorrow. But fortunately for him and very unfortunately for me, he quickly moves away, and the kidneys cease to be a target.

Instead of a thud and painful scream, I get a surprisingly loud *SLAP* as my face connects with his bare butt cheeks. I'm so mad, I smash my face into it again.

"Dude, get outta my ASS!" he laughs.

"Shut up, dude." Well, maybe this is a little funny. I'm so out of breath it's hard to laugh, but I do. Thank God the fight is over. Because drunk or not, EJ had the upper hand.

We cut off my handcuffs and find an old plastic Hy-Vee bag for EJ to make a diaper out of and walk home.

"You look like a homeless sumo wrestler," I say.

He laughs. Not so much a drunk laugh, but more of a regular EJ laugh.

"I saw Pam naked tonight," I confess.

"No you didn't!" he gasps.

"Yeah, I did and it was incredible. She's not a natural blonde," I say.

He lets out a sexually frustrated squeak, and I know we're back on track.

Winter

30. Our Winter's Discontent

Football is over (thank God) and winter is on the way. It's time for the basketball, wrestling, or swimming season to start. Pick your poison. All my boys play basketball or wrestle. I thought about playing b-ball, because I'm one of the taller guys in my class now, but I still suck at shooting the ball, dribbling it, and passing. So I may save myself the humiliation. Wrestling would be cool if it was the WWE Smack-Down type of wrestling. But it's not. It's just rolling around with sweaty dudes wearing a *singlet* (a cross between Daisy Duke shorts and a girl's swimming suit) and always having to lose weight so you can wrestle a kid who's four pounds lighter than you. That doesn't sound fun to me, so I'm going to swim back and forth in a pool for two hours every day, wear a Speedo, and take in as little oxygen as possible (can't wait!). I'd never admit it, but I kind of like the Speedo. It feels like you're naked. My boys dog me for owning one, but I'm caring less and less about what's said in the halls. Who knew you could get used to humiliation?

Coach walks up to our crew at lunch. The football coach is also the wrestling coach at Merrian High. I guess the thinking is, if you're tough enough to play football, you'll be stupid enough to join the wrestling team.

Coach looks right at me and says, "Hey, Tinker Bells,

shouldn't you two have your water wings on and your nose plugs in for synchronized swimming practice?"

I look around to see who else he's talking to. I swivel in my chair and make direct eye contact with Andre's punk ass.

Coach continues, "My toughest guys are joining the swim team?! What's the world coming to?"

I almost crack a smile, because Coach just referred to me as "tough," then Andre shuts it down by saying, "Sorry, Coach, I'm the all-city champ. I gotta swim, but maybe Carter'd wrestle for ya, 'cause he sucks."

I just glare at him and explain to Coach, "I got second."

"Yeah, distant second!" Andre laughs.

"The only thing distant around here is you and reality," I retort, but nobody laughs.

Coach breaks in. "Hey, if you don't have the strength and mental fortitude it takes to wrestle a man to the ground and bend him to your will, maybe the dive team is where you belong," he says, and then struts away.

Yeah, the dive team comment hurt, but I had to fight off a laugh when he was talking about "bending another man down." Andre raises his eyebrows at me as if to say, "What was that?" But I do not respond. I've got people I raise my eyebrows at, and people I do not. I can't waste any facial gestures on backstabbing, chick-thieving punks who call me suckie in front of other people!

Just then, Abby walks up to our table and makes me feel even worse. She purposely doesn't look at me and walks off with Andre. I grab my backpack and rummage through it for something to do. Nobody knows that I'm just hiding my red face and looking for my balls. I'm also trying to figure out why my chest gets so friggin' tight and my neck tenses up so bad every time I get near her. I can't breathe, and I feel like I'm going to fall down or do something stupid every time we pass and pretend not to notice each other. I see Amber Lee sometimes too, but I can just cruise by her without feeling much of anything. I used to think she was so hot, but not anymore. She still has a nice butt, but I can look past it now and know that she's mean. It makes the rest of her ugly to me.

I'm not seeing much of EJ either, because he's practicing a lot for basketball tryouts and he kind of has a girlfriend all of a sudden. Sarah "the Caboose" Ruiz. He talked to her! We were all shocked. He asked her, "What time is it?" one day in the hall. That's the question he came up with. Huge clock on the wall behind him; he walks up to her with a straight face and busts out, "What time is it?" She tells him, and he says, "Thanks!" and then runs away. It didn't look like he was late for something, or anything, but more like he was running away from a monster.

He retardedly asked her twice more, "What time is it?" She finally asked him, "Why don't you get a watch?" and then he replied, "Don't need one. . . ."

She naturally asked, "Why?"

And then he dropped the tightest line on her I've ever heard: "Because I like asking you." (My boy is so goofed up he fell into the smooth!) The Caboose smiled, and that's it. Now they're making out in the halls. It's not a miracle. Just ask a question and then blow them off. That's the secret. He did it so terribly that the gods of love must have shaken their heads and said, "Hell, why not throw this horn dog a bone!"

At our table in the cafeteria, EJ starts to take some heat.

A few of my boys have gone out with the Caboose over the years, and her reputation is not stellar. They call her the "Village Bike" because, as J-Low puts it, "Every boy in Merrian has had a ride on her!"

That's funny, but uncool at the same time. I want to tell them to knock it off and that she's really nice. That EJ's never had a girlfriend before, he may never get another one, and to let him enjoy this moment. But I don't.

Andre, who claims to have had sex with her in seventh grade, walks up, slaps EJ's neck, and asks, "How's your ho, pimp?"

Bag chimes in with, "What do you call the car that comes behind the caboose? The EEEJAY!" The Caboose dumped Bag back in October, but he still dogs EJ for dating her.

He laughs it off, but I can tell he's pissed. He doesn't stop seeing her, though. They go bowling and to the movies and stuff. EJ's mom is terrified because he's not so easily controlled now that he has a girlfriend. My mom's got nothing to worry about, because every girl still thinks I'm a first-class A-hole.

EJ is going to have sex before I do. I just know it. He's smart to go after a slutty girl. They'll let you practice your moves on them and figure out what the different condoms are for. I can see now that it's the only way to go. Abby's a nice girl, and if you're into holding hands and talking your face off, she's your gal. But if you're trying to get somewhere, you've got to go after a hoochie. Nutt's brother Bart tried to sell me a fake ID for fifty bucks and told me to spend more time at bars. He says that tramps hang out in bars, and they smoke cigarettes and have tattoos on their lower backs.

He claims he can spot a twenty-three-year-old ho-bag from a mile away. But at our age a girl hasn't quite made up her mind whether or not to be a skank, or the right guy hasn't come along and screwed her up. I don't have fifty dollars, so I need to focus on the high school parties and get a drunk chick, so I can be that guy who screws them up and over.

Speaking of screwing up girls, I think I just caught Abby staring at me. She tried to cover it up by waving at the goth girl standing behind me, but I look back at the chick and she obviously has no idea who Abby is. . . . Busted!

31. Too Much Info

It's Friday night, and I'm renting a movie by myself. It's pretty lame, but EJ's playing putt-putt with the Caboose, so he wins the award for Most Lame tonight. I tried to talk the boys into a bros before hos night, but nobody would go for it. Bag's out with some chick from St. Mary's Academy. It's a private religious school for girls. He says she wears a plaid skirt and she's a slut. Nutt and Doc are dating junior high girls. I would have made fun of them when I was in eighth grade, but I realize now how tough it is to be a freshman and to compete for chicks with older dudes who drive cars. I have a nice bike, but the girls don't seem to care about axle pegs anymore.

I show up at Blockbuster with five bucks and some frozen snot on my face from riding in the cold. We have a Blockbuster right next to my house, but I'm not allowed to rent movies there because I've lost a number of items over the years. My parents can't even rent there anymore; the store hates me that much. I pick up The Rock's movie from the new releases and think back to the first time I didn't see it. How the movie was better when I was making out with Abby than it was when I got to watch it. It's an action movie with some laughs, but to me it's a bitter, romantic tragedy (two thumbs way down!), so I put it back.

A cold wind cuts through the Blockbuster. A chill goes

down my spine as Andre and Abby walk through the door. This is not what I need, so I hit the deck and crawl past the foreign films. Did Abby not recognize my bike out front? Why are they here? She doesn't live anywhere near here. I peek over the classics and see Andre wearing his new letterman's jacket, picking up The Rock's movie. No way, Abby, that's our movie! Wait a minute . . . that's not Abby. It's some girl in a puffy vest kind of like Abby's, but she isn't as pretty. Did they break up and nobody told me?

I'm not really hiding anymore. I'm very perplexed, like a dog who's heard a strange noise. Andre looks over to see who's staring at him, and now I'm like a dog who's been caught digging in the trash. Not sure what I've done wrong, but I'm definitely guilty of something.

"What're you doin' here, Carter?" Andre seethes and nods his head for me to go with him toward the candy aisle.

I don't move. I just say, "Good to see you too, 'Dre."

"You spyin' on me?" he asks, and nods again toward candy.

"I may be at Blockbuster by myself on a Friday night, but I got better things to worry about than what you're up to . . . and who you're with," I reply pointedly.

He bites his lip and nods for me to follow him again.

"Somethin' wrong with your neck?" I ask.

He shakes his head in disgust and asks, "You gonna run and tell Abby?"

I shrug and ask, "What should I tell her?"

He squirms and barks, "Screw you, Carter! If you tell her, you're a punk bitch."

I just stare at him for a second. The nerve of this jackhole! He set me up, ratted me out, and stole my girl. Eye for an eye ring any bells, big fella?

"The only person you're gonna hurt is Abby," he snaps.

I fire back, "Don't you bring her into this!"

"Ya know what?" he adds. "I couldn't care less, dog. You lied about going down her pants anyhow. Bitch won't put out for nothin'."

"Hey! First off, don't call Abby a bitch. And second, I went up the skirt. Not down the pants. If you're strikin' out, that's your deal."

"Whatever, dude, she's a prude and I'm done with her," he says as he walks back to his slut.

Well, this sucks. I don't want this info. It will only hurt Abby, and that won't help me. She's not going to come running back just because Andre's a jerk. It'll just make her hate guys—and therefore me—more. I walk out of the store with my head down, jump on my bike, and pedal off without a movie or a friend in the world. Life sucks and I'm freezing.

32. Riffraff

A party at Gray Goose Lake is in the works for tonight. And though I'd rather do anything in the world than go to another high school party, I'm going because I heard there'll be girls from Hooker High. And maybe I can meet a Hooker who doesn't know what a jerk I am.

Gray Goose Lake is private. They have a guard out front to keep the riffraff out. I've never been, but I hear they have diving boards and a rope swing on their huge party dock. Apparently the guard had a heart attack on Monday, so no one will be keeping an eye on the riffraff this weekend . . . so here we come!

On my ride over to Hormone's house I stop at QuickTrip for a two-liter of Mountain Dew and some condoms (not to be used together). The condoms are for positive thinking, and the Dew is the key ingredient in my plan to look cool and not have to drink beer. I dug two Bud Light bottles out of the recycling. I'll take my backpack to the party and fill the empty bottles with Mountain Dew. It'll look like I'm enjoying an adult beverage, but I'll just be "doin' the Dew"!

The sardine ride over to Gray Goose Lake is miserable, but as we drive past the empty guardhouse I see why they keep this place locked up. The houses are old and huge.

They have long driveways and some of their garages are the size of my house. The main clubhouse looks like a jeweled mansion that's been buttoned down for the winter, but I can imagine how awesome it would be all decked out for a Fourth of July party. It would be sooo sweet if we were rolling in here in the summertime, with our trunks on, getting ready to fly off the rope swing and splash down into the cool lake water. I can almost smell the sunscreen and the hot dogs on the grill. I picture a rich girl from Hooker High strutting up to me with a bottle of Coppertone, asking me to do her back. And when I try to rub it around her bikini strap, I accidentally pop the lock open and her boobs fall out. She slowly turns around and giggles. "That always happens . . ."

"Carter, get out of my car!" Hormone yells because I'm all alone in the CRX, staring at the lake.

I snap out of my dream and yell, "Yeah, give me a sec . . . I've got a cramp!"

"Well, lock it when you get out, and don't forget your backpack," he instructs.

Man, I've got to stop sporting wood in the CRX, or I'm going to give off the wrong impression. I climb out and look around at the beautiful lake. The party deck, the rolling hills, and the frozen trees look like something out of a movie. The old wooden piers seem to be quivering in the frigid water. There's a frozen dock in the middle of the lake that's dying for me to crash through the ice and swim out to it. I didn't know we had cool things like this in Merrian. I hope that security guard has another heart attack in July so we can come back.

I stash my backpack in the woods and strut into the

party with my first beer/Dew. I'm on a mission to meet a Hooker. How jealous will the girls from my school be when they see me making out with my Hooker? I give my fives and punches to the boys and try not to look as uncomfortable as I feel when Abby and Andre walk up like freshmen royalty. I want to burst that bubble of lies, but I can't do it to Abby. I'll just drown my sorrows in Mountain Dew. Brock and Lynn roll in with a bunch of Brock's friends. EJ and Sarah Ruiz stroll out of the bushes, and EJ looks kind of different. He looks taller, maybe? Or he got a decent haircut . . . or he's had SEX! He did! Son of a . . .

"You got something you wanna tell me?" I ask him when he finally comes over to the boys.

"What?" He smiles goofily.

"You did it, didn't you?" I ask.

He's not even shocked that I noticed. "Maybe," he replies.

"You don't know if you did it? I think that's something you should be aware of if it happened," I say.

Bag jumps in with, "She might not know, but you should."

He smiles and confidently says, "Well, let's just say, if this party was for virgins . . . I'd have to leave."

I'm green with envy, but kind of proud too. If EJ can do it, anybody can! I scan the party for the lucky girl who's going to steal my virginity. Where are those Hookers?! Hopefully she's hot, but at this point I'll take a straggler.

"Where'd you get the beer?" EJ asks.

"Uh, my dad," I reply while still shopping for a chick.

"He just gave it to you?" he asks.

"No, I took it," I say. I couldn't tell him my dad gave it to me, because he'd tell his mom by accident and my folks would get a call. And I'll wind up in a class for alcoholics every Saturday for drinking Mountain Dew.

"Give me one?" he asks.

"No way, dude, I only have the one," I answer.

"Let me have a drink, then," he responds.

"Uh, naw, I-I-I really can't spare any beer tonight," I say, a little panicky.

"Since when do you like beer? And since when are you a selfish little—" he starts to say.

"Since when are you getting laid, man?" I ask, trying to change the subject.

"You're jealous, huh?" He laughs.

Well, look who's cocky all the sudden? EJ gets lucky and cocky in the same breath.

"All right, dude, why don't you slam the rest of my beer, stud," I say as I offer up the bottle.

He tips it up and fills his mouth. "Uhhhh!" he squeals, and spits the green fluid out. That's the worst—when you expect one thing and get a totally different taste! His face is awesome as he asks, "What is that? Acid Kool-Aid?"

I push him away from the boys and whisper, "Shhh! It's Mountain Dew."

"What're you, ten years old?" he asks.

"No, ass-wipe, I'm fourteen! I'm not old enough to drink beer, and I hate the junk, so I'm drinkin' Mountain Dew in a beer bottle so I can look cool. You got a problem with that? Go hang with your stupid girlfriend!" I mutter.

"Chill, Carter, I'm just messin' with you," he says. "I don't want to hang out with her anymore. She won't shut up, and she talks about the dumbest stuff. I think I'm gonna dump her."

"What? Shut up, dude," I say.

"Naw, man, since I got with Sarah I've been getting mad looks from other chicks," he replies.

"Dude, the odds of you trickin' another girl into letting you do it to her are really slim. Don't throw that fish back into the lake. I think you should marry her," I reply.

"No way, I'm gonna do it with her one more time, but then I'm droppin' her," EJ says.

"Damn, you're a hard-ass. Got what you wanted and that's it, huh, cowboy?" I ask.

"I guess," he replies.

My sister's right: all boys are jerks. I never realized it before, but if EJ and I are jerks . . . we all are.

"So how was the Caboose?" I inquire. "Were you scared?"

"No, it's awesome, man. We just did it in the woods." He laughs and gives me five.

"In the snow?" I ask.

He smiles and nods.

I pester on. "Which kind of rubber did you use?"

"Oh, uh, I didn't use one," he replies.

"WHAT?" I ask. "Are you serious? What shows are you watching, dude? You're gonna get a disease for sure, and that's if you're lucky. You just made a baby! You'll be a dumb-ass kid with a kid. I'd rather be called Slappy or Sloth than Uncle Carter! But the worst nickname for a freshman in high school is the one you got comin' . . . DAD! What were you thinkin'?!"

"I don't know." He shrugs. "She said it was cool, so I didn't use one."

"She did?" I gasp. Not only is Sarah Ruiz dumb in math, she's a tard in the bedroom/bushes as well.

"Dude, take one of these," I say, as I hand over one of my condoms. If I use one of them, it'll be a miracle. But three? Let's get real.

EJ's chick walks up with a girl I don't know. EJ doesn't even say hello. Man, the Caboose seemed kind of whatever about him before, but now that he's blowing her off for real, she's all over him. This is all so easy to understand when it's happening to other people.

She just stares at us for a minute. All I can think about is the fact that she and EJ were just doing it in the woods, so I try not to look her in the eye. Her friend is pretty cute. The Caboose finally says, "I failed that quiz in Rumpford's class yesterday," to me.

"Ruddy Gill was absent, huh?" I ask my shoes. "Only so many trips you can make to the pencil sharpener."

"Shut up, CARTER!" She laughs way too loud so EJ will pay attention to her.

She grabs his hand and says something else . . . I have no idea what . . . I'm trying to wrap my head around the fact that she's been naked in front of EJ! How many times have I been talking to someone, like a teacher or somebody, who has just had sex?! People everywhere, all over the world, are doing it without me.

"Do you know my cousin Amy?" the Caboose asks me. "She goes to Saint Mary's Academy."

Oh my, that's even better than a Hooker slut. "I-i-is that a private, religious school?" I ask.

"It sure is," Amy replies.

"D-d-do you wear a u-u-uniform?" I stammer.

"Yes." She laughs. "I have to wear the knee-high stockings and everything."

The Caboose laughs too, as my eyes roll back into my skull. This is the girl! She'll wear the skirt and the stockings and nothing else. Sarah gives it up, so her cousin must too; sluts hang out together. If a girl is a prude, the slutty girls cast her off. They move in packs. They roam the bars, arcades, and swimming pools for young studs like me to satisfy them. And I will, just as soon as I come up with a question or two.

"Is, uh . . . ?" I ask. "Um, are you . . . uhhh?" Oh man, I got nothing. EJ looks at me and crosses his arms. He knows what I'm doing, and he doesn't help at all. "Uhh . . . Amy? D-d-do you know what time it is?"

"It's nine o'clock, dude." EJ laughs. "Is your watch broken?"

I use all of my strength not to punch him in his face as I look down at my watch and seethe. "Maybe it will be . . . after I beat you to death with it."

"Ohh, I'd like to see you try that, bitch," he says. "Maybe I'll stick that watch up your ass."

I glance over at Amy. She makes a disgusted face at the thought of my Timex taking a licking and continuing to tick . . . in my butt. "Y-you know, I do know what time it is, E . . . It's time for your beat down!" I say as I slap his face, pretty hard. He slaps me back harder because he's super quick. I point my finger in his face and whisper, "Knock it off!" and wait for him to let his guard down before I slap him again: WHACK! And WHACK! He tags me back. Dang it!

"What's your problem, dude?" I ask.

"Why you stealin' my pickup line?" he replies.

"'What time is it?' is *your* pickup line exclusively?"

"Maybe!"

The Caboose cocks her head.

"What the hell do you need a line for anyway? You were just doinkin' her in the woods!" I say, and watch the Caboose's jaw drop.

EJ's eyes get really big as she and her cousin stomp off. "Dude?!" EJ barks.

I shrug my shoulders and ask, "What? You said you were dumpin' her."

He whisper/yells, "After we did it one more time, jack-ass!" and runs after her.

"Sorry," I say, and duck into the woods for a Mountain Dew refill. So that could have gone better. I've got to figure out a pickup line that I can use in tight spots like that. Something more creative than, "What time is it?"

I'm racking my brain and just putting the two-liter back into the bush when I get a shock from behind. "Well, if it isn't Peeping Tom," Pam says drunkenly. "Is that beer?"

"No, it's Mountain Dew," I respond without embarrassment.

She smiles and puts her hand on my back like she's my girlfriend. "You're so cute. Can I have some?"

"Can you handle it?" I reply.

"I think so," she says, and takes a swig.

Pam is touching my back and we are sharing fluids. She's the best pretend girlfriend ever. We walk out of the bushes together, and I pray someone sees us. Someone does. Abby rolls up on me real fast and real close.

"What's going on, Carter?" she barks.

You see? If you have a chick on your arm, they come running. "Oh, um, we're . . . we're just friends," I say all cool.

"Oh shut up! I mean with Andre," she demands. "He

thinks that you told me something. Or that you're supposed to tell me something. So what is it? What lies have you been spreading about me?"

Pam stops touching my back and looks at me for an answer. I guess pretend girlfriends don't stand by their men when the going gets tough.

"No, no. Nothin'," I say to the bushes.

"What did you say, Carter? What are you supposed to tell me about Andre?" she persists.

"All I can tell you about Andre . . . is that he's a dick-head. D-d-do you need me to tell you that?" I ask.

"No, it's just, he's acting weird," Abby whines.

Pam busts in to help out in a drunken sort of way with, "He's just pissed because you won't have sex with him."

"How do you know that?" Abby asks Pam.

Pam knows all, that's why.

"That's how they all are. They're all jerks and they're all babies," Pam slurs. "I mean, who would have thought Carter would screw you over like he did?"

"Okay, so I'll just see you guys later?" I say as I break out of the conversation. Drunkie the cover girl was selling me down the river awful cheap, and I can't stand to have Abby mad at me, so I polish off my third Mountain Dew and make my sixth lap around the party. I walk up to Doc, Nutt, and Bag and ask, "S'up?"

Doc replies, "Just chillin', checkin' out the Hookers."

I add, "Yeah, I've seen some cuties."

"Andre's talkin' to the hottest one. Did you see her?" Bag asks me.

I look over at Andre grabbing the girl from Blockbuster by the waist. That smooth son of a . . .

"Did he and Abby break up?" Nutt asks.

Doc replies, "No, he's just got hella' game. That's a hot Hooker!"

"Yeah, if you're into that sort of thing," I mutter.

"What sort of thing?" Doc asks.

I fight back a laugh and say, "Well, I heard she's got a glass eye and a peg leg."

"Shut up!" they all yell.

"That's what I heard," I say.

We all stop talking for a second to consider whether or not a peg leg would be a deal breaker for us.

Bag asks me, "You thinkin' about pickin' up one of these Hookers, Carter?"

"Yeah, but I got no game. I just can't talk to 'em," I say in defeat.

Nutt responds, "You should use the massage technique, bro."

Of course I ask what the massage technique is, and he explains it's a move his brother heard about, where you just walk up to a girl and start rubbing her shoulders. You don't say a word, you just make the move and she's supposed to melt in your hands. It makes perfect sense to me because of my language barrier with girls. I should rely on action instead.

I spot a girl that might be just right. She's by herself next to the rope swing, and the boys think she's perfect. She doesn't go to our school, and she doesn't seem to be missing a leg or anything, so they send me in. I approach from the rear. She has a decent butt and okay hair, so I turn around and shoot them a thumbs-up. I'm sure she has boobs, but she's wearing a coat, so they have little effect on me. If we were at this lake in the summertime it would be a different story, because she'd be wearing a swimsuit; and although she'd be impressed with my skills off the boards, I could never just roll up on a chick in a bikini and start rubbing her shoulders. I'm having enough trouble finding the courage to go after her puffy jacket. I'll just stand behind her for a second and plan this out.

Nutt yells from behind me, "Get in the fight, man!"

He's such a dumbass, but he's right about this! What's to plan? Take charge and grab her! My heart is pounding as I extend my shaking hands. . . .

I'm not sure if the massage technique works or not, because she just bent down and is puking into the lake for all she's worth. She'll never know what she missed out on by drinking too much tonight. I turn away quick because puke freaks me out, and I see my boys laughing their asses off. I also see Abby crying by the diving boards as Andre walks away from her. He struts through the crowd and right up to the slut from Blockbuster, who, because of me, everyone will think is a pirate until she wears shorts again in the spring. Dang, that guy is a jerk. Abby's crying hard. I think she was crying harder by the football room windows, though. Not that this is a competition or anything . . . I'm just saying. A half-moon is lighting the lake behind her, and she looks so pretty. Andre is a fool. I should try out the massage technique on Abby.

She spots me watching her cry. Our eyes meet, and she approaches me head-on. She looks so sad. Her heart doesn't deserve this. She needs a massage. She's all hot and intense as she strides toward me. She sees the error of her ways, and she needs her Carter back. It's okay, pumpkin,

I know. Stop that crying, I forgive you. . . .

WWHHAACCKK!

The sharp sting of her right hand slapping my face snaps me out of the dream. OUCH!

"Do you hate me?" she barks.

"What?" I ask, grabbing my jaw.

WHACK! She connects a left-hand slap. I grab the other side of my jaw and think some anger is being misdirected here. It's being directed at me and my face, and we've done nothing. People are drunk, but intoxicated or not, folks love a fight.

"How could you, Carter?" she asks.

"How could I what? W-w-what are we talking about?" I reply.

WHACK! Another slap. OW! She's quick. I have to get on those karate classes.

"Please stop hitting me," I say.

"Don't patronize me!" she yells. (How can I patronize anyone? I don't know what that word means.) "I thought at the very least you were my friend. All I ever did was like you, and you've done nothing but screw me over. You knew Andre was cheating on me, didn't you?"

My lightbulb finally goes on. "Oh, that?" I say.

She cocks back again, but I step aside to avoid this slap. Fourth time's a charm!

"What did I ever do to you?" she squeals. "I always thought you were so cool. I thought you were different. But you're just like all the other guys. You're worse!"

I just stare at her. I'm so embarrassed I can't speak. No stutter or anything, just . . . nothing. Everyone is staring at me. I'm beet red from humiliation and slaps. I want to tell her that she's the most beautiful girl here tonight and that I love her more than words can say; that I never meant to hurt her. That she's right about me . . . I'm not cool. I'm an insecure prick who honestly thought I shouldn't tell her about Andre and the Blockbuster slut because I didn't want to cause her any more pain. . . . But that's crap! Because if I really cared, I would have told EJ or Bag to tell Nicky. But what I really didn't want . . . what I truly couldn't handle was for anybody to make fun of me for caring.

I don't say any of that. I might have, but the police sirens start blaring in the distance and the fire drill on crack has begun. "COPS!!!" someone yells, and kids scurry in every direction like it's a surprise the cops have shown up. We *are* breaking into this place. There are two hundred screaming drunk teenagers here; the police are going to be notified. What's the mystery? It's only my second party and I can already see the pattern.

Abby darts off, and I run away from her. I'm headed for the CRX, but as I approach, it's already pulling away, and sparks are flying up from the muffler. The engine is starting to smoke, and the bumper is dragging on the ground. Ten guys have already squeezed in, and one kid is riding on top. It's just too much for the little engine. But Hormone doesn't let up on it for a second. That poor little Honda had the misfortune to come into the hands of a fifteen-year-old boy, and that's the end of the line for a car. There's no resale value. No trade-in. We're going to kill it. It's not just Hormone's first car, it's the entire freshman class's. It belongs to all of us, but I'm not getting a ride from it tonight. The cops have blocked the exit, and it's chaos! I grab my backpack and make a run for it. EJ sees me duck into the brush and ditches his new girlfriend. That boy's coldhearted, but I'm glad he's with me, because I'm scared of the woods. We're running fast. It's freezing and I'm not sure where we're going, but this is really fun. So far, getting to run from The Man is my favorite part of high school parties.

33. Truckin'

We run for a half hour or so before we finally find a road. We split the rest of the flat Mountain Dew, but basically I've consumed an entire two-liter by myself. That can't be good for you. We jump into a ditch when we hear the roar of an engine coming from behind us.

"Oh man, COPS!" EJ whispers.

No red or blue lights are flashing, but the engine sounds really mean. Nick Brock's old truck rumbles over a hill and smashes down some small trees. It's got big tires and four guys standing up in the back. The stereo is blasting and my sister is laughing in the passenger seat. It looks so tough as it blasts through the ditch and up onto the street. Then the truck drives over the road and crashes into the ditch on the other side. Not quite as cool. There's only so much a badass truck can do when its owner's plastered. Nick is punching the steering wheel when EJ and I run up.

"You okay?" I ask.

"Yeah, baby, it's all good," Nick slurs. He's thinking something over. "Hey, Carter? You got your learner's permit?" he asks.

"Hell yeah, I got it," I lie.

"You'd better get her home for meee. . . ." he says, and then falls asleep into the steering wheel.

"Wait, what? You want me to drive your truck, Brock?" I ask.

"Hell no. No way, CARTER!" Lynn yells as she opens the passenger door and falls out of the truck into the ditch. She's out cold. It must be late because it's definitely bedtime for these party people. I'm feeling pretty good, though, whatever time it is. Mountain Dew is the bomb. If it weren't for the stinging pain in my stomach and the shaking in my hands, I might use this stuff to keep me focused at school. The drunk guys load my sister into the back with them, and EJ and I push Brock over to the middle seat. This truck is awesome! I've never driven an actual car before, but a golf cart is pretty much the same thing, I hope. I put my seat belt on and turn the key—*WWWRREEEKK!*

"And that's the sound a truck makes when it's already turned on," I say to EJ. Everyone cheers from the back. "Shut up!" I yell at them like a soccer mom.

"You got it, dude." EJ smiles encouragingly.

I've got to get us out of this ditch, so I put the stick into R, and push on the gas pedal. The engine roars, but nothing's happening. I press the pedal harder. We're rocking backward a bit, but not enough to get this big old truck out of the ditch. I smash the pedal all the way to the ground, the engine screams, and the truck starts to shove itself backward. Now we're moving! We're free of the ditch and absolutely flying in reverse.

"I didn't know cars could go this fast backward!" I yell over the whining engine.

EJ doesn't say anything constructive. He's too busy yanking on the seat belt and screaming, "STOP!"

Okay, I've just got to take my foot off this skinny pedal

and smash down the other one. *EEAAAARRRRRRRTT!* The tires screech and the truck slides to a stop.

I shift the stick to D before anyone can say anything, and squash the skinny pedal again. We peel out, and EJ is giggling like a girl. The guys in the back are screaming. Not sure what they're saying, because things are loud at sixty miles an hour. It's hard to keep this truck in a straight line, and it's harder to see things coming at you at seventy miles an hour. On my bike I can see stuff and think about it before I get to it, but when you're going eighty miles an hour, the stuff's long gone before you can figure out what it was. Like the girl we just flew by looked like Abby, but at ninety miles an hour, who can tell? She definitely had a nice butt; I can tell that at any speed. I really think it was Abby, though. So I take my foot off the skinny pedal and press on the fat one, hard.

EEAAAAARRRRTT! The tires screech and the truck skids to the right. I'm pressing on this pedal as hard as I can, but we're still hauling ass sideways. I thought we'd just stop, but at a hundred miles an hour, it takes some time and rubber. There's so much smoke from the tires when we finally stop I can't even see EJ. We pull Brock off the dashboard, and I put the stick back on the R. After a minute or two of flying in reverse we get to the girl. It is Abby, and she looks as surprised to see me behind the wheel as I am to be here. She must be impressed, but I'm not positive, because we just flew right by her. DANG IT!

EEEAAAARRRRT! We slam to a stop, but she keeps walking.

"You need a lift, little lady?" I yell, with my head out the window.

EJ thinks it's funny, but maybe Abby didn't hear me. I peel out and almost run her over as we fly by her again.

"That's it, Carter, break her heart and then mow her down!" EJ yells as I hit the brakes and screech to a stop about fifty feet in front of her.

I stick my head out the window again and yell, "You need a lift, little lady?" That joke is a winner, I'm sure of it. But it doesn't even get a smile out of her. EJ gives me a disappointed look for busting it out twice.

We fly by her again. Two things at once is hard enough for me. But driving for the first time and apologizing to a girl is just too much. Without stopping, I slam the stick into P and jump out. The truck screeches, jerks, and clangs to stop. I've got to remember never to do that when I get a car.

"Abby, wait!" I yell. "Um, did you get a haircut?" (Bad question.)

"Oh, save it, Carter!" she snaps, and keeps walking.

"Can I give you a ride home?" I ask.

She just shoots me a mean look and picks up her pace.

I respond to her look. "You can hate me all you want, but you shouldn't be walking out here by yourself. You don't even have to talk to me. The rest of these guys in the truck all think I'm a dumbass too!"

"What other guys?" she asks.

I look back to the truck and discover that I've lost all of my passengers except EJ, Lynn, and Brock. "Never mind. . . . Come on, Abby, it's cold out here and dark. You've had a really bad night. The odds of some creepy dude trying to pick you up and do things to you are pretty high, don't you think?" I say.

"You're the only creepy dude I see out here," she fumes.

I forget how quick Abby is. "That was pretty good," I concede. "Look, I'll just drop you off."

She doesn't say a word, but she turns around and stomps back to the truck and opens the passenger door. EJ slides over onto Brock's lap.

"What are you doin'? Get in the back!" I whisper at EJ.

"No way, dude," he protests. "It's freezing out there, and you're a terrible driver. You'd better buckle up, Abby!"

I point at his face as if to say, "You'll pay for this later," shift into drive, and head for Abby's house. I keep the speed down to a respectable sixty miles an hour. I was hoping to have a heart-to-heart talk with Abby as we flew down the road, but I'm pretty busy with all the driving responsibilities. Gas pedal, brake pedal, steering wheel, turn signals, deejaying. There is a lot to do. EJ and Brock are blocking my view of Abby, and with EJ yelling, "CARTER, CARTER, watch the ditch! Red light! Slow down! Look out!" like a little bitch the whole time, I can't get a word in.

We screech to a stop in front of Abby's house, and she jumps out before I can say anything. No thank-you, no good-bye, just a nice view of her butt walking into the house. I like the view, but I still think it's rude.

I peel out, not because I'm angry or anything, but just because that's how you drive this truck. A dull thud comes from the back, and I turn to see my sister rolling around in the dirty truck bed. Thank God she's unconscious, because when she wakes up, I'll be in big trouble. I look back at the street and realize that I'm driving on the wrong side of the road. Dang it! I'll just calmly steer it back onto the right side of the road. What're the odds of another car coming over the top of this hill at three o'clock in the morning?

Pretty good if it's your first time driving and your name is Will Carter.

I see the headlights, and EJ screams to reinforce my theory that we're about to die. I can't move my arms or legs to do anything about it, but thank God the other car can, because I'm just going straight at this point.

Cops must take special driving classes to learn how to skid away like that just in time. Dang it!

EJ confirms it. "COP," he gasps as the police cruiser slides into a ditch.

"Ohhh, was that the cop who busted me at the party?!" I scream.

"I think I saw a mustache!" EJ replies.

"Should I stop?" I ask.

"Yeah, you should stop . . . if you want to see what jail's like!" EJ cries. "Punch it!"

I accelerate down the road and look in the rearview mirror but don't see anything except Lynn bouncing around. Maybe the cop thinks I'm a foreigner. If I were driving this truck in England, I would be A-OK, but we're in Merrian, and that cop's lights are now flashing back there like he doesn't care where I'm from. I really hope it's not the cop from the party. How embarrassing must it have been to lose a fourteen-year-old prisoner? And I'm sure that rottweiler gave him a look too, like, "You dumbass, Barney!" Nobody likes to be put down by a dog. Especially not a cop.

I bust a fast left toward my house, and the right side of the truck comes up off the ground like *The Dukes of Hazzard* (awesome). I guess before you turn you have to slow down. I've never seen my street at sixty miles an hour before. I hardly recognize it. I try to bust a right turn into my driveway, but I sort of merge into my neighbors' yard instead, and rip through their bushes. I barely miss the corner of my house and smash the mailbox into a million pieces. The truck crushes the hedges I was supposed to trim last Sunday (scratch that off my list of things to do). I try to slam on the brakes, but I accidentally smash the gas pedal again, and we fly right over a rock retaining wall my dad built last year. I see Lynn fly up into the air like a wet piece of spaghetti and crash back down into the truck bed.

"Dude, we just got air!" EJ yells as the front bumper smashes down and breaks off.

We barrel over the bumper, crush my basketball goal, blast through the wooden fence in the backyard, and finally skid to a stop, taking up a bunch of grass with the big tires. I hit the lights on the truck and shut it down. The engine is smoking and making all kinds of banging noises. It doesn't seem to want to turn off.

My dad flies out the back door in his underwear with a flashlight and a golf club. He means business. His eyes are all big and blinky, trying to wake up and figure out what's going on in his backyard.

"Hey, Mr. Carter," EJ says, like he's just come over to say hi.

"What the hell is going on out here?" Dad yells.

"Nick let me drive his truck, Dad!" I say, all proud.

"I can see that. Why did he do that?" Dad asks.

"Uh, well, he got really tired and fell asleep," I reply.

"Where's Lynn?" he asks.

"Oh, she's in the back here," EJ says. "But she's asleep too, so, shhhh."

Hearing her name, Lynn raises her head from the truck

bed. She's covered in dirt, has a bloody nose and straw sticking out of her hair. She's not sure what's going on, so she slurs, "Uhhh, heeyy, Daaadddy!" and stumbles out of the bed and staggers into the house.

"You're drunk!" Dad barks. (Nothing gets by my old man.)

Lynn says, "Shhhh!" from inside the house.

He turns and asks me, "What the hell is going on?"

I shrug my shoulders and mutter, "I was just driving the truck."

"Since when do you know how to drive?" he asks.

"Since never, Mr. Carter. He's a terrible driver!" EJ blurts out.

My dad shakes his head as he surveys his busted-up yard, broken-down fence, and the smoking truck hissing on his back patio, before he finally sighs, "Good lord, well . . ."

He might have been getting ready to say something about how everything is fixable and what's important is that everyone got home safe and how his son is a hero. That may have been what he was going to say, when that police car whizzes by with the lights flashing.

"Looking for you, by any chance?" he seethes.

"How should I know what they're lookin' for? I been drivin'!" I reply.

He throws the flashlight across the yard and snaps the golf club across his knee. He's shaking with anger, or he's starting to freeze. "Damn it! I don't know how to handle this! You were good kids, like, a month ago! What the hell is going on with you, son?"

"I honestly don't know," I reply. "Everything is just harder than I thought it was going to be, and I'm not doing very well at any of it! My life's a friggin' mess . . . I don't like girls anymore . . . I'm flunking all of my classes except drama. . . ."

"Wait, y-y-you don't like girls?" He looks like he's eaten a habanero pepper when he asks, "S-s-so you think you're gay?"

My jaw falls open, and EJ doubles over with laughter. "Ha-HAAA!!!"

I bark, "Get outta here, E!"

"I thought I was spending the night. . . . You don't wanna cuddle?" He laughs.

I angrily point toward his house, and he cackles off into the night.

Dad continues, "Not, not that there's anything wrong with being gay, son. . . . Your mother and I, w-w-we love you no matter what."

"You do? Wait, what?! Why do you think I'm gay?" I ask.

"I don't know, you just said that you were into drama and you don't like girls anymore," he barks.

"I did? Well, I guess I could be. My friends tell me I'm gay all the time, and I really do like the acting class, so it's a possibility. It's too soon to tell, though, I think . . . I'm only fourteen. But what I meant to say was that girls positively don't like *me* anymore."

He scratches his head and tries to figure out how this talk has spun so far out of control. We're both trembling because he's horribly underdressed and I'm jacked up on two liters of Mountain Dew. He seems to be wrapping it up when he says, "Well, we're behind you . . . or we're with you, no matter what you decide."

"Thanks, that's good to know," I reply awkwardly.

He turns to go back into the house but stops short. "Hey, another thing. I keep finding a porno playing on the basement VCR. Is that yours?"

"Uh, maybe," I reply.

He sighs, "Well, okay. It's just, it's always playing in fast-forward like a weird matinee show when I get home from work, and it kind of creeps me out. Why don't you turn it off . . . when you're through with it?"

"That's a good question, Dad. I think I may be retarded or something. My drama teacher says I'm 'in the moment.' She thinks it's a good thing," I reply.

"Well, knock it off," he barks. "If your mom finds that kind of thing, she'll freak out. She still thinks you're a little boy, and you'll have to see a counselor or something, and we can't afford it right now, so give it a rest. And another thing, those movies and porn in general—it's not good for you. It shows you everything wrong. That's not how it works at all."

"Oh, I know that, Dad," I say with certainty.

"You do?" he asks.

"Yeah, I couldn't go that fast if I practiced every day," I reply.

"Just knock it off!" he orders, and marches in the house shaking his head. Poor guy.

Approximately 4 1/2 hours later

I'm rudely awoken at nine a.m. by the sound of banging in the backyard. It feels like I just fell asleep. Brock and my dad are out there fixing the demolished fence. My dad is banging the hammer really close to Nick's face. It's loud, and Nick obviously doesn't like the noise this morning. My dad is kind of funny.

Lynn isn't up yet, which is best for everyone, so I put my coat on and go down and throw some grass seed around where the skid marks are worst. We have to push the old truck into the street because it won't start.

"That's weird," I say to Nick. "It was running great last night."

I put all the rocks and logs back together where I smashed the truck through the retaining wall. It looks good as new (more or less). After my dad goes inside, Brock comes up to me with his crushed bumper in hand. I start to slowly back away when, surprisingly, he says, "Sorry if I got you in trouble last night."

I think he just apologized to me for ruining his truck.

"I'm not tryin' to tell you what to do, Nick, but you don't need to . . ."

"Yeah I do; you look up to me, and I let you down by getting that drunk." It may just be the cold wind, but it seems like he's about to cry.

Everybody looks up to Nick Brock because he's so tall, but I do because he's so cool. If there was some cheesy music playing in the background I'd throw my arms around his twenty-inch neck and cry, "It's okay, Brocky, I still love ya!" Instead I kick a rock and say, "Dude, driving your truck was awesome."

He laughs. "Looks like you had some trouble with the landing. . . ."

"I didn't mean to jump it!"

He holds up the bumper and chuckles. "So we got some air, huh?"

"*Dukes of Hazzard* style, bro! If you were awake you would've dug it."

He's still laughing, so I go ahead and clear my conscience, filling him in as to why he might get pulled over in the near future and thrown in jail for resisting arrest. "I also may have run a cop off the road. . . ."

The nice big brother vibe exits the conversation, and his kind expression morphs to pissed off. Not good!

"But I may not have," I yell while sprinting away from him. "There was a lot going on!"

34. Thrash

I dive into the Merrian High indoor pool on the first day of practice and slip through the water like it's the finest silk from China . . . not freezing cold, chlorine-laden, urine-tainted Merrian tap water. Ahhh! The water feels sooo good. The world seems perfect at the bottom of a pool. All sounds disappear. It could be July again, and my biggest problem could be what trick to bust off the diving board, but my lungs start to sting and I jump to the surface to fill them with musty air. The snow remains piled high outside the windows, and Andre is jumping into my lane. The stupid swimming coach has put us together. I can see how such a mistake could be made—freshmen, football players, all-city first and second place—but this isn't going to work. We're not friends, and I'm not sharing a lane with the punk.

I swim toward Coach Barker to file a protest, but she yells out, "Eight hundred warm-up! I want it fast!" before I can get to her.

Eight hundred what? Meters? Are you crazy, lady? I was thinking of doing a thousand for the whole practice. It's the first day; let's not get carried away. But all the other guys swim off, including Andre. Oh no you don't, punk! I take off after him. Coach may call this "a warm-up," but with this jerk in my lane, it's a race to the DEATH. I fly past him: *Eat my wake, bitch!* Man, I'm doing great. I feel strong. It must be all those weights I've been lifting. I'm churning up the water faster than I ever have. The first hundred meters is a breeze, but the flip turn starting the second hundred is a little sloppy. My shoulders seem to have caught fire and are starting to burn up. I'm breathing every stroke now, and my lungs might be bleeding. Andre is gaining on me, and I'm fading fast. My arms are still moving, but I don't think I am. Andre passes me like I'm standing still. DANG IT! Oh, I've got nothing, after only two hundred meters, I'm no longer just not moving, I'm starting to sink! I grab the lane line.

Coach Barker notices and yells, "Freshman, get off of my lane line! Let's GOOO!"

Okay, bitch, I already don't like you for putting me in this lane with Andre. And now I'm dealing with the repercussions of your dumb-ass decision, so cut me some slack. I shake my head, and with all the strength I have left, I raise my thumb as if to say, "You got it, Coach!" But I don't move.

Andre passes me again, and the punk has the nerve to stop, and the breath to say, "Pussy!" before swimming off.

I just huff and puff at him. I hope he gets that I'm huffing and puffing in anger. If I could spare a scrap of life, I'd extend a finger at him too, and it wouldn't be my thumb. I let go of the lane line and get going again. Slowly. Andre passes me a couple more times, but I finally finish the warm-up. Well, six hundred meters . . . five fifty at the least. But I'm definitely warmed up!

The first practice is nuts. I can't keep up for anything. I'm giving it everything I have and cheating like crazy, but it's just not enough. Andre isn't keeping up either, but he's doing better than I am. Lap after lap, hour after hour. I would've quit after ten minutes of this crap and been home by now . . . if Andre weren't here. But that punk *is* here, pushing me forward, driving my legs to kick, and forcing my arms to thrash this water until they fall off. But I won't let my arms really fall off, because that would make Andre way too happy. I'll finish this practice doing a dog paddle if I have to, but I won't give him the satisfaction of seeing me quit.

At dinner, I eat my usual helping of Mom's famous (not) turkey tetrazzini. And I'm still starving. I'm going to need double the usual amount to fill me up. Only problem is, I can't reach the serving bowl. It's two feet away, but it may as well be a mile. I can't get it. My brain is sending the signal to my arm to get some more tetrazzini, but the shoulder's paralyzed. I'll starve to death before this arm will reach out the two feet I need it to.

I can only manage the strength to get to my room and collapse onto the little bed. I'm dead asleep at six forty-five. No pajamas, no teeth brushed, just eyelids and dreams. I'm chasing Andre all night long. He's in a car and I'm running after him. He's in a boat and I'm swimming after him. I'm on a bicycle and he's on a rocket ship. For twelve hours and twenty minutes I chase him. I'm as tired when my dad wakes me up as when I crashed onto the mattress. Running after a guy in your dreams does not make for restful sleep.

35. The Gayest Ben

I thought I knew what soreness was all about until this morning. Mom will have to send a note to school with Lynn: *Carter will not attend classes today because he is paralyzed.*

They say swimming is the best exercise. Well, whoever "they" are, they don't know Coach Barker. Her brand of swimming can kill you! But I'm going back. Andre isn't getting a lane all to himself, and he'll never know what a "pussy" I really am. My Advil breakfast does the trick, and I'm okay as long as I stay perfectly still. I feel pretty good, in fact. I didn't do any homework last night, but I just aced a math quiz. I don't need to study more; I just need to sleep more.

I try to hang out with my boys at the lockers, but a stench has filled the halls today. Like a peppermint acid spill.

"It smells like an Altoids factory exploded around here!" Bag yells.

"What is that?" I ask.

"That's the smell of gayness," J-Low says.

The football/wrestling coach walks up and starts laughing. "Whew, somebody found the Bengay!"

It reeks, but the stuff must work, because from the smell of it, everybody is using it. My eyes are watering like crazy, but my sinuses are clear as glass.

"I put some on my neck," Hormone adds. "But somebody took a bath in it!"

"Man, my neck is sore too," I say, as if someone asked. "I just took a bunch of Advil, though."

Coach gives me a disgusted look and says, "Why, did you swim into the wall?"

Everybody's cracking up like that's the funniest joke of all time, and Coach struts down the hall all proud because he made a fourteen-year-old look dumb. Way to go; why don't you go back to the chalkboard and work on some more zingers, jerk.

"Who is the Gayest Ben?" J-Low asks, like a newsman sniffing out a story.

All of the winter sports started yesterday. It could even be one of the drama geeks, because they started rehearsals for a show called *Stomp*. It would be me if I'd known about the stuff. I'm glad it's not, though, because it's so much fun looking for the biggest wuss in the school. I wonder who'll earn the nickname Gayest Ben for life.

After science class I know that I've only got one more hour before I have to go back to the pool. I've never not wanted to go swimming before, but I've never not wanted to do anything more than I don't want to swim today. I would rather eat my Speedo than put it back on. It's sopping wet when I find it wadded up at the bottom of my locker. I didn't plan very well for this yesterday. Hell, I didn't think I'd live through the night, let alone be back at this locker looking for goggles.

Andre is by himself stretching when I come into the pool. He looks like he's been working out or something.

He's all shiny like a bodybuilder in his little Speedo. I have to wear a towel or shorts. I never just rock the Speedo by itself. As I walk past the diving boards I'm hit by a wall of peppermint stench. The closer I get to Andre the wider my sinuses open. I may have found the Gayest Ben!

"It's stinky in here . . . huh, Ben?" I ask him.

He doesn't respond. YES! He's so sore from yesterday, he's covered himself in greasy antipain cream. I love it. One more Advil and I'd be in a coma right now, but nobody knows that but me! Everybody can smell Andre's pain from a mile away. The team doesn't say anything through the stretching part of practice, but no one gets very close to him, either.

We all jump in the pool a little slower than yesterday. I also can't help but notice that there are a few less dudes in the pool today.

"Two hundred warm-up. Take it slow, fellas," Coach Barker yells.

We take off, and I'm not setting any records today, but I'm going. My lane is disgusting. A cloud of grease follows my lane partner, and I get a nasty taste of minty grossness every few minutes, but I love knowing Andre hurts.

The warm-up is done, and we all rest on the wall for a second. I bet we'd have a few more bodies in the pool if we'd done a little more of this yesterday, Coach.

"Are you sore, Carter?" Andre pants.

Oh no you don't, sucker. You and me? Not friends! You are my sworn enemy. And if I'm a little sore, it's your damn fault. "Nope, not really," I say, and take off for the first set of really hard laps.

I don't talk to him during the rest breaks; I don't talk

to him ever. We may share this lane for four years, but I'll never say a word. Usually I'm the king of jacking around at swim practice, skipping parts of the drills, and not really trying very hard. But not anymore! Not in this lane. I am all business.

The biggest deal in swimming is the four hundred–meter relay team. Only four slots and it's all about your individual time. You could be the coolest guy in the world, but if you're a split second slower than the biggest prick on the planet, you're out! Andre is the fourth-fastest guy (behind three seniors), and I'm number five. So not only did the prick letter in football, but he's going to get one for swimming too. We both beat out a junior that was on the relay last year, so I get to be the anchorman for the junior-varsity squad. No letterman's jacket, but it's pretty cool for a freshman. I'm faster than ever, but it's not enough. I can get him. I will beat Andre. I could get a silver medal in the Olympics, but if Andre got the gold, it would be a total failure. I want to smoke him.

If I had a nickel for every time I had a new master plan like this written on my arm, I'd have a couple bucks. I usually stick with them for a week or two, but this beating Andre thing is really strong. I'm committed to it. Lap after lap. Day after day. Week after week. My poor body is paying the price. I'm working my tail off . . . literally. I don't have a butt anymore. I eat more food than anyone I know, but my jeans are practically falling off me. I'm getting ripped. I don't even skip when I'm sick. Every practice, I make sure to swim at least two hundred more meters than Andre does. I work my starts after practice. I get there early and work my turns. I'm focused. My dad was disappointed in me last summer after I quit mowing lawns; he said that I had "no work ethic." I didn't care about it at the time because I had no idea what he was talking about. But I think I'm getting it.

My mom is worried about me, and says, "You've got a hungry look in your eyes, young man."

I tell her, "That's because I *am* hungry!" All the time. I don't just want junk food, either. Protein and vegetables is all I want these days.

Coach Barker says, "Ding Dongs and Coke won't make you swim faster." If they did, it would be cool. But they don't, so I don't even bother with them anymore.

I swim in all the events and all the meets my coach will let me, but it's hard on me. Not just on my body, but my spirit is taking a beating as well. In the summer, I win. I won almost every race I entered, except when I swam against Andre. And then I'd at least get second. But I'm not even close to winning any of these races. Neither is Andre, though. My dad tells me not to sweat it and to "just swim against the clock and try to beat yourself."

I keep track of my time, but I'm not trying to beat myself. I'm trying to beat Andre. I was three seconds slower than him in the hundred-meter freestyle at the beginning of the season. And now I'm one and four-one-hundredths of a second slower than him. That doesn't sound like much time, but it's a lot in the pool. It just sucks because when I shave some time off, Andre does too; it's a vicious cycle. I hate him, but I sometimes wish he sat next to me in math class or something. I'd study until my brain fell out to get a higher score than him on a quiz.

❀   ❀   ❀

The state championships are coming up, and practices are getting even harder. I guess our relay team has been invited to go, and it's a big deal. Andre and the rest of the seniors get to spend the night in a college dorm together, and they have to shave their heads. I'm so jealous it hurts. We have the junior varsity championships here at Merrian High next week, and it's my last opportunity to beat Andre before State. It makes me work even harder than I was before, because I know if I can beat him, I'll be the one with the shaved head!

Everybody shaves off their body hair before the JV championships. The razor is supposed to shave time as well as hair. Apparently, my leg and armpit hair have been slowing me down and I didn't know it.

The team gathers in the shower room after practice and lathers up. By the time I finish swimming my extra laps, Andre's head is completely shaved and he's almost done with his legs. I guess somebody's pretty confident that I won't beat him at the JV championships.

Won't that be embarrassing when people ask, "Why did you shave your head, Andre?"

And he has to reply, "Oh, I was supposed to swim at State, but after Carter smoked me, I didn't get to go!"

I've got to catch up. I want to beat him at everything, leg shaving included. So I slap the cream on my legs. I grab a razor out of a bag and another one off the floor. Andre is only using one razor; I'll use two. I rip the blades up my legs over and over again. From the foot to the knee, from the thigh to the Speedo. Top to bottom. I've got more hair than I thought I did. This is taking some effort. I'm ripping through it, though, and gaining on Andre. The blades get clogged, so I rinse them out real fast and keep moving. I space off for just a second to notice a river of blood running down the drain. Man, that is gross. It's like a horror movie. Somebody in here is cut—bad. That has got to hurt. No one is screaming, though. I'd be crying like a bitch if . . . Man, is it hot in here? Like steamy/fuzzy. I'm feeling kind of tired all the sudden. Shaving really takes it out of you. Maybe my leg hair is like that guy in the Bible whose strength is in his long hair and when his chick cuts it off, he gets really weak. I'm just pushing myself too hard these days. I can't even catch my breath. I can't wait to just go swimming for fun and not kill myself in the pool for three hours a day. I really want to go back to Gray Goose Lake and hit that roooope swing. It'll be soooo niiicccee. . . .

"CARTER! Carter, get up, dog!" someone yells from far away.

"Mom, get out," I yell, all groggy. "I'm up!"

Andre is slapping me in my face, so I try to defend myself with a retardo karate block.

"Carter, you're bleeding, dude!" one of the seniors yells.

"Where is bleed come for?" I mumble, and pass out again.

I don't remember much else. I don't have to go to the hospital or anything, but I lost a lot of blood. I'm just going to say it: fourteen-year-olds should not handle razor blades. If I did get checked into the hospital they'd think I was one of those self-mutilator kids. I am when it comes to beating Andre, but I didn't mean to carve myself up like a turkey.

36. Take Your Mark

Stripping off my jeans before the JV championships is as painful as it is disgusting. I'm covered in a poison ivy–looking rash and have bloody racing-stripe cuts and little mohawks up and down my legs. It only takes fifteen minutes to put my Speedo on, but once I tie the drawstring I start to get excited and focused on the race. I wrap a towel around my waist and head out for warm-ups.

"HHHAAAWWWWWEEE!!!" I scream as my bloody cuts collide with the chlorine and sizzle. Normally it wouldn't be a big deal to scream at a swim meet, but for some reason a lot of people are here today. It's not just parents, either. The JV cheerleaders are supposed to come. Which is kind of dumb. I wouldn't kick them out or anything, but our sport takes place underwater; we can't hear anything. No "GO"s, no "FIGHT"s, no "WIN!"s. I guess the cheerleaders thought it was stupid too, because the drill team just showed up instead. Man, that's a slap in the face. What are they going to do, bust out a big dance number? It's hard enough to walk on a wet pool deck . . . hip-hop is going to be impossible.

Abby files in toward the end of the herd. She looks like someone is holding a gun to her back, forcing her to come to this swim meet, like, "Hey, Abby, how many guys have broken your heart? Oh, only two dudes? Well, how about you get your ass in this natatorium and shake it for both of 'em!" She looks cute despite her deer-in-headlights expression. Andre is doing his Mr. Clean impression, talking to his Hooker slut right in front of Abby. What a jerk. He yawns and kisses his girl good-bye. He looks all relaxed, and I'm a nervous wreck. We're in the same heat for the hundred-meter freestyle, and I know this is my chance. I want to win so bad it's making me sick. How sweet would it be to pull this off in front of Abby?

The butterflies in my stomach feel like they're on crack when the lane assignments are called out. Mr. Clean is right next to me in lane three. My hands are trembling as I try to put my goggles on. I look over at Andre as we step up to the blocks, and he yawns at me. Oh no you didn't! Mr. State Championship relay team member has decided this little JV meet is beneath him. Oh, I can tolerate the drill team stomping and mooing over there, but this slap in the face, I cannot. Now you're going to get slapped, dog!

The starter calls out, "Swimmers, take your mark." Andre better take his mark and get set to be smoked.

The start bell chirps—*AAARRTTT*—and I'm off like a shot. All of my anxiety and frustration are released in the first four strokes. My cut-up legs are kicking the water as if it's Andre's face. I pull the water toward me like I'm pulling Abby back to me. I grunt and snarl under the water. I don't need air; I've got anger, frustration, and loneliness for fuel, and I've got someone to blame for it all in the next lane. My flip turns are money. I'm cooking! I glance to my right after the third flip turn, but I don't see him. Dang it, he's so far ahead of me I can't even see him. NOOO! He was all relaxed and ready to fly, and I was all tense and ready to sink. My muscles are crying out for mercy and air, but I dig down and demand more. Let's GOOO! He can't beat me. He can't embarrass me like this in front of Abby. I smash into the wall like I'm trying to break it down. I pull in a full breath of air and rip my goggles off, but I'm all alone on the wall. That's weird. Everyone is looking at me and shouting. DANG IT, you stopped too soon! I must've counted the laps wrong. It's just four laps, but I really suck at math. I pull my goggles back on and turn to see the coolest thing ever. Seven guys slamming into the wall and gasping for air . . . behind me. Andre included! I beat him. I smoked him! The crowd isn't yelling at me . . . they're cheering for me. YES! I pump my fist like Tiger Woods.

Andre (Mr. Fourth Place) lazily sticks out his hand, and I instinctively slap it five. I kind of lose my balance when his big arm shakes me off my feet. I fall toward him, and he gives me a man-shake-hug. Get off me! We don't high-five, and we sure as hell don't hug. He doesn't get to be a gracious loser. He needs to concentrate on just being a loser.

He slowly climbs out of the pool and holds his head low. I've beaten him soundly in front of his ex-girlfriend and his soon to be ex–Hooker slut. She'll totally dump him for being such a loser. I almost feel sorry for him until he YAWNS again! No way; he's pretending to yawn just to cheapen my victory.

I shaved 1.04 seconds off my time; I'm now exactly as fast as Andre. I haven't beaten his time, but I have smoked the man. If I'd beaten his time, I'd get to go to State for sure, and I'd be shaving my head soon and wearing my letterman's jacket.

I was really psyched up for this race. I should have been

shaving my legs this whole time. I had no idea how much that fuzz was holding me back. My mom gives me a kiss and my dad high-fives me. They know how hard I worked for this, and they're really proud of me. All the drill team chicks are clapping and cheering for me. Out of the corner of my eye, I even see Abby smiling, but she quickly looks away when she catches me watching her.

Two days later

The following Monday, the gossip in the hall is that Andre's mom had to take him to the hospital after the race. I'm guessing that he had a bad case of *In Your Face!* and needed to have a doctor look at it.

Bag walks up to the boys and me in the hall and asks, "Yo, did you hear about Andre having mono?"

"What the hell is mono?" I ask back.

"They call it the kissing disease because you get it from saliva, and I guess you can die from it."

I jump around the hall yelling like I just won a million dollars. I know I shouldn't be this stoked—a guy is dying in the hospital—but I'm going to State! I'm so happy, it doesn't even get me down that he's surely going to use this "mono" excuse to explain his defeat or the fact that he got the disease from kissing too many chicks, which is a pimp-ass problem I wish I had.

The seniors on the relay team are all waiting for me after my seventh-hour health class. They pick me up and carry me down to the locker room, where Coach Barker is waiting out front to congratulate me with hair clippers, shaving cream, and a razor in her hand. Awesome! I want to tell them my new rule about razor blades, but there's no time. In swimming, everything goes fast, and head shaving is no exception. I only thought it hurt to shave your face or legs . . . but the head tops them all! When your head gets cut, it doesn't stop bleeding. The arms or the knees know what's up when they get slashed open, but the melon doesn't expect it. It just bleeds and bleeds. I should go to the hospital, but instead I jump into the pool and swim my butt off for a few hours. And let me tell you, nothing gets the heart racing like swimming. And nothing helps pump blood out of a fresh wound like a racing heart. I may die, but I beat Andre and I'm going to State, so whatever.

We finish practice and I can't wait to see myself in the mirror. I bet I look so tough. But I don't. Have my ears always been this big? Did they get a growth spurt that I didn't notice? In a stiff wind I could take flight with these babies. If I learn to use them properly, I could be very useful as a spy someday. And with these cuts on my head and being so skinny lately, I resemble a special guest on a Jerry Lewis telethon. People would jam the phone lines trying to help poor Carter in his brave battle with whatever horrible disease makes your ears swell, causes you to go bald, and gives you lesions on your head.

And good God, it's cold! I never knew it, but the hair on your head is good for more than just combing, washing, and putting gel into. It really keeps you warm. No wonder Andre got sick. Well, kissing too many chicks was his downfall, but the case of pneumonia I've got coming is going to be a direct result of not having any insulation on my bean.

37. Tickle Me Chemo

The Friday night before the state championships, I'm relaxing at the movies with Nutt and EJ. I'm wearing a new Burton skullcap that my mom picked up for me. All the Dumbo and Tickle Me Chemo jokes are behind me as we figure out the best way to sneak into Keanu Reeves's new movie. I like to watch his movies just to try and figure out how it's possible that that dumbass is a movie star. I mean, if he can do it, anybody can.

We catch Doc, Hormone, and Bag coming out of the new Kate Hudson romantic comedy. Busted!

"S'up, ladies? Did you have a good cry?" I say as we all duck into the arcade.

"Shut up, dude," Doc says. "We thought it was a different movie."

"Sure ya did," EJ fires back.

I've got to get us off this Kate Hudson subject or it'll slip out that EJ and I already saw it. "We're gonna go see Keanu stumble through some dialogue. You wanna join?" I ask.

"Naw, we're rollin' to a party at the Chopper's house," Hormone says.

"The Chopper, huh?" I ask. She's a junior on the drill team. Her real name is Christy Schauper. She works the snack bar at the pool, and she gave me free soda a few times, so she's cool. She has a bit of a Village Bike reputation, and she usually wears her hair in two pigtails. After the Skeleton hooked up with her, he called her pigtails handlebars and coined the name Chopper.

"Can we come?" EJ asks.

"No, we cannot," I say to EJ. "I have the biggest swim meet of my life tomorrow, and I hate parties. They all turn out the same and . . ."

"Abby's gonna be there. It's like a drill team party. You may not be welcome," Doc says.

"Drill team is like a gang. You can't just dog one and then show up at their party," Bag adds.

"Oh," I say.

That info right there is enough to get me out of going to this party, and I can go watch Keanu do his thing. But Abby did smile at me the other day. Or she, like, smiled because of me. Or we were in the same room and she smiled. My point is, I'm getting somewhere, and the drill team chicks don't hate me so much anymore. I could stop by.

"Those fatties don't determine where I go, fool," I say, all snide.

38. Ride the Chopper

We roll into the Chopper's house without knocking, because we're that cool. Plus the fact that she might not let us in because of my reputation as an enemy of the drill team. I give a couple of nods and a few "S'up?"s, but I don't know very many of the faces. Drill team parties are not nearly as wild as other parties. I don't have my Mountain Dew–filled beer bottle tonight, but I just keep telling people, "I'm swimming in the state championship tomorrow, and I can't pollute my body."

I don't see Abby, so I do a lap around the party. I look in the kitchen and downstairs, but no Abby. I shoot upstairs, but there're just people having sex up there. The doors are shut and noises are coming from all the rooms. I check the bathroom at the end of the hall, but nothing. So I head back to the stairs, when Christy Schauper comes down the hall. She's drunk. Really drunk.

"Heeyy, what are you doin' up 'ere?" the Chopper slurs.

I just look at her for a sec. I'm not positive she's talking to me, because she's kind of looking over my shoulder.

"You're on the swimmy team, right?" she asks.

Yep, she's talking to me. "Uh-huh," I say.

"You're the cute one in the little Speedooo," she garbles.

Wait a minute, is she talking to me?

"Yeah, we cheered for you, and you won. And, and you're the freshman that screwed over my girl Abby!" she continues.

"Yeah, that's all me. My name is Carter," I say.

She walks up, and I can smell her before she gets very close. Alcohol and cigarettes, a.k.a. "slut perfume."

"Oh, I know your name, Carver," she kind of yells.

Eww! When she said "Carver" it produced a cloud of stank that drifts into my face. Yuck.

"So, h-h-have you seen, um, Abby?" I ask, turning away from her stink hole. "Is sh-sh-she here?"

This chick is giving me a cross-eyed look that's freaking out my stutter.

"She was here until you walked in, but then she split," she says.

"She broke out because of me?" I ask.

The Chopper doesn't answer. Instead she grabs my face and smashes her drunk, stinky mouth against mine. Okay, so Chopper and I are making out. Did you see the formula? I'm not into her, and I asked her a question. Foolproof!

The taste is not pleasant. But my horny mind can block out anything. And it would be rude to pull out of a kiss just because she's smelly and I'm not into her. I wouldn't call her ugly, but I bet people say she looks like her dad. If any of my boys come up the stairs, I'll be totally busted in a full-on lip-lock with the Chopper. I could never come up with a reasonable excuse for this. I'm trying to concentrate on the kissing while not breathing out of my nose at the same time.

"You're a good kisser, for a freshman," she babbles.

"Uh, thanks. You've kissed a lot of dudes, I bet," I reply.

"Oh, I want you soo bad," she says like a porn star. At

least I think that's what a porn star would sound like. Does this mean I'm going to get to do it? Right here, right now, with the Chopper? She pulls away and gives me a kind of cross-eyed sexy look. It doesn't take much to rev a fourteen-year-old engine. Yeah, let's do it, baby! She opens a bedroom door, but I guess people are already using the room, because a guy's voice shouts, "Get outta here!"

This is her house, but she shuts the door. She kisses me really hard again and tries another door. But this one is locked. And so is the last one. Dang it. Well, I guess that's the end of that.

"Let's go out to the shed," she says as she grabs my hand and leads me downstairs.

I'm hoping "the shed" is her pet name for some secret, sexy, love room in the house.

EJ's eyes get really big when he sees us come downstairs holding hands. He's as confused about what he's seeing as I am. We've only been here for five minutes and I've somehow lassoed the Chopper. Or been lassoed; I have no idea.

He shoots me a look like, "You are making a BIG mistake, old friend." But that's an easy look for him to shoot. He had sex with the Caboose four times. I'm still shackled to my virginity like a ball and chain. The Chopper and I are going out to the shed to chop it off. Oh man, this is not how I thought this would go. And EJ has witnessed the whole thing. I'm screwed!

She takes a swig from a liquor bottle as we walk out into the freezing-cold backyard. She lights up a cigarette, I guess to be sexy, but it's just more stink on the pile to me. She kisses me again, and I really wish she'd stop doing that. It tastes like she's been drinking gasoline. The cigarette isn't just gross, it could be dangerous. We walk around her house, and I get my first glimpse of our love nest. "The shed" is just that: a metal hut where her dad keeps the lawn mower and junk. I can see my breath, it's so cold. Hers is so foul I bet you could see it in August. The shed is lit by a single strand of Christmas lights. Which I guess is romantic. My heart is racing as she flicks the cigarette into the yard and shuts the metal door with a clang.

Oh boy. I'm trying to appear relaxed while she spreads out a blue plastic tarp. But my trembling body is telling a different story. I'm shaking because I'm nervous, but I'm also freezing. I've got my skullcap on, but without any body hair or a coat, it's friggin' brisk. The Chopper must not feel pain, because she's starting to disrobe. The Christmas lights barely illuminate her struggle to get her T-shirt off. Her boobs are big, but her bra could be cuter. It's kind of a flesh-colored number that my mom would wear (Sears catalog, page 47). *Get your mom out of your head, freak!*

I guess the T-shirt is caught on one of her dangly earrings, because she's stuck. Maybe I should help. She's just kind of stumbling around the shed with her bra exposed and her hands above her head. Okay, that's pretty funny. She looks around to see who's laughing at her. She reminds me of my dog when you put a sheet over his head and he struggles to get out. That really gets me laughing, and she can hear it, dang it.

"Are you laughing at me, freshman?" she slurs from under the shirt.

"No, I just thought of something else that was funny," I cover.

"I ought to beat your ass!" she yells.

What? "Is that like, dirty pillow talk, or do you really want to fight?" I ask.

"Oh, you think you're funny, Carver?" she slurs.

"My name is Carter." I laugh. "Not Carver." (Although that would be a good nickname with all these cuts on my head.)

When I'm nervous, I laugh. I can't help it. I'm supposed to be having sex here, but I'm trembling and giggling my head off in a shed with a girl called the Chopper whose head is stuck in a T-shirt.

"Ha-haaaaa!" I cackle uncontrollably. Oh man, this isn't going right.

The Chopper is a mean drunk, because I think she just took a swing at me. She's pissed, but she can't see very well and is coming at me now!

"Hey, hey, simmer down, Chopper," I say in an effort to calm her.

"DID YOU JUST CALL ME . . . CHOPPER???!!!" she barks.

Well, that backfired. Some nicknames are given to your face, and some are only used behind your back. I'm guessing "Chopper" is reserved for behind-the-back use only, because she charges me and yells, "You mother . . ." She's coming fast, but I step out of the way just in time to dodge the Chopper charge and—*BAANNGGG!*—she smacks into the metal door, face-first. Her T-shirt didn't seem to soften the blow at all. I'm guessing she's knocked out, because she bounces off the door and does a lazy spin into the weed whacker and takes out a rake on her way down. That had to hurt.

The Chopper's KO'd in the first round. The door did

the most damage, but that weed whacker didn't do her any favors. She's just lying there and starting to bleed.

I'm not exactly sure what the protocol is here. I'm definitely not having sex. I really want to just break the hell out of here, round up my boys, and split. I doubt she'll bleed to death, but she'll definitely freeze if I leave her out here. I'm not in love with ol' Chopper, but I don't want her to die.

"Christy?" I say, shaking her. "You okay?"

No response. I can tell she's breathing because her stink stack is still pumping fumes into the air. Yep, this is me, "gettin' lucky"! I've got to get her into the house. This is going to be awkward. What's really embarrassing is that I can't lift her. First I try to carry her all romantic, like the cover of a trashy book at the supermarket, but my arms can't do it. There's this exercise that we're always supposed to do for football called squats, where you put a bunch of weight on your shoulders, then literally squat down and try to stand back up. I hate doing it. I'm always skipping it, but I wish I'd done it a few more times, because then maybe I'd have a snowball's chance in hell of lifting this chick. Man, she's heavy. After a few minutes I get her over my shoulder. I push up with all my might. My legs tremble, but I start to feel some movement. I'm getting her; I'm squatting the Chopper!

"Uuhhh!" I grunt as I lock my legs out. Yes! Now I've got to try to get her into the house. One step, two steps . . . DANG IT! I should have opened the door first. I fumble with the latch for a second, but the Chopper is slipping. I need to raise this latch. Then I see the big dent in the metal door where her head rammed into it.

I start laughing and lose my balance. The Chopper and

I fall to the ground. I instinctively do a spin move so she doesn't crush me, and I land on her instead. (Who says chivalry is dead?) Poor Chopper was looking for love when she came up those stairs tonight, but she found me instead.

I manage to get her back up on my shoulders again, but I smash my head into the rake in the process, knocking my new skullcap off and slashing one of the cuts on my head open. Now I'm bleeding too, dang it! I'll have to come back for the hat, because I'll never be able to do another set of Chopper squats.

I stumble across the yard. What seemed like a few steps when we came out here now feels like a mile with a drill-teamer on my back. I thought I'd be out of breath about now, but I never dreamed it would come from this activity. I can feel the hot trickle of sweat pouring down my face. But when I catch my reflection in the sliding-glass door, I can see it's a stream of warm blood running from the top of my bald head, down my forehead and nose, then dripping off my lips. I look like Frankenstein's evil helper, Igor, carrying a virgin back to his cave. Well, Chopper's no virgin, and I never thought I was evil until I tap on the glass with my foot and yell, "Open up!"

Bitchy Nicky opens the door and lets out a blood-curdling scream: "EEEEEEE!"

I stagger past her and into the house. Now, I'm positive I didn't see a record player spinning earlier, but I swear I just heard one scratch to silence when I cross the threshold. Choppy and I must really look a sight, because no one's talking. I try to set her down gently. But I'm so worn out, I just drop her to the kitchen tile with a thud. Everyone gasps.

"Oh come on, she isn't exactly light!" I protest.

And sure enough, the damn earring releases its death grip on the T-shirt, and her blood-soaked face pops out for all to see. Everybody screams.

"Oh my God! What did you do to her?" Nicky yells.

"Uhhh, she . . . fell? Into the door. Out in the shed," I say innocently. I'm sure I don't look super innocent with all the blood rolling down my face.

"She fell? She fell?! That's what they all say, isn't it?" Nicky scowls.

"Who? Who's 'they,' Nicky? She rammed into the metal door with her shirt over her head, that's it!" I exclaim.

"Why would she do that?" Nicky pesters. "And why did you shave your head; you look terrible!"

"I'm swimming in the state cha—"

Bag jumps into the conversation with, "What were you doin' in the shed with Chopper, Carter?"

"Not now!" I bark.

There will be an open season of endless burns coming my way as a result of this stunt. But now is not the place, and it isn't even close to the time.

"Oh, Carter!" Nicky seethes. "I just thought you were a jerk, but you're evil, you know that? You're a dangerous menace. And I'm going to see to it that you go to jail!"

Now, I have no doubt that Nicky is going to be an awesome lawyer or judge someday, but she's only fifteen years old—she has no real authority at a drill team party. She can't send me to jail. I don't think. I mean, what would be the charge? Most terrible lover, ever? If that's a crime, then I'm going down, but I don't think it is. A couple of drill team chicks pull the Chopper's shirt back down and are cleaning up her face. I grab a few paper towels for my bleeding head and apply pressure. I'm on my own at this point.

The Chopper finally stirs, and she's calmer than the last time she was awake, but she's still mad.

"What the hell? How the . . . ? What did you do to me, Carver?" she yells.

Nicky jumps in to cross-examine. "Yes, what did he do to you?"

"What's it to you, bitch?" the Chopper asks.

"Thank you! You ran into the door and I carried you inside. That's it!" I tell her.

"Why is your head bleeding?"

"I cut it yesterday and it just got reopened. I'm swimming in the state cham—"

"You carried me into the house?" the Chopper asks, kind of touched.

"Yeah," I say. "No big deal; you're not heavy."

She smiles. (Now, that's a gentleman.)

The mood of the room seems to have lifted, so I say, "Hormone, can you take me home? I gotta go to bed."

Spring

39. The Boys of Spring

Spring is in the air. I know this not because flowers are blooming or birds are singing again, but because it's time for spring tryouts. The sports we get to choose from are: baseball, track and field, tennis, and golf (all of my boys play ball, and Nick Brock too). I played T-ball when I was little, but I never played baseball. The Little League season is in the summer, and my swimming schedule never allowed time. Plus, my dad thinks baseball is the most boring game ever. He's right, but I really want a Merrian High baseball hat, because they're awesome. They're fitted and black with a red *M* written in cursive on the forehead. You can't buy them; you have to be on the team to get one.

It's not so much that I want to "play baseball," as much as I want to "be a baseball player." Chicks dig them. My sister has never seen a baseball game in her life, but if there's a baseball player giving an interview on TV, she stops dead in her tracks and watches, like she's the editor of *Sports Illustrated*. The guys who play baseball and wear the fitted hats never shower. They chew tobacco. They're always dirty, and they totally get chicks.

My itty-bitty glove from T-ball isn't going to cut it, so I borrow EJ's dad's mitt for the tryouts. I should've bought cleats, pants, and some black paint to put under my eyes, but I didn't have time. The state swimming championships were on Saturday, and the first day of baseball tryouts are on Monday. I could have picked the baseball junk up on Sunday, but I had to watch TV all day. Seriously. I may or may not have been a little depressed and needed to take my mind off something. The state championships may have gone awesome. It's possible that I swam so fast my relay team won the state title, and all the senior guys carried me out of the pool on their shoulders, yelling, "CARTER, CARTER, CARTER." Or I may have jumped off the block a moment too soon and disqualified the whole relay team. And ended the seniors' high school swimming careers with a disappointing failure, removing any proof that they'd made it to State and destroying any chance that I had of getting a varsity letterman's jacket as a freshman. Any of these things may have happened. I don't really recall. I've blocked that day out of my memory completely.

I show up to the first day of baseball tryouts without a letterman's jacket (you do the math). My baseball costume is pretty sweet for somebody who's never played. I've got on Bag's LA Dodgers shirt, Nutt's KC Royals jacket, Levi's NY Mets hat, and my football cleats. I definitely look like a ball player. I've never actually watched an entire baseball game before (my ADD won't allow it), so I don't know all the rules. I'm terrified that a ball will hit me in the face, but I have no doubt that baseball is going to be my thing. I love all the gear, but you don't get your official uniform until you make the team. They cut the losers on Wednesday after practice.

My boys are trying to help me out with the technical stuff. EJ runs up to me and yells, "RELAX, dude!" Brock tells me to "Keep your eye on the ball" when I whiff for the thousandth time. Nutt keeps reminding me to "Look where you're throwing!" when I whiz the ball over his head. I'm more focused on looking cool and am hopeful that the skills will follow.

When I throw the ball I just want to sling it as hard as I can. I've got to show the coaches that I'm worthy of a hat. That I've got "wheels for feet" and a cannon attached to my shoulder. That I'm "raw talent" or "moldable clay" that they can shape into the greatest baseball player they've ever coached. I grit my teeth when I make a throw, I sling my whole body around and fire the ball. I really don't aim, so the ball never arrives quite where I mean it to. And my feet always leave the ground, which they tell me is bad. Sometimes I fall on my face from the effort. It's cool to hit the ground when you catch the ball, like a Derek Jeter diving catch, but with me, it's more like there's just too much going on with the running and the opening of the glove, and I just fall down. I hope the coaches haven't noticed. They have to have noticed the raw talent, though. Every time I throw the ball, a kid yells, "CARTER!" as it sails past him. I haven't actually hit the ball yet, but Brock keeps telling me I'm taking some good cuts.

By Wednesday, I'm really starting to get the hang of it. I hit a couple of foul balls. They don't count as hits, but I think they show major progress. My arm cannon is getting some control, and I borrowed a sweet Yankees shirt from J-Low. I can't see why they would cut me from the team. I probably shower too much, but I could work on that.

We meet in the baseball room (a.k.a. the football room) after practice. All the older guys and freshmen pile into the room. It's tight, but we're a team. We're a unit. The coach has a clipboard in his right hand and a tape measure in his left. They're going to measure our heads right now. I could have my hat by tonight!

The door closes and the coach rattles off the same spiel he probably gives every year. "Fellas," he says, taking off his hat, "this is the worst part of my job. But we only have so many slots, so we gotta cut a few of you. It's not that you're not . . ."

I figure I've got a few minutes, so I look out the windows and think back to when this room was the football room. When the air was crisp, you could smell burning leaves, and a lynch mob was waiting for me out there. (Good times.) I can still hear Abby sobbing, and the drill team girls with their torches and sticks. Beating their bare chests and demanding my release so they could drag me back to their village and have their way with . . .

"Cory Day, Gene Arioli, Nick Brock, Paul Skelton, Ben Kriesman . . ." the coach continues as he looks down at his clipboard.

Dang it! I have no idea what's going on. Is he reading out names of guys who made the team or are they the names of guys cut from the team? Is Nick Brock getting cut from the team? I'll quit if they cut him.

Coach continues, "Emilio Johnson" (EJ), "Josh Loos" (J-Low), "Bill Kasson" (Doc), "Andre Durlan" (thorn in my side), "Todd O'Connell" (Nutt) . . .

Okay, he's calling out a lot of names. I doubt this is the list of guys getting cut, because all those guys are really good. I'm not hearing my name, though. Say it. Say "Carter!" Raw talent, remember? I'm your Play-Doh. I could be great if you'd just say "Carter." This is my crew. Just because I suck at hitting and throwing a ball, you can't cut me from my friends.

"Kurt Harmon" (Hormone), "aaand Matt Sparks" (Bag), "and that does it," the coach says as he looks up from the clipboard.

Dang it! Did I just get cut? Or did he call out my name when I was spacing off? Usually I snap out of an attention-deficit dream if I hear my name, so if he said my name, I probably would've noticed.

"If you weren't called, I'm sorry. It was a tough decision, but we only have so many slots. If you were, stay put; we're gonna take the hat measurements. But if you weren't called . . . go ahead and get your gear," Coach says.

What does that mean, "get your gear"? I think, loosely translated, it means, "Get out, losers," because that's what I heard. Guys are leaving the room with their heads low. A couple of guys are crying. Being rejected sucks. I'd probably be crying too, if I were positive my name hadn't been called. But he might have. I don't want to leave this room. The walk of shame is just too much. I could smack off of a thousand diving boards, but I can't walk out of this room in front of all my boys and Nick Brock, too.

The coach gives me a nod. "You okay, kid?"

"Yeah," I say. "Um, my name is Carter? Did you call my name? 'Cause I was spacing off there for a sec, and I didn't hear it."

"No, I didn't call your name," the coach says flatly.

"Ooohhhh," I say, like air being released from a balloon. "So . . . I should go?"

"Yeah, sorry," he mumbles.

Everyone is staring at me as I make my way out the door. I want to turn around and scream, "Take your dumb hats and balls and bats and shove 'em up your fitted, dirty asses!" But I'm so busy trying not to cry that I'll have to save the speech.

Tom Hanks claimed in some movie that there was no crying in baseball. But there sure is today. A bunch of guys are out in the hall sobbing. I won't be one of them. I won't waste my tears . . . at least not in front of these dudes. I'm going behind the drama wing to ball my eyes out.

It just hurts so much to be told you're not good enough, or that you can't do something that you really want to do. That you're not allowed to be a part of something. I don't want to care about this stuff, but I do. What am I supposed to do now? My friends are going to be talking about baseball all the time, and I'll feel stupid, and they'll feel that I feel stupid and not want to talk about baseball in front of me, and then they'll avoid me so they can talk about it without worrying about my issues. And there I'll be, alone, without a hat, without a girl, and without hope. I was really counting on using the baseball-player vibe to get a girl to like me. But now I'm back to square one.

I'm a loser, and the baseball coach must have sensed it. He decided that even though I had raw talent, I was more trouble than I was worth. I try to clean myself up quick because I see my drama teacher leaving the building. Of course Ms. McDougle sees me and walks over, because I haven't been humiliated enough for one day.

She smiles and asks, "Hey, Carter, did you get cut from the baseball team?"

"God, was it on ESPN or something?" I cry. "Does

the whole school know what a loser I am?"

She just looks at me. "Uh, no I just saw the baseball glove, and you looked sad. I didn't even know it was baseball season."

"Oh. Yeah, I got cut," I say.

"Well, I'm sorry to hear that. I'm sure that doesn't feel very good. Have you thought about auditioning for the spring play?" she asks.

"Oh, I can't do a play," I say, and wipe my face.

"Of course you can. You might be great," she replies.

"No, I don't mean I couldn't do it." I laugh. "I mean, I can't. My friends would never let me live it down."

"That's ridiculous; you should just come and audition. You'll have a blast," she says.

"Oh yeah, Ms. McDougle, that's just what my self-esteem needs . . . to get cut from something else. Thanks, but I'll pass," I say.

She crosses her arms and says very seriously, "You know you're one of my best students."

"No I'm not," I reply flatly. "I'm getting a D in your class."

"That's because you never do the homework and you bomb the tests. But with the moment-to-moment *truthful* acting work, you're really one of my best," she says.

"Really?" I ask. "Like, raw talent?"

"Um, sure," she replies. She may just be trying to make me feel better, but it's working. I'm one of the best actors in the school, huh?

"My friends would really make fun of me if I did a play."

"You are one of the most popular boys in the school, Carter. Who would make fun of you?" she asks.

"Naw, you only think that because all the kids you hang out with are drama geeks," I say. "I'm not really that cool. Comparatively, maybe, but realistically, not really."

"Well, I won't beg, but I bet you'd have fun. The show is *Guys and Dolls*, and we need guys. You might get to wear a fedora and a zoot suit. You don't want to play a gangster?" she asks.

Wait a minute, a costume? This might be okay. I could totally be a gangsta! If I had any hair, I'd slick it back.

"Your 'cool' friends don't even need to know that you're trying out for the play," she continues. "Or you could work on the lighting crew or help build sets."

No chance of that. Not after a costume has been brought into the equation. I'm doing it. I'm totally auditioning for *Guys and Dolls*!

40. Porn! the Musical

Bad news must travel fast, because the troops are armed with Kleenex and sympathy when I walk into the house. I guess I'm supposed to be freaking out about getting cut from the baseball team, but I'm not feeling so bad anymore. I hate being rejected, but I'm pretty stoked about this whole theater thing. My mom looks like she's ready to cry for me, and my sister just looks mad. Big shock.

"I can't believe those jerks cut my brother from the baseball team!" Lynn barks. "I'm gonna give that coach a piece of my mind. Nick said you were doing really great, too."

"Please don't talk to anyone. Nick was lying. I'm no good at baseball," I say.

My mom jumps in with her usual "Yes you are, honey. You're great at whatever you try to do."

"No." I laugh. "It's cool, though. I think I'm gonna try out for the spring play instead."

Lynn's jaw drops. Exciting development. She looks more concerned about this than the baseball cutting. She squints her eyes really small and says, "Oh no you're not! Only dorks do theater, and you're not a dork. You're my brother!"

Mom pulls her off me with "That's not true, Lynn! If he wants to do a play, I think that's great."

"No, no, no, it's not 'great.' It's not good. It's not even okay. It's not remotely socially acceptable," Lynn howls. "He'll be shunned! He's popular, thanks to my constant effort and guidance, but I can only do so much. Him being on the swim team was very difficult, but I can't do anything for him if he's singing and dancing in front of God and everybody."

"Shut up, Lynn; nobody is singing or dancing," I protest.

"The spring play is a MUSICAL, you doofus! Singing and dancing is all you'll be doing. Mother, people will find out and he'll be ruined. I've seen it happen before. This guy Jeremy in my class was very cool in junior high, then he went down into that drama wing our freshman year, and he, well, he just never came back," Lynn yells.

"It is not a musical! It's this play about gangsters and looking tough. It's called *Guys and Dolls*, for God's sake!" I exclaim.

My mom kind of winces at my stupidity. "Yeah, honey, that's a musical, with lots of singing and dancing. Not that there's anything wrong with that. *Guys and Dolls* was also a very popular movie . . . your grandmother's favorite. Marlon Brando was so beautiful before he ate himself, and I think Frank Sinatra was in it too."

"Nuh-uh, Mom, it's about gangsters. Frank Sinatra? Wasn't he a hit man for the mob in real life? And Marlon Brando was *The Godfather*. You see? The show is about tough guys," I protest.

"Yeah, tough guys who sashay and prance around singing every couple of minutes," Lynn says.

My mom's laughter makes me think that Lynn is right. Dang it! Ms. McDougle set me up. I jump on my bike and fly down to Blockbuster. I didn't even know they had a musical section. The cover of the DVD doesn't look very promising. It's definitely Ol' Blue Eyes and the Godfather. They're all young and cool and dressed in gangster suits, but they look way too happy and their mouths are open really wide. Dang it, they're singing for sure. I grab a copy of Keanu's last movie as I approach the counter to try and disguise the musical, because the girl at the counter is hot. I've got shame in my eyes as I place the movies on the counter. It's like I'm trying to rent porn.

She smiles. "*Guys and Dolls*, huh? Are you trying out for the musical at Merrian High?"

This must be some big deal if random hotties know about it.

"Uhhh, no. I just wanted to see this movie. 'Cause I like singing and dancing. I don't do it myself or anything. I'm more of a supporter of singing and dancing than an actual participant," I clarify.

She raises her eyebrows like I may have given her too much info and says, "Okay, that'll be five eighty-nine."

Dang it, I only have five bucks! I grab the *Guys and Dolls* movie like I'm going to put it back, but I don't want to rent Keanu's stupid movie. I really want to see this singing-gangster flick. It's too built up now. I've got to see it.

"Um, I'm just gonna p-p-put Keanu's movie back," I say.

"Okay," she replies with a smile. "You do go to Merrian, right? You used to date Abby?"

I have been identified. "Yep, my name's Carter," I reply in disgrace.

"Yeah, I thought I knew you. I was at Christy Schauper's

party, and I have choir with Abby," she says judgmentally.

"Well, you know, I might try out for the musical," I say real quick. I don't need to hear how Abby cried for a week in choir class. And how she thought I'd murdered the Chopper.

She nods and says, "You should. We need guys."

This chick is a drama geek? I've never even seen her before. If this chick is what's going on down there, I may start spending more time in that drama wing, no matter what. If none of my boys has spotted this chick before, who the hell is going to notice me down there? I'll just tell people I've got detention. Three months of detention will only help my bad-boy reputation.

She smiles and says, "Break a leg" as I walk out.

That was uncalled for. "Bitch," I say under my breath as the door closes.

I race home and pop it in the basement DVD player. There is some singing and dancing right at the start, but it's not too bad. The clothes are super cool and I like the way they talk. There are a lot of old-timey jokes, and what they're singing about is getting chicks and how guys only do stuff to impress them. I'd like to play this fat guy for sure, but I'm not even close to fat anymore after swimming my ass off for the last few months. And there's this cool little guy who pals around with the fat guy, but I'm way too tall now. I may just get to be one of these guys with no lines, who just walks by with a newspaper or something. But I'll still get a costume, I bet. The story is getting going, and Brando (Sky Masterson) is trying to trick this Goody Two-shoes chick to come to dinner with him in Havana, Cuba. Because that's how gangsters roll. He's charming her and asking her a bunch of questions like a player, but she's a tough cookie. He's not just going to bag this chick by asking questions, and he knows it, so he just busts out a song right in front of her! How dope is that? See some chick at the mall and just start singing to her. Brando more raps than sings anyway. If Marlon Brando can do it . . .

I hear some commotion upstairs. There are footsteps and loud talking, then the basement door flies open and my mom yells down, "Sweetie, your friends are here."

Oh noooo! I grab the remote as fast as I can, but the fear of my boys catching me watching a musical makes it shoot out of my hands and sends it crashing to the floor. Batteries fly everywhere. Feet are stomping down the stairs. I've got to shut this thing off! Brando is really going for it when he talk/sings, "Yes, I'll know when my love comes along!"

Shut up, Marlon, my boys are *coming along*, and I'm dead meat if they see you. I slam my hand into the machine to get it to shut off, but he's still crooning away. I'll kick the screen out of this TV if I have to, but these guys will not catch me watching a musical!

EJ, Bag, Hormone, Nutt, and Doc walk in. I slam the machine down as hard as I can, and the player finally shuts off.

"Carter, what are you doing?" EJ says.

"Nothing! I'm not doing anything," I say, way too loud. My face is glowing red, and I think I broke the machine.

"What were you watching, dude?" Bag asks.

"Nothin'!" I say, guilty as hell.

"He was watchin' porn." EJ laughs. "You were watching a porno!"

"YEP, guilty as charged. I was watchin' a porno! Ha-HAAAA." I laugh. It's way better to get caught watching porn when you're fourteen than to be caught red-handed with a fifty-year-old singing, dancing, gangster movie. At least with these dudes.

"S'up?" I ask as I look at them for the first time. They're all wearing matching hats. Black fitted ones with an *M* on the forehead. They look so proud. Jerks. They didn't even think about it. How is Bag's hat already dirty?

"We're going to a party at Ryan Kim's house. Hormone only has five in the CRX. You wanna come?" Doc asks.

I just look at the hats for a second. I can't be mad at my boys for making the baseball team. I'd never take that hat off if I had gotten one. It doesn't make it hurt any less, or make me feel any less left out, though.

"No thanks, I'm just gonna chill out here. . . ." I say, as Frank Sinatra pops back onto the TV, does a little jumping spin move, and starts belting out a song.

Nobody interrupts Frank. They all just watch in silence as he sings.

I unplug the set, and Frank shuts up. I turn to my old friends with a guilty look. Their jaws are open wide. The nastiest, freakiest, donkey porno would not have warranted this level of shock.

"What the hell was that all about?" I ask, like I'm as shocked as they are. "My mom, she loves this crap," I say.

EJ smirks and says, "Yeah, your mom is pretty gay."

They walk out and pile into the little car without saying much else. My sister is totally right, as usual. I haven't even tried out for this musical, and it's already ruining my life. I watch them drive away, five matching hats in a car with two seats.

41. 5, 6, 7, 8!

The drama wing is electrified. I'm still not sure I can go through with this. You can feel how nervous the drama geeks are. These kids are all trying so hard to be weird. I'm genuinely weird, so I can spot the effort a mile away. I'm always trying to be cool, but down here, weird is cool. So they, like, compete for who can say the craziest stuff or dress the most jacked up. Competition is stiff this afternoon. I'm sure I could be the man down here if I just started talking a whole bunch of nonsense or singing for no reason at all. But I think defense is my best offense in *the wing*. I sign up to audition for Nicely-Nicely Johnson, Benny Southstreet, and Liverlips Louie. I think those are the coolest names, and if I try for all three, I might just get a part.

They have three rooms set up for the auditions. One room is for dancing, and everybody has to go into it, and then, depending on what parts you sign up for, you go into different rooms to read for them. The little parts are in a classroom and the big parts are in the theater. It's mostly older drama geeks that are trying out for the big parts. I think a drama nerd actually growled at me when I looked at the sign-in sheet for the Brando part. Kids are screaming in the halls, yelling, and just being really obnoxious. I think one guy has makeup on. Some kids look like they're trying not to look nervous, but mostly, everybody looks freaked out. I'm numb.

I just came out of the classroom where I read for Benny Southstreet. I think it went pretty well. I don't stutter when I say somebody else's lines. They had me sing half of the Happy Birthday song and told me to go on to the dancing room.

What am I doing here? Why are all these kids being so loud? It's like they're looking for deaf kids to be in this play. I guess you have to be loud when you're onstage, so they're practicing? But I've been around some deaf people who speak, and they have no idea how loud they are, so they just go for it when they try to talk. That's more what it seems like. Either that or they're trying to intimidate me. I know I'm an outsider, and I'm getting looks that seem to confirm my status. They're trying to ice me. And it's working, because I'm terrified.

I go into the dance room with about ten other dudes. They call out my name and stick the number twenty-one on my chest. I see a piano and an old lady wearing a leotard. I've got to quit staring at her boobs, because now a guy is playing the piano all of a sudden, and she's jumping around and counting to eight over and over again.

"Five, six, seven, eight and one, two, three, four," she yells, and kind of step, hop, kicks, and wiggles around the room. "*Chassé, arabesque, pas de bourrée, chassé, grand battement, pas de bourrée*, ball change, and that's it!" she says.

That's what? It's not English. Where the hell is Ms. McDougle? They didn't talk or dance like that in the movie. Gangsters don't wiggle! She does the moves a few more times, and the other guys seem to be getting it. I pretend like I'm getting it too, but I'm totally clueless.

"Okay, let's break off into groups," she yells.

Three guys to a group, and we're supposed to remember the *pas de bourrée* stuff on our own. And then what steps go where with the counting. Brando didn't *arabesque*! He just looked cool and kind of strutted around.

My group is called first (of course). The piano starts and the other dudes are *chassé*-ing and *pas de bourrée*-ing around pretty well. I'm just sort of jumping in place.

The music stops and the leotard lady yells, "Number twenty-one, you're missing the *grand battement*!"

Oh? Am I missing the *grand battement*? Terribly sorry. I thought I was missing something. Uh, by the way, what the hell is a *grand battement*? Is that the wiggle, the kick, or the march?

The piano man starts going again, and we're off. Leotard lady yells, "Five, six, seven, eight!"

I jump a few times and then start running around the room.

"No, no, NO! Twenty-one, you're coming in on the half step. You're missing the one count. Go again!" she barks. (I'm missing a hell of a lot more than the one count.) "Five, six, seven, eight," she yells.

I march in place for a second then step, kick, wiggle.

"Nooo, Twenty-one! You're not feeling the music," she says, shaking her head in disgust.

I just glare at her. Who has time to "feel"? I'm too busy over here counting and wiggling to feel a thing. "What?" I ask, a little pissy.

"You're missing the steps because you're not feeling the music, young man. You're being too timid!"

"I'm being 'too timid' because I can't remember the damn steps and I don't speak Japanese!" I bark back.

Oops, I just yelled at the leotard lady. She seemed to like it, though, because she says, "Don't even concern yourself with the steps; just feel it, and come in when you're ready. The steps will follow. Why don't you go by yourself this time? I think the other boys are negatively affecting you," she says

Yeah, they're the ones "negatively affecting" me.

I ask her, "So, feeling is more important than the steps, here?"

"Yes, feeling is everything in dance. Passion is paramount in the theater. The steps are just steps, the words are just words, everything is nothing without emotion!" she says.

This lady is pissing me off. Why the hell did she teach us all the march, step, wiggle crap if it doesn't mean anything? Was all that *chassé* crap just busywork? I got your feeling, bitch!

I yell out, "Play the damn thing, piano man! Five, six, seven, eight," and the piano goes. I take a deep breath and close my eyes. I'll just wait until I feel it. I've got to block out this whole room. I've just got to imagine those dancing gangsters in the movie and let them flow into my body. Those dudes could dance . . . and so can I!

I feel something, so I step out with some flair and stomp, march, step, kick, wiggle. I kick out my leg and jump around in a circle. The piano doesn't stop, so neither do I. I toss my head around and spread my fingers out really wide and shake them. March, step, wiggle, waggle! I gyrate my hips and bust a squat move I've seen on MTV.

That's probably the wrong feeling, but it's a feeling, and "feeling is everything in dance"! So I go for it! This is way better than that old march, step, kick, wiggle (and way more fun). I swirl my arms around in a circle and spin around again. I sprint across the room and try to slide on my knees. But I more just slam my knees into the floor and stop cold. I throw my hands out like that was my big finish. Then the piano stops and I turn to the leotard lady.

She's staring at me in disbelief. So is everybody else. Maybe I felt too much. She breaks the silence. "Okay, I think we've seen enough. Number twenty-one, you are free to go. Next group . . . please!"

Dang it! I walk out shaking my head. Man, that was embarrassing. Thank God none of my friends saw. But actually it's kind of nice. To make a complete ass of yourself and not have anybody dog you for it. You can't be too much of a geek in the drama wing. In fact, I may have just out-geeked the biggest geeks in the school.

I feel her before I see her. The right side of my head gets really hot, and I look over to see where the tractor beam is coming from and who's shooting it at me . . . ABBY!

"What are you doing here, Carter?" she seethes.

"Uh, Ms. McDougle asked me to try out for the spring—"

"For what part?" Abby demands.

"Uh, the fat guy," I say, because I can't remember any of the characters' names I signed up for. She's really jacking me up with that stare!

"You're not fat," she barks.

"Oh, thanks. Neither are you," I say.

She glares at me and shakes her head. Maybe she

didn't catch that as the compliment I was throwing.

"You don't need to worry about it, Abby." I laugh. "I just got kicked out of the dance room, so . . ."

"Why would . . . What did you do, Carter?" she asks.

"Nothin'. I was just feeling the music, like the lady told me to. I may have freestyled a bit. Busted some jumps and spin moves that she wasn't ready to handle," I say.

Abby laughs. I made her laugh again!

"I don't think I'll get to be in the play is my point. I might sign up for the lights or building the sets or something," I say, all cool, like a guy who has a tool belt in his truck. Chicks love that. But if she ever sees me hammer my thumb into a board and cry like a bitch, it'll ruin it. She almost smiles, but then she pulls back and gives me the usual scowl.

"I heard about you and Christy Schauper," she says.

"Who?" I ask.

She shakes her head and clarifies. "The Chopper, you jerk!"

"Jerk? I saved that chick's life. She would've frozen to death in that shed if I hadn't carried her big ass into the house," I reply.

"Oooh, only after you were . . . Uhh, Carter! You are unbelievable!" she bellows.

"What? W-w-what do you want from me? I'm doing the best I can! I screw everything up, yes. But I never try to. I'm sorry, but it's not my fault if a chick throws herself at me," I say.

She stomps away in a huff, and fumes, "Stupid jerk, I can't believe I ever . . ."

Dang it. I can't win with that girl. Well, I believe I've

had enough embarrassment for one day and walk toward the doors. For a guy with rejection issues, I seem to set myself up for it an awful lot.

As I pass the door to the theater, I hear screaming and yelling, so I stop to check it out. It sounds like an episode of *Cops* is being filmed in there. A girl is screeching like somebody is beating her trailer-park style. So I cut through the drama classroom and sneak in the back way, to peek through the curtains. A drama geek girl and a drama dork guy are holding papers and yelling at each other . . . as loud as they possibly can!

He yells, "'I'll make you a proposition!'" all stiff.

Oh, I know this. He's yelling the Brando lines, but not nearly cool enough.

"'And what's my end of the bargain?'" she says like a piece of wood with a megaphone.

This is the scene in the movie where Brando is trying to get the Goody Two-shoes to go to Cuba with him. They fight a little more, and then a piano kicks in and they start singing. The girl must be nervous, because her voice is all crackly and off-key. The dude doesn't sing anything like Brando.

Ms. McDougle is writing stuff down. I bet she's writing "These kids SUCK!" and "Kill me now!" but they finish screwing up the song, and she says, "Hey, guys, that was awesome! Thanks so much for coming. We'll post the cast list after school tomorrow. Really great job."

What? Is this some alternate universe where "great" means "crap"? Because those two knuckleheads missed the whole point of the song! Wait a minute! She said I was one of her best students the other day in the parking lot. She must just throw those compliments around, because I got the boot from the leotard lady in five seconds. And, homework or not, you wouldn't give your "best student" a D!

She pulls the same "That was great" line with a bunch of other kids. I'd call them a lot of things, but "great" wouldn't make my list. It seems like nobody has seen the movie. The guys aren't tough enough, and the dolls aren't mean enough to the guys. The girl is supposed to hate this guy at first because he's a real player in her eyes. And she's a hater. She thinks he's a no-good sinner! He gets her with his charm in the end, but that doesn't happen for an hour or so. Plus, nobody is singing the song right. It's not about singing pretty, it's about being smooth! These auditions are like great reality TV, though. I can't not watch. It's interesting to see how so many people can say the same lines so totally different. And totally wrong! They're all so nervous.

Even upperclassmen you'd think of as supreme drama geek royalty, like Jeremy (the guy my sister used to be friends with), are screwing it up. He's been in every show since he was a freshman, so he walks in like he owns the joint. His clothes look expensive and his hair is perfect, but his mouth is so dry, his top lip keeps sticking to his teeth and jacking up the way he talks. He sings really well, but almost too well, like he's showing off.

I had no idea how many drama geeks there were. More than a hundred kids must have come to screw up tonight. The hottie who works at Blockbuster walks in, and I thought she'd be great. She has to have seen the movie, right? Wrong! I want to yell "Booo!" when she starts to sing. I wish I had one of those old-timey hooks to pull the stinkers offstage and save Ms. McDougle the trouble of lying. "That was really terrific! Thanks so much for coming." I know why she's such an awesome drama teacher now: she's a great actress. It may be eating her up on the inside, but it doesn't show one bit. It's after ten o'clock, and that notebook has got to be full of "This idiot is even worse than the last!" or "Crappy . . . but not too crappy."

The helper girl comes in looking really tired and finally says, "Okay, we have Abby and Trevor. The last pair of the evening."

Abby walks in looking really pretty. She's wearing her black dress. I guess she keeps that thing in her locker. She looks hot but nervous. I want to run out there and tell her, "Relax; all the other kids suck!" Her partner, Trevor, looks like no exception to the rule. He may top all others, though, because he looks like he might puke. Awesome!

He's auditioning for Sky, and has the first line. He's supposed to say, "I will need a lot of personal help from you." But this kid is doing everything he can to hold down his dinner, and he isn't letting the line come up, either.

Abby waits for a second and then jumps in with her dialogue. " 'I think not, Mr. Masterson. Tell me, why are you here?' "

Oh, Abby is good! Good and sassy. But the green goblin standing across from her isn't saying a word. His line is supposed to be, "I told you. I'm a sinner." But I think he's stopped breathing. I know he's not dead, because his hands are shaking the pages together, making a flapping noise. He looks around like he's in a dream. He might be, like, one of those serious method actors Ms. McDougle talked about in class. Maybe he's really deep into the character and he's digging up the emotion. Nope, he's digging up his lunch! He covers his mouth and runs out of the theater. YES!

Abby must really be nervous, because normally she'd be laughing at that doofus.

"Well . . . ?" Ms. McDougle says. "Is anybody else still here?"

The helper girl looks panicky as she replies, "No, everyone is gone."

"Oh well," Ms. McDougle responds. "I guess that's it, Avery. Your résumé says that you've had a lot of dance training. I think you did really great. Thanks so much for coming."

Who the hell is "Avery"? I think Ms. McDougle is beyond tired. She should at least listen to Abby sing.

"My name is Abby," she sheepishly replies.

"What?" Ms. McDougle says absentmindedly. "Right, Abby. Look, we're out of boys. Thanks for coming, though."

Abby's lower lip starts to tremble. Don't do it, kid. Fight! Demand to sing. You can't be any worse than the rest of them.

"Okay." She softly surrenders and drops her head to leave. She walks offstage and looks so sad. Her shoulders start to shake as she steps down.

"Nope. Can't do it," I say as I step out into the blinding light. "Would it be okay if I read the Brando part with her?" Man, I really hate to see this chick cry. This is going to suck!

"Sure," Ms. McDougle replies.

"No," Abby says with a tear rolling down her face. "It's not okay. I don't want to read with him."

Ms. McDougle ignores Abby's protest and asks me, "Why didn't you audition for Sky in the first place, Carter?"

"Oh, um, it's nice and calm in here, but outside those doors, it's chaos. A kid growled at me when I got too close to the sign-in sheet. I just want Abby to get to the singing part," I say.

"No, no, I really don't want to read with someone who's not in the theater," Abby says, all snide.

WELL! Try to do something nice and what do you get? Sass! "Oh, get over yourself, Avery!" I say. "Get up here and read the stupid part!"

She shoots me a mean look and marches back down toward the stage. She may be coming to hit me again, so I don't even wait for her to get up onstage before I cock my head, point my finger in her face, and fire the first line. "'I'll need a lot of personal help from you. Why don't we have dinner?'"

Her jaw drops, she turns red, and seethes, "'I think not, Mr. Masterson. Tell me, why are you here?'"

Abby is great! "'I told you. I'm a sinner,'" I say.

"'You're lying!'" she snaps back.

I don't even have the script in my hand. I've seen the scene so many times that this junk is just rattling out of my mouth. I crack a smile and say, "'Well, lying's a sin. You need sinners, don't you?'"

The smile pisses her off. "'We're managing.'"

I get close to her face and quietly say, "'Why don't you let me help you? I'll bet I can fill this place with sinners.'"

She pushes me back and yells, "'I don't bet.'"

I pick up a script off the piano because I can't remember what comes next. She's not looking down at her script. She's just staring at me. "'I'll make you a proposition,'" I say coolly.

She just glares. "'And what's my end of the bargain?'" she asks, all snide.

"'Have dinner with me,'" I respond like a pimp. Oh man, I'm the gangster of love! This is where I trick her into going with me to Cuba. Abby and I go back and forth for a while. Some of the lines are wrong, but the "feeling" is definitely right. I'm being so cool and it's pissing her off so bad. I think she smiled at me once, though. I like this! I call Abby "doll," "dame," "broad," and "baby." She hates it, but what can she do? It's in the script!

I say, "'Why don't you change your pitch to, "Come to the mission one and all, except guys. I hate guys!"'"

She tries to say her line. "'I don't hate anybody.'"

But I totally cut her off with, "'Except me. I'm relieved to know that it's just me personally and not all guys!'"

Oh, it feels good to yell at Abby. And she seems really into yelling at me. I bad-mouth all the guys she's dated and all the "squares" she'll date in the future. She yells how she would never have someone like me as a boyfriend. She fumes that she would never date a degenerate, a hustler, or a guy who's one of the devil's first-line troops!

I tell her, "'I'm not interested in what he'"—her boyfriend—"'will not be'"—like cool. "'I'm interested in what he will be.'"

The piano starts and I'd forgotten about the singing part. Abby sure didn't. She opens her mouth wide, and angels fly out: "'IIIIII'LLLL know when mmmyyy looove cooomes aaalooong . . .'"

Wow, she's awesome! And she's not just singing the words, she's still yelling at me through the song! I miss my part to sing because I'm just staring at her. Dang it!

She gives me a worried look, but I jump in and talk/sing, "'You'll know at a glance'"—I'm just talking in time with the piano—"'By the two pair of paaaannts . . .'" Oh boy, I just sang that one! I didn't explode, either; I might do another.

She busts in and sings, "'I'll knooow by that calm steady voice, those feet on the groouund.'"

I bust out laughing because these lines are cheesy. Abby glares at me, then smiles.

She sings, "'I'll know . . .'"

And then we both sing, "'When my looovvve cooomes aaallllooonnnnggg . . .'"

I sang pretty quiet, but Abby let it go. Awesome. The piano carries out the last note and fades to silence. I guess that's it. Nobody is saying anything, though. I'm just looking at Abby, who's staring back at me. I look down at my script, and it says *Sky kisses her*. So I do. *BANG!* No leadoff peck, either. I just give it to her. None of the other hundred kids must have seen this in the script, because nobody kissed anybody all night. She's not expecting it at all when I crush the script into her boobs. I miss kissing Abby. She's shocked at first, but then I feel her give in to me. She's into it because I'm that guy. Gangsta!

We kiss for about a minute, and it's so nice. I could care less if Ms. McDougle and her helper are uncomfortable and they want to go home. I'm kissing ABBY! We break apart for some reason, and I slowly open my eyes just as she opens hers. That's a look of love if I've ever seen it. Then her eyes get a little smaller and a little more serious. Her mouth crinkles up and her body leans to the left. Then she spins really fast to the right and I hear a loud *SSSLLLAAAAPPP!* and feel a sharp pain in my face. Bitch just slapped me! My jaw drops open from the shock.

"OOOWWWW!" I say as I grab my face. "What the hell was that for?"

Abby may be skinny these days, but she still hits like a heavyweight. She just glares at me. I look down at my script, and there it is, in black and white: *Sarah belts him one across the chops.* Dang it!

Abby drops her crumpled script and says, "Jerk" under her breath.

Now, I know that's not in the script! The audition must be over. I have no idea if that was good or not, but it was definitely fun. Ms. McDougle's not saying anything, though. She's not scribbling. She's just staring at us . . . kind of mean, actually. I bet she's mad I kissed Abby. She should be pissed at Abby for clocking me. But Abby definitely sang the song better than any of the other chicks.

Ms. McDougle opens her mouth to speak. I should just say it for her: "That was great, thanks for coming. . . ." But she doesn't say that. She just stares at us with an open mouth for a minute. Then she starts chewing her pencil like a woodchuck. Well, this is uncomfortable. I guess we should go? I walk past Ms. McDougle and her helper. Abby is behind me.

"Hey, when can I sign up for the light crew?" I ask.

"Oh, shut up, Carter!" Ms. McDougle barks. "You're both freshmen, right?"

"Yeah," Abby says.

"If I can squeeze a D out of Mr. Rumpford, I'll be a sophomore in two months," I say.

"Shut UP, Carter!" she says, breaking the pencil with

her teeth. "What the hell am I supposed to do with this? Get out of here, both of you!"

Okay, Psycho. Ms. Positive Feedback McDougle seems to have just gotten her ass kicked by Ms. Tired Angry Bitch McDougle.

Abby and I break out quick. "Sorry about that," I say as the door shuts.

But she's back to hating me again, and she just stomps away. Dang it! I thought that I was helping Abby by doing the audition and kissing her. I thought those were all good moves, but I'm thinking now that I was wrong.

42. Casting Couch

The next day I sneak toward the drama wing like the theme music to *Mission: Impossible* is playing. I can't let my boys see me! The light crew sign-up is today, and I don't want to miss out. I run in so fast no one could have known it was the Race Carter flying past.

I fling the doors open, and about a hundred drama geeks are gathered around a bulletin board fighting to get a peek at the cast list for *Guys and Dolls*. A bunch of kids are hysterically crying. It's all very dramatic! I can hear them talking . . . because they're the loudest people on earth. They yell, "It's all political!" They scream, "It's ridiculous! It's absurd! That's my part! Ms. McDougle is an idiot! My mom won't stand for this!"

I watched all these kids audition. They couldn't have expected Ms. McDougle to put them in the show. If they were that bad at the auditions, how God-awful would they be in front of five hundred people?

I see Abby shaking her head and crying. A couple of drama girls are gathered around her, laughing and smiling. Man, chicks are ruthless! She must not have gotten a part. No, wait . . . she's smiling now. Maybe she did. I have no idea. Girls are nuts. Maybe I didn't screw her up. I bet she'll play a Hot Box Girl. They dance in the play and wear slutty outfits.

A few kids are really excited and jumping around

laughing right in front of the crying kids. Man, that's uncool. Go celebrate somewhere else. Anywhere but right in front of the bulletin board. This area is reserved for screwups like me who don't get to be in the show. High school is cruel no matter what wing you're in.

I'm getting a fair amount of attention since I walked in here today. It's kind of unsettling. They're probably staring at me because my hair is sticking up all over the place these days. Or maybe they're pointing at me because I ran in here like the building was under attack. Whatever it is, people are definitely looking at me . . . kind of aggressively. Maybe the drama geeks let it slide that I was down here yesterday, but two days in a row is too much. It would suck to have to tell my boys I got beat up by the drama department.

That guy Jeremy prances right up to my face and asks, "Do you know who I am?"

I don't think he expects an answer, so I just go, "Uhhh . . ."

He bellows, "I am Jeremy, the president of the Merrian High Thespians. I have been the lead in the past three shows. I am not, however, the lead in *Guys and Dolls*. Can you please enlighten me as to why?"

"Uh . . . a-a-are you really asking for my opinion?" I ask.

He seems shocked that I know how to speak, when he narrows his eyes and hisses, "Certainly."

"Well, you should really think about drinking a little water before you audition. Maybe even take a bottle onstage with you. . . ." I say hesitantly. He nods his head like I've just given him some decent info, so I add, "You also don't seem tough enough to be a gangster, and you sing beautifully but you totally missed the point of the love song . . . and maybe too much hand waving."

His eyes well with tears, and his confidence drops.

"But hey, what the hell do I know . . . I'm just a freshman," I say apologetically, because he's sobbing. "Hey, do you know where the light crew sign-up is?"

His jaw quivers and his lower lip is shaking when he asks me, "Are you Lynn Carter's brother?"

"Yeah," I reply. "How'd you know that?"

He takes a deep breath to collect himself and mutters, "Oh, she was just the last person to make me cry."

"Yeah, she does that. . . ." I say.

A girl stomps up from behind and cuts me off with, "I bet you think you're pretty cool, don't you?"

I'm sure she doesn't expect an answer to her question, so I walk into the drama classroom. Lots of crying in here too. Three girls are sobbing in front of Ms. McDougle's desk. "A freshman? You can't be serious. You can't let a freshman play Sarah! She's never done a show here before! The drill team is no substitute for THE THEATER!"

Ms. McDougle can only take so much of this. She finally fires back, "None of you were guaranteed parts at all! The freshman gave the best audition. I'm sorry you're disappointed. I've had my heart broken many times over many parts, but that's also part of THE THEATER. The only fair thing to do is give the parts to the best people at the auditions. And Abby gave, by far, the best audition."

Did she say Abby? I also think I heard "drill team."

The drama girl fires back, "Fair . . . FAIR? What's fair is that you and Abby and this whole production are destined to fail, and I will be there to laugh when it does. Ha-HAA-HAAAA!" (Psycho!)

Abby got the lead! That is so awesome. She won't get to

wear the Hot Box Girl outfit, but she's probably happier about getting the lead part. What the hell was she crying about in the hall?

As the psycho girl passes me, she stares me down. She's coming fast. I try to jump out of her way, but she rams me into the wall and barks, "No-talent, freshman jock jerk!" and stomps away.

"Ouch," I say. "This place is tough on self-esteem."

Ms. McDougle laughs. "Well, here's the man now. The boy who's made my life a living hell."

"Who's the man? What'd I do?" I say, walking up.

"How are you holding up? Are you excited?" she asks.

"Yeah, sure," I say, all nonchalant.

"I think you'll be great," Ms. McDougle adds.

"You think? I mean, I've screwed in a few lightbulbs, but I've never, like, hung one before; so sure, I'm stoked," I say. "Where is that sign-up sheet?"

"You're not doing light crew, Carter," Ms. McDougle says.

"Why not?" I ask, a bit pissy.

"I think you'll be a little busy," she says sarcastically.

"What kind of crap is that? You can't cut me from light crew. I'm signing up, whether you or any of these drama nerds like it or not!" I say.

Whoops, I just yelled at a teacher. I shouldn't have done that. McDougle's my favorite teacher. She's pretty and she never talks to me like I'm some stupid kid. It almost seems like she respects me . . . or something. That's probably why I just yelled at her. If she'd just treat me like a punk, like all my other teachers do, I'd never have had the courage to go off on her.

"You're going to be performing in the play, Carter. You can't do lights too," Ms. McDougle says.

"What? I'm what? Nuh-uh!" I say like a dope. "W-w-which, what part? Do I get a costume? Am I gonna play the fat guy?"

"Sky Masterson," she says, shaking her head.

Sky Masterson? Sky . . . Masterson? Which part is? Wait? "THE FRIGGIN' BRANDO PART?!" I yell. "You gave the lead part in the spring play to a freshman? Are you crazy?!"

Ms. McDougle just laughs.

"What's funny? This isn't funny! I mean, thank you very much, but seriously, no way!" I shout.

Now she's mad at me. "Get over here!" she yells, and pushes me into a dressing room.

I'm having some difficulty breathing.

"Mr. Carter, a hundred people auditioned for that part and did not get it. You're being very insensitive!" she yells.

"I'm being? I-I-I'm k-k-keepin' it real! I can't do it!" I protest.

"Of course you can! I wouldn't have cast you if you couldn't. You were the only guy who got the character of Sky. You and Abby have chemistry. I had to give you two the parts no matter how much crap I'll get for casting freshmen."

"So Abby is really gonna play Sarah?" I ask.

"Of course. You two were head and shoulders above the others. It was REAL and passionate. That's what people come to the theater hoping to see, Carter."

"They do?" I ask.

"Yes. I hear we have to work on your dancing, though."

"Naw, I can dance. I just can't count," I reassure her.

43. The Play's the Thing

We do what they call a "table read" with the whole cast. We don't have a table big enough for thirty-two kids and ten adults, so we're smashed into a giant circle of folding chairs, reading the play out loud. I've never liked reading in front of people, so this is going to be painful. But Abby's here. I thought she'd run up to congratulate me, or say thank you, give me a big kiss, show me some boob . . . something. But she didn't say a word. Ms. McDougle made her sit on my right because most of the talking is between her (Sarah) and me (Sky). Jeremy is sitting on my left because he's playing my best buddy, Nathan Detroit (Sinatra). Everyone is shoulder to shoulder in the circle, but I've got elbow room to spare. In fact, I think this whole circle hates me. I try to look like I don't care and just read the script. My head is buried in this sucker like I'm a pro actor who can't be bothered. Dang it! I have sooo much to say. Too much! Good lord, we've got to cut this down, McDougle. Give some of my lines to the fat guy. He loves to talk.

I don't have any lines at the beginning, so I'm trying to figure out what's going on in the show. I'm also very busy sweating and shaking in anticipation of reading my lines. Is it hot in here? My first scene is with Jeremy. We make a bet that I can't get Abby to go with me down to Cuba. I'm supposed to be all cool. Well, Sky may be cool as a cucumber, but Carter is a mess! My mouth is full of dust and I'm dyslexic all of a sudden. I can't stay with the lines. I'm going all slow but still screwing everything up. Everybody is staring at me like I'm an idiot, including Abby and Ms. McDougle. Sweat is pouring off my face when we get to the scene between Abby and me. Finally I know what's going on, and we're off and running! I don't even have to look at the script; I still remember it from yesterday. We're going at it. Back and forth, *bam, bang, boom.* It's great. People are laughing. This is fun. Abby looks all serious at first, but I get her to crack a smile a couple of times.

The helper girl says, "Skip the song and go to the top of page twenty-one. . . ."

I flip to page twenty-one, and the first words are *Sky kisses Sarah.*

So I slide over and plant one on her. *BAM!* It shocks the hell out of her, and the whole drama department gasps. It's in the script, people! They gasp again when she slaps my face . . . as hard as she can. Everyone claps, so I do a little bow in my seat, which makes them laugh. They've instantly stopped hating me. Hell yeah! So this is THE THEATER!? What the hell was I doing screwing around with football, swimming, and baseball? This is where it's at! I do another scene with Jeremy about gambling, and it goes great. He and I are joking around and he gives me a playful shove, and the whole room seems to be having a blast. What a great place this drama wing is! I want to run out onto that baseball field and laugh at my boys running wind sprints and scratching their crotches. They have no idea how miserable they are, or how much fun being in the spring musical is.

I'm so proud, my face hurts from smiling. I've never felt this kind of pride. Of course, I can't really tell my boys about any of it, because they'd make fun of me endlessly; but secretly, I feel great.

I'm almost as stressed about my boys finding out about the play as I am about learning all the lines, dance moves, and lyrics. My sister has everyone under strict orders not to talk about the play to anyone, but it's difficult to keep something like this under wraps.

I'm walking down the hall with EJ and Bag when the hottie who works at Blockbuster walks right up to us and yells, "Way to go, Sky!"

I just walk right by her like I don't hear a thing. I want to smile. I want to say, "Thank you!" I want to say, "We should hook up sometime," but I just look like a deer caught in headlights as I duck into the stairwell.

EJ asks, "What the hell was that?"

"H-h-how should I know?" I say. "That chick's always walkin' up to people and saying random junk. Like, 'Way to go, clouds!' or 'How about the moon?' I think she's on drugs. Um, I'll see you guys later. I got detention."

"Again?" EJ asks.

"Yep," I say, without even looking at him.

"You're a degenerate, Carter!" Bag laughs.

He has no idea. I'm not just a degenerate, I'm a gangster! A singing, dancing, kissing gangster. The drama department hit man. Belting out the hits from three o'clock to six o'clock, every night. Firing out jazz hands and slapping down *pas de bourrées*—I love it! I just go for it down in the drama wing. I like these kids, no matter what Lynn says.

I don't talk to them in the halls or anything, but I wish I could. They're all smart. They discuss movies and books. I can't say anything about the books, but I can throw in my two cents when it comes to movies. They debate *themes* and *character arcs* and stuff I've never even thought of. The only thing my boys talk about these days is baseball, and I hate being the only one without a hat.

I'm still an outsider down here, but then, I feel like an outsider everywhere I go. It's cool because Sky Masterson's an outsider too. He hangs out on the outskirts of society and doesn't know how to deal with people on the *inskirts*. Usually he just uses dames for sex, but he accidentally falls head over heals for Sarah, and he cleans up his act for her. He sacrifices his tough-guy reputation to prove he's worthy of this chick. He's all about honor and not letting people down. When Sky gives his word, he always comes through, whether he's making good on a bet or making himself good for Sarah. I wish I could drop all this wisdom on my boys, but they're too busy learning how to hit a curveball.

After a month, Abby still won't talk to me outside of the lines in the script. My favorite person and damn near best friend lately is Jeremy. He's a bit girly, but he's really cool. He has a sweet car, and I try to copy his hair and the clothes he wears (a little). He's a great dancer, and he helps me out after rehearsals. He kind of translates the moves into thoughts and ideas instead of all those funny words and counting. I'm starting to get it.

I know all my lines with Abby like I know my own name. I won't give her the satisfaction of hearing me yell "Line?!" when I forget. I did it a bunch at first, and she'd always smirk. So I study them like a madman now. I have to leave enough time to space off, so I don't have any free time at all. I haven't seen a movie or been stuffed inside Hormone's CRX in six weeks. Weekends, nights, mornings—I'm working on this play. I want to be great. I want to show those drama nerds who think a freshman could never handle the lead part in the spring play that they're wrong. And I will!

Thankfully, my ADD is keeping pretty quiet these days. I tend to drift off when I don't have lines, so that's my main battle right now. Most of the time, when it gets dead quiet onstage, I'll know that I've missed my cue and rack my brain for where the hell we are and what it was I was supposed to say. Sometimes I just flex my jaw like a tough guy taking a dramatic pause and fire out the missing line like I was keeping it a secret. After the rehearsal, Ms. McDougle tells me, "Carter, take out the pauses in the group scenes." Like I'm not trying to stay focused harder than I've ever tried to do anything in my life. If I could concentrate on the junk I'm supposed to, life would be a breeze.

Rehearsals are especially tough now that the Hot Box Girls have gotten their skimpy costumes. In one of their numbers, they play farm girls and wear Daisy Dukes that show the bottoms of their butt cheeks. Does the costume designer want me to fail?!

I'm supposed to say, "I've got a little more than dough riding on this one," and then the music starts for my toughest song, "Luck Be a Lady Tonight." But all I can think about are those girls wiggling around offstage. The piano man probably notices what I'm gawking at, because he starts playing, snapping me out of the daydream.

This song is about gambling, and it goes really fast. I usually get lost somewhere in the middle, but I'm keeping up so far. I'm singing to the dice, so that when I roll them, they'll do what I want them to do. And so that Lady Luck won't be a coldhearted bitch tooo-night!

I roll the dice and kind of walk around all cool with my hands in my pockets. The leotard lady wants me to prance and gallop more, but I keep telling her, "This gangsta' don't gallop. I strut!" She's starting to get it. Abby just shakes her head.

I wish I could sing as well as Abby when we sing "I've Never Been in Love Before." It's a love song, and I feel it deeply. I look into her eyes, and in that moment, I really believe she loves me, too.

There are a few places where I'm certain she's *not* in love with me. She gets to slap me twice in the first act. She lives for those moments. Ms. McDougle is into realism, so we don't do "stage slaps" in the Merrian drama department. Which is great for the audience, but I'm going to be one of those old boxers who gets loopy from taking too many shots to the head. Abby lets me have it every time—HARD! One time she hit me so hard, it knocked the next line out of my head. I see little birds flying around, and Ms. McDougle goes, "Carter! 'I'll drop in again.' Say the line today, please!"

I know the line, lady. I just need a standing eight count before I can deliver it!

I shake it off, and Ms. McDougle says, "Okay, guys, take it again from the slap, please."

Before I can even get myself together, *WHHAAACKKK!* Abby lets me have it again. DANG IT, woman!

"I'll drop in again in case you want to take a crack at the other cheek!" I scream.

Ms. McDougle's only note for me after rehearsal is,

"Carter, you're wincing before the slap. You can't anticipate it, buddy."

Oh, am I, "buddy"? Yeah, I'll have to work on that! Maybe I could join the Marine Corps in my downtime to toughen up a bit!

Other than that, I'm having more fun doing theater than I've ever had doing anything else. I feel smarter and more confident, and I find myself laughing all the time. Also, it's probably my imagination, but sometimes when people talk to me these days, there's this weird tone in their voice I've never heard directed at me before. . . . I think it's respect.

44. Springing Leaks

Five days before we open the show, Nick Brock is at my house having dinner with the family. It's great when he comes over, because my sister is so nice to everybody. I can't help but laugh at her when she says, "Mother, could you please pass the delicious casserole?" instead of the usual, "Give me some of that crap in the bowl before I starve to death!"

I'm talking to Nick about his truck repairs and how baseball is going. I tell him I haven't seen any of the games because of my detentions, when Lynn breaks in and says, "Could you please lower your voice?!"

"Oh, am I talking too loud?" I ask.

"Yes you are, and it's very obnoxious, so please stop," she politely condescends.

"Lynn, he is practicing his projection, and he's doing great!" Mom defends.

No. No helping, Mom.

"Well, Mother, all I'm saying is: it's annoying. And he should be aware when he's being annoying. I'm just trying to help him, like I try to help everyone," she says.

"It's funny," I say to Nick, "because sometimes I'll forget if it was Mother Teresa that did something or if it was Lynn."

Brock laughs, takes a bite of casserole, and asks, "Hey, what's 'projection'?"

Oh boy. Brock is not going to like this.

Lynn jumps in with more assistance by yelling, "Nick, don't talk with your mouth full!"

Good ol' Lynn. Helping me. Helping Brock. Two birds, one bitchy stone.

"Nick," my mom says, "projection is when people in the theater speak loud enough and clear enough for the people in the back row to hear what they're saying."

Mother, zip it!

"Why would you need to work on that, man?" he asks me.

"Um . . ." I say.

"Well, Carter doesn't want anyone to know it, but he's the lead actor in the spring play!" Mom blabbers.

Momma, noooo!

"Really?" Brock asks. "Lynn, why didn't you tell me that?"

"Because it's mortifying, that's why! We don't talk about his drama problem in public," she says.

"Well, I think that's awesome. The spring play is a big deal. You know, I tried out for the winter play when I was a sophomore, but I got cut. Congratulations," Nick says, all seriously.

"*You* got cut from something, Brock?" I ask in disbelief.

"Yeah, I took drama classes and everything back in the day, but I choked at the audition," Nick continues. "The play was called *The Diary of Anne Frank*. I really wanted to play this kid Peter Van something."

My dad chokes on his water. "*Anne Frank*? The Holocaust *Anne Frank*? No offense, Nick, but you're like, six foot five? It'd be pretty tough to imagine you as a little Jewish boy. . . ."

"William!" Mom barks. "I imagine Nick would have been very good in the part."

Brock gets quiet and thinks about what might have been. I bet he would have been a kick-ass Peter, the little Jewish boy. It would have added flavor to the family if they'd had a muscle-bound linebacker eating all the food in the attic. I should feel bad for feeling this way, but I really like hearing that Nick Brock screws up. That he's been cut from things and my sister yells at him too. I gain strength from his pain.

"Well, I can't wait to see the show," Nick says.

Oh? Nick's going to see the show. "Cool," I say half-heartedly.

Not cool! I don't mind singing and dancing with the drama dorks, but I never really thought other people would come. God, if Nick Brock comes, that'll mean my sister might come. Jeez, I don't like that! What if other kids wander in? Like, my boys hear about the Hot Box Girls and come down to gawk. I doubt if they'll be as supportive as Nick. I can't worry about it, though. I've got to save my stress, and focus on doing better in the show.

45. Dance Fever, Punk

I run into the drama wing with my backpack over my head at my usual breakneck pace, to find Jeremy laughing with Abby on the steps of the theater. His arms are wrapped around her waist, and her arms are draped around his neck. She's cracking up and staring into his eyes. He passionately kisses her on the cheek and she squeals with delight. Well, well, well! What do we have here? A backstabbing drama nerd with perfect hair, riding the Village Bike. I thought Jeremy and I were going to be good friends, but I guess Abby has just given me my next nemesis. (Andre's hair is growing back a lot faster and cooler than mine. He hit four home runs in a single baseball game, and he and EJ hang out sometimes now, but I don't have time to care about him anymore.)

Granted, Abby and I never actually speak outside of the dialogue in the play, but it should be pretty obvious that she's my girl, Jeremy! How do I kick this guy's ass? Do I outdance his punk ass? Whack him singing-gangster style and haul him off in the imaginary trunk of my cardboard Cadillac? Man, I don't want to hate Jeremy. He's, like, my best friend lately. He's always showing me how to dance, sing, and dress better, and he drives me home after late rehearsals. The Andre feud almost killed me, so I'll just let him have her. If anybody is good enough for my Abby, it's Jeremy. I can live with this.

"S'up?" I ask through clenched teeth.

Abby doesn't respond; she never does. But Jeremy projects, "Hey, hey, Mr. Car-ter!" Like that knife in my back shouldn't hurt a bit. But I'm okay with this!

We do a run-through of the second act, and I'm totally off. I know these lines—I do!—but I can't seem to remember them at the right time today. I grab the script whenever I get offstage and look them over. I have most of my scenes written on my arms, but I'm still having trouble with them. The last scene in the play where everybody gets married is up, and I see Jeremy and Abby look at each other and share a knowing giggle as we *chassé* into position. My blood starts to boil. Are they laughing at me? That's my imaginary girl-friend you're mackin' on, pretty boy! She's about to become my pretend wife! For the first time in my life I wish I was at football practice and I could smash his junior, dance-fever punk ASS into the fake walls! I hate these older dudes and their stupid cars, and . . . (dead silence).

Dang it! I bet it's my line. I'm missing my line. What is it? Where the hell are we? The show's almost over. Everyone is looking at me. A skinny kid named Tony is standing in front of me dressed like a priest.

I flex my jaw and say, "Uhhh?" all smooth.

Abby whispers angrily, "You do!"

I do what? When? You're not helping . . . LIGHT-BULB! I yell, "I DO, DO!" really fast, and we break out dancing again. But the music stops just as we get going, and Ms. McDougle jumps up onstage like a pro wrestler.

She throws her clipboard down and yells, "Carter, you are killin' me!"

Dang it! No one is safe when I'm around. Football, swimming, math class, you name it and I'm there, like a ninja assassin.

"What the hell is with you today?" Ms. McDougle barks. "Concentrate, please! We have two days. Two rehearsals until five hundred people fill those seats! All of your friends and family will be watching. How are you going to react?"

Family maybe, but I don't think my friends will be a problem.

She yells, "Everybody out! Carter, Jeremy, Tony, Kara, and Abby—do the wedding sequence until you drop! I've got to work on the latest costume catastrophe. And Carter, please, stay focused!"

As she stomps out of the auditorium, I give her an awkward wave and say, "You got it, Ms. McD, I'm focused like a Nikon camera!"

"Killin' me!" she cries as the door slams.

"Okay, what the hell are we doing, guys?" I ask.

Everyone glares at me. We rehearse the wedding scene and the final dance number for three more hours. Man, this stuff is tough. I've worked as hard as I possibly could on this show. It's all I've done for two months, and I'm still screwing up. I haven't done homework in forever. Good thing I never do it, or I'd really be screwed.

I'm exhausted as I unlock my bike to ride home in the dark. I feel someone watching me, and turn to find Abby about twenty feet behind me leaning against a lamppost. She is so pretty, and she doesn't look away when I meet her gaze, so I ride over to her and say, "Hey."

She replies, "Hey," and I try not to smile too big.

"Do you need a ride?"

She looks at my axle pegs, shakes her head, and says, "No, my mom's on her way."

"I'm sorry I keep screwing up the show. . . ."

"You're not screwing up that bad," she replies. "I think it's the same with me and Jeremy and everybody else; you just need to get out of your own way."

I nod my thanks and try to think of something funny to say or a question I can ask, when her mom's headlights come into view. Abby picks up her backpack and walks to the car. Her mom glares at me from the driver's seat like she's figuring out how much trouble she'd get into for "accidentally" running me over. I hop on my bike and ride off in the other direction, to be on the safe side.

46. Let Yourself Go

Opening night! I can't believe it's here. Man, I'm more nervous than I've ever been in my life. It's not that I'm worried I won't do a good job; I'm worried that I'm going to die. A heart attack at fourteen . . . is that possible? You'd think I'd been eating out of Taco Bell's Dumpster for the last week the way I've got diarrhea. Only one boys' bathroom in the drama wing, and the dorks are a little fussy that I'm murdering it. I've got my fly gangster suit on, my hair is just long enough as of yesterday to slick back, and I look so cool! I'm dressed for the funeral if I do croak.

I watch Jeremy put on his makeup and just do what he does, but when I try to put on the mascara, my hands are shaking so bad that I keep poking myself in the eyeball. Abby must have seen me struggling, because she's fighting back a smile when she takes the wand out of my hand and orders me to "look up" before applying the junk to my eyelashes. I thank her as Ms. McDougle yells at us to come into the classroom for a pep talk.

Fifteen minutes before the curtain goes up

Everybody involved in the show, from the lighting guys to the mothers who helped sew the costumes, are all holding hands. Jeremy calls it the Dildo Circle—so many hands are trembling it sends a vibration all through the line. Ms. McDougle talks to us with a shaky voice about what a great thing it is to do a play, and how THE THEATER matters. How live theater is the closest thing people get to living out their fantasies. She tells us to enjoy this moment because we may never get to experience anything like it again. How proud she is of us and how we should reach for the stars tonight, and stay relaxed and let ourselves go!

She wouldn't be so proud of me if she knew what I was about to do to this bathroom. DANG IT! The door's locked. Crap! I'm not just saying that; I mean "Crap!" I'm going to ruin my fly gangster suit if I don't find a toilet now. I break out of the drama wing, sprint up the stairs and down the hall. I think it's a no-no to be outside of the wing in my costume, but I'd rather not do *Guys and Dolls* with a runny steamer in my pants.

The school is empty, and thank God the boys' restroom is too. If it had a hundred people in it a minute ago, they would be long gone the second I start letting myself go. WHEW! That is terrible! And that is it. Nothing left in the tanks, Captain; you've got a show to do.

I look in the mirror on my way out, and I may be a little pale and shaky, my eyeballs may have sunken into my head a bit from dehydration, but I have never looked so cool! I love this. I'm ready for this. For the first time in my life I have no reason to second-guess myself. I've worked way too hard to possibly get all caught up in my head and fumble through this play and wreck it all. Nobody would be shocked if I did, because, "It's just Carter up there, and that's what Carter does."

Well, not tonight! Not this Carter; I'm going to do it right. I'm going to be great. I kick the bathroom door open like the singing gangster I am. I step out into the hall like the biggest badass this school has ever known, when I hear a chillingly familiar voice. Not the voice of God, not my own voice, but a voice I know almost as well.

"Carter, what are you doing?" EJ asks in disbelief.

I look over at the last guys you'd ever expect to see at school at 7:55 p.m. on a Thursday night. Eight matching baseball hats, same matching expression: profound dumbfoundedness. EJ, Bag, Doc, J-Low, Levi, Hormone, Nutt, and Andre.

"Hey guys, w-w-what're you doing here?" I ask as I walk by.

"Just came to see if it was true," Doc says.

"Abby said you were in the spring musical, and we told her she was crazy," Bag adds.

"When did she tell you?" I ask.

"About three weeks ago," EJ explains.

"Why didn't you ask me about it?"

"Because we never see you anymore, dude," Bag adds.

I just look at them with my hair slicked back, gangster suit on, and makeup applied, when Nutt asks very seriously, "Well, are ya?"

I have to laugh. "No, dumbass, I just get dressed up like this sometimes and come up to school to goof around."

The guys laugh like they've forgotten why we're all standing here uncomfortably. Hormone adds, "Ms. Holly is givin' extra credit for seein' your play."

"Makeup, huh?" EJ asks.

"Yep," I say, without a hint of embarrassment.

Andre looks like he's doing the potty dance, he wants to burn me so bad. He finally comes up with, "Doin' a play is gay."

I nod my head and say, "Yeah, that was a good one. Well, you guys better take your seats. The show's about to start."

As I walk away, I hear them chattering like a gaggle of hens. And I don't care. I can't believe it, but I don't. This is it. This is *me* for the first time in my life not caring. Because I'm not doing this for them, or my family, or Ms. McDougle, or even Abby. I'm stepping out onto that stage tonight for one person—me—that's it. Because this is who I want to be. Not, like, an actor or a singer or dancer, but a guy who does what he wants to do because he wants to do it. Life has made, and will make, me do a lot of stuff I don't want to do: football, swimming, studying, parties, work, etc. So I think when you tap into something that you really want to do, you have to fight for it, even if the fight is with yourself. I just overcame my one true enemy, and I feel like a new person walking down this hallway. One week and six days before the end of the year, and I finally feel like a fresh man. This is the person I've been creating with every step and misstep that I've taken this year. I've worked harder for this feeling than I ever imagined I could, but these steps are completely effortless.

As I look out onto the stage, the lights come up, the music starts, and the show begins. It's going better than it ever did in rehearsals. I think back to how bad we were at the beginning—to how everything was so clunky and retarded. I never thought we'd get to this place. The fat guy and his pint-size sidekick are cracking everybody up. The show is better than perfect so far, and it's amazing to watch. It makes me feel good to know that everybody screws up, but if you just keep going you can get through anything, and you just might be great when you get there. I never thought I'd live through this year at all, and here I am, about to star in the spring musical! I'll probably always care what people think of me, and want to impress them, but when I walked away from my boys to do a singing, dancing, gangster musical, I realized it didn't need to be the driving force of my life. I felt a shift, and it feels great. Like, I'm ten feet underwater, looking up at a perfect blue sky in late June. It feels like freedom.

"CARTER, you are killing me! Get on stage," Ms. McDougle whisper/yells.

She can't see the epiphany that just happened here. All she can see is that Jeremy said my cue line and I'm staring up at the lights smiling. I step out onstage with my heart racing like I've just sprinted a hundred yards on crack, but I know I'll be okay.

That's about all I remember. I'm suddenly staring at the back of a curtain, and the audience is going wild with applause. I'm trying to catch my breath and figure out what's going on. I know I stepped out there and said my first line. I know I talk/sung pretty much when I was supposed to, and I danced up a storm, because I'm drenched in sweat. We just did the wedding scene and sang the big finish number really well.

We step into the curtain-call position, and I take Abby's hand in mine. She smiles at me as the curtain rips open. The audience jumps to its feet, and I realize that the show is really over and we must have kicked ass, because EJ and the rest of my boys (even Andre) are clapping their hands off! Pam is cheering two rows behind my dad. Mom's crying, and Brock is jumping up and down like a girl. My sister grabs Brock by the shoulders and shuts down the jumping with brute force.

We finish the bowing, the curtain closes, and Abby tries to let go of my hand. I squeeze it tightly and look over at her. I don't want to let go. I don't want this feeling to end. When she finally looks up into my eyes, they're filled with tears. She gives me a smile, and I release my grip. Abby turns to walk away, then spins around and jumps into my arms. She's squeezing me so tight that my ribs might break, but I'd let her break every bone in my body before I'd let her go.

"You were great," she whispers in my ear.

"You too," I wheeze.

Jeremy runs up, throws his arms around us, and yells, "FIERCE!"

We rock back and forth for a while before he starts to kiss Abby on the cheek a bunch of times. I'm not mad, but I don't want to be a third wheel, so I let go of Abby and pat Jeremy on the back before retreating into the dressing room to peel my costume off. My gangster suit feels like I've been swimming in it for the last couple of hours.

It happened like that for the rest of the run. Diarrhea every night. My family was there for all of the performances. Brock never missed a show, and neither did EJ. And then it was over. I'm glad, because I'm exhausted, but when the curtain closed for the last time on Saturday night, it felt like somebody died. I don't get to be Sky Masterson anymore and the thought bums me out, terribly. I'll miss him. I'll miss the drama nerds. I'll miss kissing Abby every day and putting on that suit and strutting around. I can't just bust out a song and dance whenever I want to. I could, I guess, but I don't really want to be "that guy."

When things suck, time stands still, but when you have an epiphany and you're having the time of your life, it goes by in fast-forward.

47. Knockout

It's Sunday afternoon and the *Guys and Dolls* closing party is in full swing at Pizza Barn. Lots of kids, lots of hugging, and lots of noise! The drama kids must not even know about the arcade in the back room. They're probably all too smart to be into video games, so I break off for a second and pop a quarter into the old Punch Out game. I doubt if anybody has even played this thing since I wasted a quarter on Amber Lee back in August. I knock out the first opponent like I play this game every day, and am stretching my wrist and warming up my punch finger for the next digital chump that needs a "Mighty Blow!" when I feel a tractor beam coming from behind me. I could've knocked out the next guy, but I let go of the controls and turn around to grapple with a more worthy, prettier adversary.

"KNOCKOUT!" the machine yells as my guy falls to the canvas.

Abby smiles and groans, "That's got to hurt."

"You could take 'em, I bet," I say.

She nods, and we stare at each other for a couple of seconds. We're cool again and I know it, so I ask, "You waitin' for the Punch Out game?"

"No." She laughs.

"So you're just back here stalkin' me?" I ask.

"Ohhh? It's like that? I could go," she replies, all sly.

"No, I'm just kidding. I don't want you to go. I'm done playing games," I say.

She seems a bit uncomfortable, but, like, in a good way. She finally asks me, "So there's a party after this, at Gray Goose Lake. Are you going?"

"I don't know. Gray Goose Lake kinda makes me nervous. I got knocked out myself last time I was there," I say.

She nods and says, "Yeah, I guess you did. But you're tougher these days, right? I've slapped you at least fifty times since then."

"Yeah, that's true; I'm pretty much a total badass now," I reply.

"So it wouldn't even be a big deal if I pop you, for old time's sake," she says as she cocks her hand back.

I grab her forearm and pull her close to me. "It's lucky you're pretty . . . so it doesn't matter that you're not funny."

I'm really close to her, and we both stop kidding around. I'm not sure if it's a green light, but the back room of the Pizza Barn gets really intense for a second as I look into Abby's eyes. She shuts it down by looking away, and starts another round of jokes. "I understand if you're scared to go back, though."

"No, no, I could maybe stop by. Did that security guard die or something?" I ask.

"No, Jeremy's house is out there. It's a drama party," she clarifies.

"Oh, ohhh, so are you gonna ride over there with Jeremy?" I ask, and break away from her.

"Well, I wasn't planning on it. I saw your bike out front

and was wondering if anybody was riding on your pegs tonight," she replies.

"No, my pegs are free so far. But, wait . . . I'm confused. Aren't you *with* Jeremy? It seems like he's your boyfriend. I see you guys kissing and dancing all the time and giving each other massages. So what's this?" I ask.

"Oh, Carter, I love Jeremy," she says, shaking her head. "He's amazing. He's my new best friend. He's got style. He can sing and dance, and he has a car, and . . ."

"Did you know he has a peg leg?"

"He's also gay." She laughs.

"Oh . . . What? You mean, he's gay, like, he's a dumbass?" I reply.

"No, I mean he's homosexual, like, he's attracted to boys," she clarifies. "You're gay, like, a dumbass."

Man, she's quick. I grab her by the waist and joke, "How great would it be if you were funny?"

She gets closer to my face and softly says, "Pretty great."

That's a green light if I've ever seen one, so I lean in and give her a kiss. I do the leadoff peck like I'm supposed to, but it's just a formality. We kiss for about twenty minutes when she pulls back and says, "We better get going."

"Where?" I ask like a dope.

"Gray Goose Lake, remember?"

"You were serious about that?" I ask. "It's really far."

"Yeah, but you're a total badass now, right? So we should get moving."

I shake my head and say, "All right, I hope you like back sweat."

She laughs, "We can jump in the lake to cool off when we get there."

"Oh, I don't have my trunks," I reply.

She turns as she's walking out of the back room, grabs my hand, and says, "Maybe you don't need them. . . ."

I almost fall down as we walk into the main room. Jeremy runs up, hugs Abby, and says, "You two were back there for a long time!"

Abby laughs and tells him that we'll see him later on tonight at the lake.

"Do you guys need a ride?" he asks.

"NO, NO! I got it," I reply as we head for the door.

I'll regret not taking the ride after about five miles, but if I've learned anything this year, it's that nothing good comes easy, focus is everything, and hard work sucks when you're doing it, but the payoff is usually incredible. I'm pretty focused on getting to that lake, not needing my trunks, and possibly seeing Abby naked!

I unlock the Redline 500a and throw my leg over the seat. Abby climbs on the pegs, and we roll out like the coolest thing on two wheels. Her arms are wrapped around me tight as we pedal through the streets of Merrian and talk about the upcoming summer and how great it'll be not to be freshmen anymore. How sweet it'll be to go off that rope swing, and how great it is that Jeremy is Abby's new best friend. I just ride and listen to her talk about how Nicky and Amber will always be her girls, but that she kind of deserves better (than those bitches!). And how tough this year was for her, but that she wouldn't change anything about it because this bike ride might not have been possible without all the heartache.

I tell her that I'm sorry for any role I might have played in that heartache, but I too am so glad to be on this bike with her, and I probably wouldn't change any of my screwups either.

We may have cruised out to the lake in about an hour, just in time for the sunset, stripped down to buck naked, and swung out on that rope swing twenty feet in the air before splashing down into the clear, refreshing water. We may have made sweet, passionate love on the bank of Gray Goose Lake, on the party dock, in an open boat, in the woods, in the lake, and maybe on the rope swing itself! It may have been incredible, everything I ever imagined it would be. Or we may have ridden the wheels off that damn Redline piece of crap for three hours before realizing we were going the wrong way, sweated out all of our fluids, and gotten severe leg cramps. We may have had to call my dad in complete disgrace to pick us up and take Abby home, without ever making love anywhere or going to any lake or party. Either scenario could have happened. Anything is possible.